LITTLE EVILS

I0684740

Don D'Ammassa

Managansett Press

This book is a work of fiction. Names, places, and events are not based on real people or places. Any resemblance is purely coincidental.

"All Flesh Is Clay" first appeared in *Blood Muse*, 1995
"The Dead Beat Society" first appeared in *Shock Rock*, 1990
"Dominion" first appeared in *New Mythos Legends*, 1998
"The Guard Tower: first appeared in *2 AM*, 1991
"Little Evils" first appeared in *Chilled to the Bone*, 1991
"Present in Spirit: first appeared in *Peter Straub's Ghosts*, 1993
"Splicer" first appeared in *Hotter Blood*, 1990
"A Tight Situation" first appeared in *Deathream 21*, 1993
"Twisted Images" first appeared from Necronomicon Press, 1995
All other stories appear for the first time in this volume.

Managansett Press First Edition 2015

LITTLE EVILS

CONTENTS

ALL FLESH IS CLAY

"Nikki tells me you've been stealing mud from the cemetery again." Laura Merriam poured herself a glass of wine and seated herself with exaggerated dignity in Greg Clark's favorite chair.

"Clay, not mud." He continued to work the material with his hands, not even glancing in her direction, still searching for the shape he knew existed within it. "Use artificial media and your results are shaped by the falseness. That's why we moved here, you know. Managansett has some of the best natural clay in North America. It works with you instead of against you; you can almost feel it responding. And it fires as well or better than anything you can get at Block Artists Supply."

Laura's tabby ambled in from the patio, jumped up onto her lap, butting its head against her breast, demanding attention. "All right, but why the cemetery? You could pick up as much as you want down along Reservoir Road and no one would mind at all. I know for a fact that the police have been receiving complaints about vandalism in the cemetery and if they catch you in there some night with your shovel and wheelbarrow..."

Greg sighed, his hands frozen in position, and he willed the muscles at the back of his neck to relax. "The texture and color are better, that's why. I'm not robbing graves, Laura, I'm just taking some clay. I know there's been some trouble, disturbed headstones and the like, but it's been going on for years. Give it a rest, will you?"

Laura switched gears easily, spoke next with genuine concern. "Not going well?"

He shrugged, gestured toward the clay. "It's a bust, I think, probably a man judging by the size, a big man, powerful. But I just can't see the details yet. Sometimes I almost think I have them, and then something feels wrong."

She pushed the cat off her lap and leaned forward. "Looks too big for just a head."

"Well, I'll be taking a lot off once I know what's hidden there, but you're right. I think these are shoulders," he traced two symmetrical lines with his fingers, "and part of the chest will have to be modeled as well, if for no other reason than to give the composition some stability. It wouldn't do for it to fall over in the middle of a showing."

Laura laughed politely and stood up. "Well, I'll leave you to it. I just came over to remind the two of you about dinner tonight."

"We'll be there."

Greg worked for another half hour after his neighbor left, but with no more progress than before. Frustrated, he wrapped the amorphous shape with damp cloths and went upstairs to shower, rapping on his daughter's door on the way.

"Don't forget we're eating at Mrs. Merriam's tonight."

Nikki muttered something unintelligible that Greg chose to interpret as assent.

Nikki troubled him, though he was reluctant to admit it, even to himself. She'd never been a fast learner, and her graduation this past year from high school had been more an act of mercy on the part of her teachers than proof of any achievement on her part. Her guidance counselor had made noises about Nikki being "socially challenged", but Greg was undisturbed by his daughter's reluctance to date regularly. On the other hand, she had difficulty retaining even the simplest of information, and drifted off into reveries from which it often took considerable effort to rouse her. She needed focus, he believed, something that would capture her imagination completely.

As he showered, he traced shapes where the steam condensed on the walls, human heads and shoulders.

The clay remained perfectly malleable the following morning, moved obediently under his probing fingers. For the first time since he'd started, he felt a degree of confidence, drawing inspiration from a dream he'd had the night before. It was a static sort of image, but remarkably clear in his memory, a foursome for dinner, himself, Nikki, Laura Merriam, and the fourth, a man, a very big man, powerful, commanding, dominating the entire conversation without saying a word.

Greg's fingers found the forehead in the clay, smoothed the brow, worked up over the crest of the head, tracing the outline of the hair. Thick hair, straight lines, long and full. It fell to the shoulders, which were massive. He stripped clay away and discarded it to one side or the other, littering the floor of his studio with divots that slowly dried and crumbled.

Thick muscles from shoulder to the neck, a strong chin though somewhat pointed, long aquiline nose above a full, sensuous mouth that was just a bit too wide for the face. Greg hesitated, started to smooth off the corners, but that seemed wrong somehow so he left them the way they were. The eyes then, fairly large but set close together and deeply recessed. High cheek bones but not rounded, angular. A face almost craggy, not entirely handsome but infused with raw power.

Greg stepped back only when his fingers were cramping from the exertion. Fully a quarter of the original material had been discarded now, and what remained was undeniably the bust of a man, though the features were still too rough to more than suggest an identity.

He was startled to notice that he'd worked for four straight hours.

Although he burned with the need to return to the sculpture, Greg forced himself to drive into town and complete his scheduled errands. The post office box yielded two royalty checks, three bills, and four pieces of junk mail that he discarded in the lobby trashcan. Then the dry cleaning, some groceries, and a brief stop at the hardware store for a better shovel.

Except for one bag of perishables, he left his purchases in the car when he arrived back at the house, put those away quickly, and returned to the studio. Laura's tabby was on the patio, batting at the glass door with one paw. Greg ignored the cat, instead removed the wraps from his sculpture. The clay remained soft and workable and the underlying shape seemed to have acquired more clarity during his absence.

In fact, something had definitely changed, though even to Greg's trained eye, the difference was subtle. After fifteen minutes of intense study, he decided that the lips were fuller than he'd intended, and the left side of the mouth was slightly distorted, suggesting a sneer. The angle of the eyes seemed wrong. Maybe the clay was too soft, wouldn't hold its form. He raised one hand, planning to erase the changes, but then let it drop. For some reason, it seemed inappropriate to interfere. If that was the true shape concealed in the clay, then he would liberate it, not fight it.

He spent the remainder of the afternoon working on the half torso, quitting only when the sun dropped abruptly behind the horizon.

"You shouldn't work so hard, Dad. It's not like, you know, we need the money or anything."

Greg regarded his daughter solemnly across the breakfast table. "A real artist doesn't work for the money, Nikki. He does it for the art itself."

"Oh, right," she rolled her eyes, "like you'd give it all to charity if that meant you could work in peace."

He shook his head. "No, I'm not that altruistic. But art isn't just something I do, Nikki. It's what I'm all about. It helps me to define myself, recognize who I am. I put my heart and soul into my work because in a way, it's all a part of me, an extension of my mind, if not my body. Some day you'll find something you care about the same way, and then you'll understand."

There were more changes. Greg walked around the emerging bust several times, rubbing his chin thoughtfully. The mouth was more distorted than ever, the cheeks had receded, losing the fullness he'd originally given them, and the hair was longer, as though the clay had stretched. There was an odd smell as well, faint, almost undetectable, but it persisted until mid-morning. It smelled like liquid copper.

But as soon as he put his hands on the clay, he knew that things were going to go well. The thick material almost seemed to anticipate his thoughts, moving of its own accord, flowing in harmony with the emerging face. Greg skipped lunch and worked on into the afternoon, stopping only when he staggered with exhaustion and his hand slipped through the clay, making a ragged line across one ear. He repaired the damage slowly and carefully, then collapsed onto the sofa.

The face had a definite personality now; the eyes seemed to positively glower across the room. The mouth, even the tilt of the chin, implied superiority and contempt. Greg decided that he didn't particularly like the man he'd found hidden in the clay, but he'd never before had a sculpture go so quickly, so easily.

When Greg entered his studio the following morning, he froze for several long minutes, then returned to the kitchen, his face as dark as that of his creation.

"Nikki! Have you been fooling around in my studio?"

She glanced up from her poached eggs, clearly startled. "What do you mean?"

"If this is some kind of joke, I don't appreciate it." His voice was barely under control, trembling with rage. "I've put my heart into this project and I won't tolerate anyone messing with it, do you understand?"

"Are you accusing me of doing something to your old statue?" Nikki pushed back her chair and glared at him. "Don't you think I have better things to do with my time than play in the mud?"

"It's not mud!" He caught his breath. "Look, maybe you just went to look and bumped into it or something and then tried to fix things. I did the same myself as a matter of fact. Just try to be careful from now on, all right?"

He spun on his heel and left before she could answer, went to assess the damage.

The changes were too radical to explain away as problems with the consistency of the media. Both sides of the mouth were misshapen, almost as though something had been concealed within and had recently emerged. Air bubbles? No, he'd worked the clay too thoroughly to miss even one this size, let alone two. And the brow lines had been drawn together across the gap, a solid bar over the nose. The cheeks had sunk even deeper, flat planes under the high ridge. And the forehead was slanted further forward, or perhaps the eyes had sunk deeper. The overall result was an almost canine cast to the features. This was no longer the face of a man; it was the visage of some preternatural beast.

The clay resisted his efforts, slowly hardening with exposure to the air, and it took most of the day to reclaim the lost ground. When he was satisfied that he'd done all that was necessary, Greg checked to make sure the patio door was secured, then locked the studio door when he left.

Nikki's door was closed but she didn't answer when he knocked. Probably sulking. Greg felt a passing regret; in retrospect he'd probably accused her unjustly. Nikki lacked the talent to make the alterations he'd just reversed. Nor could he believe that someone had broken into the house just to bedevil him. It had to be some idiosyncrasy of the clay, some reaction he'd never encountered before.

He showered and lay down on his bed, falling asleep almost immediately despite the early hour.

Greg Clark's dreams were dark and crowded. It was the same as before, the four of them sitting around a small supper table, but the unknown fourth was even more dominant, his face darkly furrowed, features distorted and lupine, eyes glowing embers. Their unknown host lifted a covered pan and removed the lid with a flourish revealing three still beating human hearts.

Greg woke in the darkness.

It was a hot August night, the air thick and moist. They were far enough from the downtown that there were no traffic noises, although in his experience, there wasn't much traffic anywhere in Managansett after ten o'clock. A faint hint of music drifted in from somewhere in the night. Perhaps Nikki was playing her radio.

His throat was dry. Greg slid off the bed and padded barefoot out to the kitchen to get a drink. The music was louder here, a single human voice, but it wasn't coming from Nikki's room. It originated on the opposite side of the house, from his studio.

Greg moved silently through the unlit rooms.

The studio door was ajar. He slipped his hand into his pocket. The key was still there and, insofar as he knew, there existed no copy. He closed the distance carefully and peered through the opening.

There was a woman in his studio, a naked woman in fact, humming to herself. He could see her body clearly as she stood in front of the patio window, outlined against the nearly full moon. At first he thought it must be Laura Merriam. She'd lived here for years, knew the Talbots before they'd moved away. Presumably they'd given her a key for some reason and she'd never returned it. The coppery smell was back as well, stronger than ever.

But then he realized that it couldn't be Laura. His mysterious guest was considerably shorter, her figure less ample, and her hair waist length. Laura's barely brushed her shoulders. Greg opened the door slightly, then gasped with recognition. It was his daughter.

Just as he recognized her, she moved closer to the bust, touching it with her own, wrapping her arms around the clay statue.

He opened the door wide then, afraid she was going to lift it from the workbench and throw it to the floor, but instead she used the leverage to climb up onto the tabletop, straddling the lump of clay, wrapping her legs around the torso.

Greg gasped out a protest. What was she trying to do? She could destroy several days of work in a moment if she wasn't careful. But Nikki neither saw nor heard him, even after he'd entered the room fully and moved to stand close enough that he could have reached out and touched her shoulder.

She was making love to the statue, rubbing her breasts and thighs over the worked clay. Dark streaks crisscrossed her body where it had touched the moist media. Her head was thrown back in a bizarre parody of ecstasy as she raised and lowered herself rhythmically. Greg felt himself growing aroused and shock at that discovery spurred him to move.

She reacted to his touch as though a switch had been thrown, collapsing so abruptly that he barely caught her head before it struck the floor. He carried Nikki back to her bed, assured himself that she was breathing normally, covered her with a blanket, then poured a brandy before returning to the studio to see how much damage she'd done.

The bust was back the way it had been that morning, before he'd erased all the distortions he'd discovered. The eyes seemed to be watching him thoughtfully as he paced back and forth. Experimentally he placed his hands on the clay. It was unusually moist, perhaps augmented by his daughter's perspiration. That thought was enough to send him half running from the room. The agency that allowed for such clearly non-random changes in the clay was something about which he chose not to think at all.

Nikki was using the garbage disposal when he entered the kitchen the following morning. She greeted him cheerfully and pointed to a full coffeepot. As far as he could tell, she had no recollection of the events of the preceding evening, and Greg couldn't imagine how he could ever bring the subject up. But something had to be done, didn't it? Even if it was simply a complex form of sleepwalking, and an expression of her unfulfilled sexual drive, it was potentially dangerous. What if she'd left the house? What if someone had seen her?

"How're you feeling this morning, honey?"

"Ummm, me? Fine, I guess. A little stiff and sore. Guess I slept the wrong way. You working again today, you know, on it?" She inclined her head toward the studio. Greg regarded her thoughtfully before answering.

"Maybe later. I thought I'd go up to the mall and walk around for a while. Feel like coming?"

"Nah, I'll pass, thanks. Think I'll just go get some rays down by the pond."

Greg pointedly did not unlock the studio, but on the other hand he had absolutely no desire to go to the mall without Nikki. There was something else that had just occurred to him, something he needed to do right now.

He was on his way out the door when the phone rang. It was Laura Merriam.

"Hi, Laura. What's doing?" Greg wasn't sure in what direction his relationship with their attractive, unmarried neighbor was moving, and was even less sure about his preferences in the matter. He hadn't remained celibate since his wife's death six years earlier, but neither had he ever wished for another close relationship.

"Oh, nothing much. I was wondering if you'd seen Gingham."

"Gingham? Your cat?"

"Got it in one. Seriously, is he hanging around there looking for a handout? He went outside yesterday afternoon and never came back."

"Has he been fixed?"

"No, I've been meaning to but I just never got around to it."

"Well then, he's probably out having a very good time. He'll come back when enough of his libido has been drained away."

Greg parked in the small lot behind the Managansett Police Station and walked into the lobby. The desk sergeant glanced up incuriously. "Can I help you, sir?"

"Is Chief Dowdell in?"

"Yes, he is, but he's quite busy today. Can someone else help you?"

"Would you just tell him that Greg Clark is here and would like a moment of his time if possible?. It's personal."

Five minutes later, he was sitting in a small office whose walls were completely covered by layers of paperwork, wanted notices, circulars, correspondence, even advertisements.

"Never had much use for filing cabinets. Out of sight, out of mind, I always say. What can I do for you, Greg?"

Greg's late father had been Dowdell's college roommate, and the two men had remained close friends up until the elder Clark died of leukemia in 1980. It was Dowdell who first told Greg about the abundance of natural clay in the area, and although the two men spoke only once or twice a year, they considered themselves friends.

"You know I live out near the cemetery?"

"Sure do. I know where pretty much everyone lives in this town. Know about your late night requisitioning habits too." He winked.

"I understand there's been some trouble out there lately. Gravestones overturned, things like that. I was wondering if there was any, well, danger I should be aware of. Nikki wanders around there on her own sometimes."

Dowdell shrugged. "The world seems a lot less safe a place these days, although statistically I guess we're no worse off than our grandparents. If you're asking me if you should keep her out of the graveyard, I'd say no, she's as safe there as anywhere during the day. After dark, well, that's another story. You might bear that in mind yourself as well."

"What exactly is going on out there?"

Dowdell shifted his weight. "I don't exactly know. Lots of disturbed graves, but no real damage. The bodies aren't being stolen. No one's spray painting obscenities on the burial vaults, and as far as we can tell they're not smoking pot behind the mausoleum any more. But there's lots of little things. Like all the dead birds..."

Greg raised an eyebrow.

"Yeah, dead birds. I even sent one over to a vet to check out but he couldn't find anything. And some of the neighborhood pets have died as well. I thought this all ended back ten years ago."

"Ended? You mean this has happened before?"

Dowdell nodded. "It's bad ground, according to the town records. That's the exact phrase, 'bad ground'. There used to be a farmhouse there, young couple just starting out, but they both died within a month of one another. The next owner kept losing livestock and moved out less than a year after buying the place. About a dozen other people tried to use the land before they all just gave up and the town took over the land to use as a cemetery."

"Have you tried the EPA? Maybe there's some kind of toxic chemical in the soil."

"Had some fellas from Brown University up here a few years ago. They couldn't find anything, and one of them had a stroke and died while he was walking around the graveyard. I'm not a superstitious man, Greg, but I'm not a stupid one either. I stay away from there, and suggest you do the same."

He spent the afternoon in the town library, but other than confirming what Dowdell had told him, he learned nothing new. It was late afternoon by the time he started home, and when he had parked in the driveway, he walked next door, wondering if there was some way he could bring up the subject without having Laura Merriam decide he had a screw loose. But he was spared solving the problem because no one answered the door. Her car was in the garage so apparently she'd gone for another of her frequent walks, probably searching for the elusive Gingham.

He unlocked the studio door and stepped inside, then gasped. Even from a distance, he could see the changes in the bust. The eyes were darker and more menacing than ever, the cheeks so sunken they seemed cadaverous, and the hair had flared wide into a mantle around the head. But most obvious of all was the mouth, because the two discontinuities at either side had altered more radically. Two indistinct but easily identifiable fangs protruded from the clay.

Greg stepped outside, closed the door, and locked it with shaking hands.

"Nikki? Are you in there?"

Her door was closed but not locked. He turned the handle, hesitated, then opened the door. There was chaos inside, but it was familiar chaos, film magazines, CD's, junk food bags, discarded clothing, the familiar debris of a teenager's life. The bed was unmade and empty, though cluttered with stuffed animals.

The pond! She'd said something about going down to sunbathe by the pond. Greg half ran from the house, trying to remember exactly how to get there. It was somewhere beyond the maze of gardens gone wild behind the Sheffield Library, he remembered. There was an access road somewhere, but he'd be better off traveling by foot.

He ran most of the way.

It was nearly dusk when he returned to the house. There'd been a handful of teenagers at the pond, and they'd been sulky and resentful of his intrusion. They admitted knowing Nikki by sight but insisted she hadn't been there.

The house was quiet.

Greg stripped off his dripping shirt and dried himself with a towel, then went to the kitchen for a beer only to discover that he'd finished the last. Frustrated, he grabbed a glass and ran cold water at the sink, grunting with annoyance when the water backed up from the drain. Something must be clogging the garbage disposal. He leaned close, got a whiff of the familiar coppery smell.

There was a muffled thump from the studio.

He used the key to unlock the door, moving as silently as possible, then edged it open. Nothing seemed to have been disturbed, but the wheelbarrow had been drawn up much closer to the workbench. Someone had been inside.

Greg opened the door all the way and stepped across the hearth. There was a sound to his right. He turned, started to raise an arm as the shovel sped toward the side of his head, but he was much too late.

"I'm sorry, Daddy. But I was afraid you'd stop me before I was done."

Greg blinked, trying to bring the room into focus. His body felt wrong, uncomfortable, but it was a few seconds before he realized why. He'd been tied into a chair.

"Nikki? What the hell? Let me out of this." He twisted and turned but the rope held him easily.

His daughter was awake this time, and to his relief, fully clothed. But her eyes were unusually animated, almost feverish, and she wouldn't meet his gaze, instead kept glancing around the room.

"I think I know how you feel now, you know? I mean, when you talk all the time about having something really important to do with your life, and getting lost in your work, and really, like, putting your heart into what you do. I know I kind of messed up what you were planning, but it was important, you know, and like I think made something real, didn't I?"

She turned to face the sculpture, and Greg followed her eyes. And gasped. Twice, in fact. First he was shocked by the latest alteration in the bust. All of the fine detail work he had expected to do over a period of weeks seemed to have been accomplished in a single day. The bust was finished except for the glazing and firing. The subject matter might not be the most pleasant, for the beast man was even more menacing than before, but there was no question that someone -- Nikki? -- had turned his rough work into a masterpiece.

That was the first gasp. The second was because he saw what Nikki had been doing all day. Judging by the size of the new sculpture, she'd brought at least four wheelbarrows of fresh clay up from the cemetery. The legs were massive columns, the powerful arms and hands were tipped with clawlike nails, and the chest was broad and full. The figure lacked head and shoulders, of course, because those had already been done.

"What...?"

Nikki ignored him. "The blood was the secret, you know. I couldn't figure out what I was doing wrong until I cut myself with the trowel and bled a little. The clay works a lot easier when you mix some of it in. I'm really sorry about Mrs. Merriam's cat, but I couldn't think of any other way to get some more right away and it needed to be done. There was just enough to finish the head."

"How did you do the body so quickly, Nikki?"

"Well," Nikki dropped her head, "I'm really sorry about that too."

That's when Greg noticed that there was someone tied in one of the other studio chairs, someone not moving. Laura Merriam.

Greg closed his eyes and struggled to remain calm. "Nikki, you have to untie me now. Your work is done."

"No. There's something missing still." She sounded suddenly like a little girl, petulant, frustrated, self concerned. "It's not, you know, complete? Remember how you told me you like to think you breathe life into your work? Well, I want to do the same thing, but I don't, like, know how. Help me, Daddy, please. Tell me what to do next."

"Honey, it looks fine to me. Maybe if I could look at it more closely? Why don't you just untie me..."

But Nikki was no longer listening. She was, in fact, shedding her clothing. Greg tried to look away, afraid to see, afraid not to.

Naked, she picked up a trowel, bent over the wheelbarrow, dipped into her last load of clay, then moved to face the statue.

Greg closed his eyes to hold back the tears he knew were coming, tried to ignore the sounds of his daughter making passionate love to a body made of earth and blood.

The sounds stopped and he opened his eyes.

Nikki had fallen away from the statue, lay on the studio floor staring sightlessly up at the ceiling. The left side of her chest was a ruin from which the blood was still spurting. Greg's immediate feeling of great loss was subsumed by absolute terror when he noticed that bust and body were no longer separate, that the thing he and his daughter had made together was now whole.

It stood up, its dark, striated body naked but no longer made of simple clay. Absently it rubbed at its own chest, where a fresh wound was fading visibly.

"What?" Greg stared into that malevolent face, not expecting an answer, but just before those now too solid fangs tore the life from his body, he had an answer.

"Nikki finally found something she could put her heart into," it said.

REVERTS

Eric Nicholson was a very troubled boy. All the signs were there, some of them pretty obvious, but no one noticed, or wanted to notice, or did anything about it if they did notice. His parents were caught up in their own concerns, both busy professionals who admitted to their friends that they hadn't really planned to have children, but wasn't it nice that Eric turned out to be such a brilliant student. He was in fact extremely intelligent, an avid learner, and perhaps that explains why none of his teachers ever sounded the alarm. After all, he always did his assignments, never caused disturbances, never talked back. He was just shy, not antisocial.

Eric had no friends except for Natalie, but he didn't even meet her until he entered high school. He spent most of his time alone, either studying in the library, wandering around the town of Managansett, or amusing himself alone at home. His parents worked long hours and were sometimes gone overnight. They hadn't used a babysitter since his infancy since he was "so responsible" that he could certainly take care of himself. He was also allowed to choose his own clothing, which was almost always black, although he couldn't be described as a goth by any stretch of the imagination. Eric wore gloves constantly, even during the summer, and didn't like to be touched by other people. Gym class was the closest he ever came to being troublesome at school, but Mr. Nelson, the gym teacher, simply made allowances for his peculiarities and the other boys accommodated him. Eric was so weird that it was unusual for anyone to try to bully him; it was as though they sensed something seething under the surface, something unpleasant.

It is possible that the situation might have changed when Eric was ten years old. Mrs. Wellstone caught him torturing a cat in the woods behind her house one day. Unfortunately, she was so shocked that she never spoke of it, although she occasionally told her neighbors that there was "something wrong" with the Nicholson boy. Word might have gotten back to Eric's parents, but the Nicholsons had no more time to socialize with their neighbors than they did with their son, and James might not even have considered such behavior undesirable. He was an odd duck himself. Mrs. Wellstone decided that it was an isolated incident, or at least she convinced herself that that is what she had decided. If she had spent more time in the woods, poking around with a shovel, she might have found one or more of the several dozen dead and mutilated animals buried behind her property.

During seventh grade there were a few minor incidents with other children that might also have raised a flag, if anyone had been paying attention. Eric suddenly became more gregarious, but not with children his own age. Instead he concocted elaborate role playing games for the younger kids. Sometimes they didn't really understand the story lines Eric suggested – the Spanish Inquisition or Rasputin and the Tsars – but they were flattered that one of the older boys would spend so much time with them, and he was much better at creating scenarios involving pirates, headhunters, and gangsters than they were. If he was sometimes rougher than necessary, he always apologized afterwards, and no one ever thought twice about it until Dawn Grant ended up with a broken arm. The police asked some questions that time, and Eric was very apologetic about the "accident" and promised to be more careful in the future. And he was. He stopped playing with the younger children altogether.

Over the course of the next three years, Eric was one of the few unchanging elements in a constantly changing world. Oh, he grew a bit taller and leaner and his voice deepened, but he still dressed much the same as he always had, dark clothes and white gloves, and he stayed at the top of his class academically. There were no fresh graves of missing pets behind Mrs. Wellstone's house, but only because he had found a new burial ground just off Reservoir Road. His parents spoke proudly of his accomplishments, when they remembered to speak of him at all.

Natalie Granger and her family moved to Managansett during the summer preceding Eric's junior year. She lived only a few houses away, but they never actually saw one another until school started in the fall. Not only was she in several of his classes, but she quickly distinguished herself as a brilliant, though quiet student. Comparisons between her and Eric were inevitable and that focused attention on the two of them that neither welcomed. Eric had become tall and slim and his features might have been called handsome if he'd changed his hairstyle, dressed more thoughtfully, and wiped the perpetually sullen expression from his face. Natalie was considerably shorter and just the slightest bit too heavy for her frame. She would never have been called beautiful, but she dressed well and her aloof attitude imbued her with an aura of mystery and desirability.

Lots of boys asked her out on dates. She turned them all down.

Others may have believed there existed an academic rivalry between Eric and Natalie, but there was never any sign that either of the teenagers shared this perception. It is not clear that they ever even spoke to one another that fall or winter, although the following spring was another matter entirely. That was when the world changed for Eric Nicholson.

Over the years Eric had refined his technique with animals many times. He was now able to prolong their suffering for as long as he desired using techniques which we need not discuss here. Suffice it to say that his study of anatomy had been rigorous. He knew where he could inflict intense pain without causing rapid death, how to identify and stimulate the nerves without destroying the surrounding tissue. He had also become adept at luring family pets away from safety by means of raw meat and other enticements, and how to do so without being observed.

Eric's favorite killing ground was near the reservoir, where a scattering of failed farms had left the landscape sprinkled with abandoned buildings in various stages of disrepair. In the basement of one tumbledown farmhouse, Eric had built a workshop. There were several makeshift cages of various sizes, and rusting cabinets were filled with a diverse collection of restraints, ropes, chains, gags, as well as more sophisticated tools including knives, hammers, spikes, vices, bottles of acid mostly purloined from the school science lab, lye taken from his parents' house, even a small battery powered generator fitted with clamps and probes.

One Saturday morning, Eric indulged himself by inflicting the last stage of pain on Ted Murphy's beagle. He found the experience rather disappointing because the dog was too weak from the previous day's exertions to display much reaction. Frustrated, Eric had finally used a razor to slit the unresisting animal's throat. It was only then that he realized he was not alone.

Somehow Natalie Granger had entered his hideaway without making any sound that might have announced her presence. She was standing only a few feet away, watching Eric with a very strange expression on her face. Their eyes met and Eric felt a sudden chill of fear that made him tremble violently. He had been so careful and now everything was in jeopardy. He had no idea what to do, what to say, how to repair the situation. Natalie nodded slightly, to herself rather than to Eric, turned and disappeared as soundlessly as she had arrived.

Eric staggered back and sat down on a rotting bench. It was a cool morning but he was drenched with perspiration and his hands were shaking. His stomach churned and he had to fight down the urge to vomit. He sat there for the next hour, then rose and shakily made his way home. His parents were away, which was fortunate because even they would have noticed the change in their son. Eric went to his room and fell on the bed and didn't move for the next twelve hours.

When nothing had happened by the following morning, he felt slightly better, but as Sunday passed into history his sense of dread returned. Even if Natalie had kept what she'd seen to herself, how could he face her? How could he share a school room with her, knowing that she held this terrible secret over his head? Eric relished the power he had over the lives he extinguished. How could he tolerate finding himself similarly impotent?

His parents greeted Eric through the closed door of his room that evening and then went about their own affairs, never suspecting that a crisis was brewing only a few feet away. Eric spent a sleepless night and almost asked his parents to call the school and excuse him as too sick to attend, but he was intelligent enough to know that this would only delay the inevitable. So he dressed as he always did, double checked to ensure that he'd completed all of his homework assignments, and started the half mile walk to Managansett High School.

Their first class together was American History. Eric entered the room cautiously and looked around. There was no sign of Natalie. He didn't know whether to feel relieved or to regret that the confrontation was to be delayed again. He was still standing in the classroom doorway, trying to gather himself together, when someone jostled him slightly from behind. Eric hated being touched, even inadvertently and impersonally, and he turned and stepped back instinctively.

It was Natalie. She stared directly at him, smiling slightly, then winked conspiratorially and walked past him and over to her seat. Eric stood frozen, shaken, until he realized that it was going to be all right after all. She wasn't going to tell on him. He still wasn't happy that she knew his secret because it gave her leverage, but at least the world wasn't going to end. Not yet.

He took his seat and, if anyone had been looking, they would have been startled to see that Eric Nicholson was smiling, if somewhat tentatively.

Eric was nothing if not cautious. He didn't return to his workshop for two weeks, although he did scout around for new subjects. The frequent disappearance of household pets in Managansett was usually blamed on the red foxes and coyotes occasionally seen in the woods surrounding the reservoir, and most families who still had pets kept them indoors or chained in their yards. Eric had released one chained mongrel, but decided it was too risky to repeat. There was, however, a high degree of turnover in the newer neighborhoods south of Main Street, and there were always a few families who had yet to learn of the high pet mortality rate, or who just didn't care.

When he found a tabby hunting in a small woodlot, Eric had acted instinctively. He always kept a bag of catnip in one of his pockets and that had sufficed to lure the animal close. A quick blow at the base of the skull stunned the animal, a skill he had practiced to perfection, and he walked briskly to the workshop with the unconscious animal concealed inside his jacket. It started to recover just before he arrived, and he hastily locked it in one of the cages.

"I wondered when you'd come back here."

Eric spun around, face white, and saw Natalie emerge from the adjoining room. "I wasted two Saturdays sitting here reading."

His mouth opened and he tried to say something, but he'd never had a talent for conversation even under less strained circumstances. Natalie laughed at him, amused by his distress. "Relax, Eric. I just came to watch. I like your style."

It was a match made in Hell.

Although it would probably be inaccurate to describe the relationship that developed between Eric and Natalie friendship, it was certainly an alliance of similar interests. They paid several visits to the workshop during the balance of the spring and the early part of the summer, so many in fact that the simmering awareness in Managansett at large bubbled up into active concern. By early August, they reluctantly decided to go on hiatus. There were too many eyes watching the town's animal population. Throughout their joint endeavors, it had always been Eric who did the actual work. Natalie was the passive observer who never actually inflicted any pain.

She was also the one who suggested that they aspire to higher things.

"Did you ever think we might lure some kid up here?"

Eric was shocked and titillated at the same time. He had fantasized along those very lines, but never seriously considered translating them into reality. "Are you crazy? We can't kill anyone."

"Who said anything about killing? We could just, you know, hurt them a little. Scare them."

Eric shook his head. "I don't know. They'd go home and tell their parents and then we'd be in deep shit."

Natalie laughed softly. "Well, we'd have to disguise ourselves, of course. And we couldn't let them know where we'd taken them. Maybe we could say it was a game, blindfold them and take them to the secret room. Or we could go someplace else if you know somewhere safe."

Eric was reluctant, not because he cared about some sniveling little kid, but because he was terrified of being found out. Natalie didn't press the issue, but she hinted about it over the course of the next few weeks, and by the end of August, Eric was so frustrated by the continued vigilance of the townspeople for their pets that he was more than usually amenable to suggestion.

"All right, let's do it."

It wasn't as hard as Eric had expected, at least initially. They took turns hanging around the playground near the elementary school. Eric wasn't fussy about whether they took a boy or a girl, but he wanted one whom he could easily subdue physically. They finally decided on Lisa Willard because she often took a short cut home through the woods behind the Sheffield Library. The first time they tried to intercept her, they were frightened off by the presence of two high school jocks drinking beer nearby. The second time, there was no one around.

Natalie had created their disguises. Her long red hair was tied up in a bun and concealed under a slouch hat. She wore dark glasses, had painted a false moustache on her upper lip, and was wearing one of her father's ankle length coats and a pair of her brother's boots. Eric had not wanted to give up his own dark clothing, but Natalie had insisted. He had rubber inserts in his cheeks to fill his face out, which he hated because they felt funny in his mouth. She'd given him a stocking cap and a fake ponytail and an old sweatshirt she'd stolen from someone's laundry line. Eric had insisted on wearing gloves, but she'd substituted leather ones for his usual pair.

Unfortunately, their disguises gave them such a sinister appearance that twelve year old Lisa Willard refused flatly to go anywhere with them. Instead, she tried to run past Eric, who instinctively grabbed her by the wrist. She screamed at him and tried to pull free and Eric's emotions got the better of him. He tried to twist her arm behind her back but she was stronger than he expected, pulled him off balance, and he fell, taking her down with him.

He heard her arm snap and then she was screaming. All he could think of was to shut her up so that they wouldn't be discovered, and he pressed her face down into the dirt and leaves and held her there until she was quiet. And motionless.

"Well, that didn't go the way we planned it." Natalie's words were casual but her tone was not. Her voice was husky and excited.

Eric got to his feet, tried to make an inarticulate apology, or at least an explanation, but Natalie told him to shut up. "We have to get out of here. If anyone asks, we were together studying at your house, right?"

He nodded.

That evening, Eric couldn't sleep. His thoughts were mixed. On the one hand, his memory of that moment when he was crushing the life from Lisa Willard was exquisitely pleasurable. On the other, the possibility that they might be discovered was terrifying. Pleasure has a way of cooling with time. Terror enjoys much greater longevity. By the small hours of the morning, Eric couldn't lie still. He paced his room in a cold sweat. The possibility that they'd left behind some clue to their identity grew from a worry to a conviction. In dismay, he closed his eyes, clenched his fists, and wished fervently, with all of his being, that they had never followed the girl into the woods, that they'd stayed at his house and finished studying for the biology exam instead. He fell asleep with that thought in mind, or at least that's what he thought happened.

"Are you all right, Eric?"

He opened his eyes. It was daylight. He was dressed. He was also sitting in his own living room with a biology book on the table in front of him. Just beyond, Natalie Granger sat in an armchair with her loose-leaf binder open in her lap.

"What?" It was all he could manage.

"You spaced out for a minute there. Are you okay? I want to finish this chapter up and go home. It's getting late."

Disoriented, Eric looked around the room. "What time is it?"

"It's almost four o'clock. Do you want to take a break or what?"

"I don't know." He shook his head. "I was thinking about, you know, what we did in the woods."

Natalie frowned. "I don't understand. What are you talking about?"

Eric felt a rush of anger. "I'm talking about Lisa Willard."

"Who's Lisa Willard? I never heard of her."

For the next couple of days, Eric walked around in a daze. Sometimes he thought that he'd imagined the entire incident. Lisa Willard was alive and well and Natalie appeared to have no memory of accosting her, although she still spoke about the possibility of abducting someone. Eric became very distressed whenever she raised the subject and her enthusiasm subsided. At first he thought he'd dreamed the whole thing, but as the days passed, Eric began to wonder if something very strange and wonderful had happened.

He decided to put it to the test. At first he planned to do so in isolation, but he changed his mind. For one thing, he'd come to rely on Natalie's presence. His activities were so much more rewarding when there was a witness, someone to share in his triumph and power. For another, he hoped that she would somehow provide verification that he wasn't just losing his mind.

One Wednesday night, he called Natalie and asked her to meet him downtown. She arrived, frankly puzzled, but he just told her to stay close to him. He waited until there was no traffic, then took the broken brick he'd concealed in his pocket and threw it hard at the front window of Mason's Hardware Store. The glass shattered spectacularly and an alarm began to sound so quickly that Eric was momentarily frozen. Then he started running along Main Street with Natalie following in his wake.

They hid in the shrubbery around the library and watched the flashing lights arrive.

"Why in the world did you do that?" Natalie's whisper sounded more exasperated than horrified.

"Wait." He closed his eyes, clenched his fists, and wished with all his might that he'd never thrown the brick. He opened his eyes. Nothing had changed. He felt a moment of panic, clenched his eyelids shut again, and repeated the process.

This time when he looked around, he and Natalie were standing in front of the hardware store, its window intact. Natalie gave him a puzzled look. "So why did you want me to meet you here in the middle of the night?"

Over the course of the next three months, Managansett was subjected to a reign of terror that never penetrated the public consciousness because, in a sense, it never happened at all. Eric and Natalie would indulge their dark desires, after which Eric would wish that things would revert to a safe moment before they did anything for which they could be punished. This gave them an additional advantage since they could prey on favored victims multiple times. He would have preferred it if Natalie had been able to retain her memories of their experiences, but at least he had her approving company during the many reverted escapades. Sometimes the reversion happened as soon as he wished for it, sometimes there was a slight delay, but time always snapped back to a point before they had committed themselves to whatever act of cruelty they had planned. Natalie looked at him strangely a few times, but if she was disappointed by his sudden apparent unwillingness to play their game to the fullest, she never mentioned it.

He became increasingly inventive and daring. More than a dozen children and half as many adults had died under his hands, some more than once, only to be restored when he was ready to resurrect them. Although Natalie was sometimes daunted by his audacious plans, she had never refused to accompany him and Eric was startled to realize one day that he could actually tolerate her touch, if only briefly, on his bare skin. They had never kissed, but they held hands from time to time, while their free hands were occupied with their victims. On three occasions they were arrested, but that no longer mattered. Eric simply reverted reality to a moment before their crimes had been consummated.

It was a wonderful time for Eric, until two problems started to interfere. One was inevitable. He was getting bored. His newfound ability meant that he didn't have to wait for a safe opportunity to strike. He could act whenever the impulse came to him, and never face any consequences. There was no challenge, no sense of danger. The second problem was even more troublesome. Natalie began hinting that she wanted a more physical relationship. She touched his hand constantly, even when they weren't indulging their dark desires, and when she leaned over to whisper suggestions, her lips brushed his ear or cheek and her color heightened. Eric was very fond of Natalie, but there were limits beyond which he would not proceed. The flesh was a dirty, perverse thing and that was why he so thoroughly enjoyed its mutilation and destruction. He had thought Natalie shared his superiority to physical urges, but apparently he'd been wrong. She was not as strong as he'd thought her to be.

Eric tried to make it clear to Natalie that he wasn't interested but she persisted. Eventually he decided that she'd have to be taken out of the picture, suffer a fatal accident. There would, of course, be no point in arranging her death if he reverted reality afterward. He would miss her, but she had really left him no choice. Once the decision was made, he discovered that he was looking forward to it. She had always been the junior partner, but she had shared his power over others. Once she was gone, it would be his and his alone.

He planned things very carefully. It would have to be in the deserted farmhouse, of course, the place where they had met. It seemed fitting to him. He had ordered handcuffs through a mail order catalog so that was all right, and most of the tools he'd need were already out there. There was also an old well on the property that they'd uncovered in order to quickly dispose of the animals they'd killed, back when animals were still sufficiently exciting.

Luring her out there was not a problem either. She agreed to his suggestion without the slightest hesitation. Eric wasn't at all concerned that she'd tell anyone where she was going. Their visits had always been intensely private affairs, just for the two of them. Overpowering her was another matter entirely. Although he was taller than she was, Natalie was at least as heavy and every bit as strong. On those occasions when it had been necessary to physically subdue their victims, she had always taken charge. He could stab her unexpectedly, of course, but he didn't want her to be seriously injured beforehand. Natalie might even appreciate his concern that her ordeal be as protracted as possible. So her stole some of his mother's sleeping tablets and dissolved them in a travel mug of coffee. Natalie really liked coffee and he'd brought some several times in the past.

She thanked him for the coffee, remarked that it tasted a little funny, but showed no sign of alarm. By the time they reached their destination, she was unsteady on her feet. "Are you all right? You look sick?" Eric's heart was racing with excitement.

"Kind of dizzy. I just need to sit down for a minute." In less than a minute, she was unconscious.

Eric used the handcuffs to secure her to one of the support beams and tied her ankles with rope. He readied his tools, planning his campaign in detail, waiting for the drug to wear off.

It took a lot longer than he expected. She didn't open her eyes until it was almost dark outside. At first she seemed puzzled rather than alarmed when she found herself bound to the post. Then she finally realized the truth, turned and looked directly at him. "Eric! I thought we were friends!"

Eric sighed, not insincerely. "We are. I wouldn't do this if I didn't think it was necessary. You'd understand if you were in my place."

"I certainly would." And she smiled.

Eric picked up a knife and weighed it in his hand. And suddenly it was an empty coffee mug that he was holding and it was full daylight again. He blinked in confusion and his head began to spin. When he turned to look around, his knees felt wobbly and he stumbled.

"How are you feeling, Eric?" Natalie was leaning against a tree. Eric recognized the tree. They were about halfway between his house and their hideaway.

"Dizzy." It was an effort to speak, an insurmountable effort to understand.

"You should be. Before I switched mugs, I added a little something of my own. Shame on you, Eric."

He shook his head, but the buzzing behind his eyes refused to go away. "Don't...understand."

Natalie laughed. "It's really very simple. You thought you were responsible for the reverts, but it wasn't you at all. I let you think you had the power because I knew you wanted to feel as though you were in charge. I liked you. It was my gift to you. But then you had to go and spoil it all."

Eric wanted to protest, insist that he really was the one in charge, that the world revolved around him, but he had trouble organizing his thoughts, keeping his eyes open, standing upright, thinking at all. His eyes closed and he couldn't open them.

When he woke up, he was in the farmhouse basement, wrists cuffed to the post, ankles tied although she'd spread his legs apart rather than tied them together. He was also naked.

So was Natalie. "I thought about it and decided that this was probably the worst thing I could possibly do to you. And it's going to be a lot of fun."

She touched his body with her hands, and then her mouth, and later with what Eric thought of as her dirty parts. She made his body do horrible things that revolted him so much that he vomited repeatedly. He felt despoiled, humiliated, and horrified. Even when she finally stopped, moved away and put her clothing back on, there was no sense of relief.

And then she picked up one of his knives and introduced him to an entirely different world of sensation.

Natalie disposed of Eric's body in the well and then covered it over. For a while she had considered reverting things so that she could do it all again, but her existing memory was so exquisite, so pleasurable that she decided there was no room for improvement. It was, after all, a perfect ending.

THE GUARD TOWER

PFC Carl Gallegher began setting up the M60 machine gun and arranging the ammunition cans on the top level of the guard post while the other two men assigned to this station for the evening stowed their sleeping gear in the hollow base of the tower below his feet. With less than two months service in Vietnam, Carl was almost always the least senior member of any guard complement when he drew the duty, so he'd had considerable practice arranging everything so that, in the unlikely event of an inspection by the Sergeant of the Guard, they would not be gigged and draw extra duty the following day.

Corporal Martin "Maggot" Michaelson's head appeared at the top of the ladder and he pulled himself easily up into the upper level of the tower, glancing quickly around to make certain Gallegher had done everything necessary. He carried his M16 rifle casually, wrapped in clear plastic to protect it from sand and dust. The weapon was extraordinarily difficult to keep clean and although it was technically against regulations to have it covered while on duty, most officers tended to look the other way under the circumstances. "Good job," Michaelson assured the younger man, and Gallegher found himself glowing under that momentary praise. At the same time, he chided himself inwardly for valuing Maggot's opinion. He despised the foul mouthed, uncouth and sarcastic Michaelson, who seemed to enjoy himself most when those around him were discomfited.

"What shift am I taking?"

First shift was the best, from dusk until about 10:00. The remaining two ran four hours each, and the middle was the worst, too early to sleep well beforehand, and the four hours that followed insufficient for a real rest.

"What do you think, nubie?" Michaelson walked over to stare out through the narrow slit toward the beach and the South China Sea. Gallegher had stopped resenting the derogatory term for a new arrival in the country, but felt that by now he should have outgrown the term. Several hundred yards to their extreme right was a small ARVN camp, known to the stateside contingent as the "toy soldiers", and beyond that the thatched roofs of the village of Phu Hiep. "The Chief has the first and I'll take dead man. You get your choice of what's left." He snickered in a moist sort of way that Gallegher found repulsive.

Michaelson crossed to the field phone, lifted the receiver, and wound it up. After a few seconds, he apparently heard a response from the other end, because he identified himself and the guardpost number. He made an unpleasant face a moment later, then replaced the receiver. "Goddamned lifer," he said softly, and Gallegher did not feel inclined to ask what had happened.

"Why don't the ARVN's have guard towers?" Gallegher chose to ignore the problem and change the subject. "They don't have anything but a fence facing the ocean."

Maggot spat out into the darkness once again. "That advisor character told the Captain the beach was sacred." The contempt in the man's tone left no room for doubt about his own opinion. "He claims there's no reason for us to worry, that the Cong wouldn't hit us from this side because they honor the old religion. Stupid shit; he's probably one of them himself, wanting us to be blind on one side."

Another head popped up from below, glanced around with an intent look that Gallegher never ceased to find disconcerting. Corporal Arthur "The Chief" Stone did not at first appear particularly prepossessing, a diminutive body, underweight, almost gaunt, large ears framing an angular face, deep set eyes that never remained still. "The Chief" would probably not even have been allowed to enlist in happier times; his leanness was nearly anorexic, and his personality was extreme even measured against the rather liberal standards of behavior that were c onsidered acceptable in this particular theatre of war.

Gallegher stepped back and away, one hand partly raised in an unconscious warding motion.

"What's up, Chief?" Maggot leaned out through the slit in the wall and spat down onto the sand twenty feet below.

Stone climbed up slowly, his body awkward in appearance but his movements slow, powerful, certain. He scanned the small

enclosure with intent eyes, silent, face expressionless.
Apparently everything passed muster, because eventually he moved
quickly over to the front wall of the guard tower and looked out
over the beach.

"Soft duty, Chief." Maggot scratched at his crotch with one
hand while undoing the buttons of his fatigue shirt with the
other. "Watching a goddamned beach, no less."

"They could come in by boat, I suppose." Gallegher didn't
believe he had had the temerity to speak, but the words were
undeniably his.

The Chief gave him a contemptuous glance. "What do you
think, a goddamned sampan assault? Shit. Goddamned nubies
playing soldier."

Stone was back down the ladder almost before Gallegher had
time to register the insult. Michaelson was laughing. "Don't
piss your pants, kid. The Chief's that way all the time. He's
only friendly when he's shooting something, or someone."

Gallegher attempted a comradely smile, wasn't certain how
well it came out. Secretly he loathed and feared both men.
Maggot was a farm boy and The Chief came from some place in
New
York City, the Bronx if he remembered correctly. Both were short
timers by now, with less than a month left in Nam before they
were rotated stateside, although rumor had it The Chief had
already agreed to re-up for another tour. Gallegher came from an
upper middle class family in Managansett, Rhode Island, and had
never realized how sheltered a life he had led until exposed to
the bewildering variety of personalities to be found in an
infantry unit.

Michaelson pushed away from the side of the guard tower.
"Stay here for a minute, will you. I need to take a piss before
I settle down for the night."

"Sure, Michaelson." Gallagher had never been able to work
up the courage to call the other by his nickname. Almost
everyone in the unit had one; it seemed to be a kind of badge of
honor. He had inquired about the origins of some of them, but
when he learned that Stone had acquired his nickname after
reportedly scalping a corpse while he was assigned to short range
reconnaissance, he had stopped asking. Certainly there was no

way he was going to ask "Maggot" Michaelson how he had picked up
that label. He was afraid he might not find the answer
palatable. The truth was that Michaelson had a famous appetite
and was a consummate expert at scrounging food. Someone had
commented once that he was like a maggot; leave some food around
and sooner or later he'll show up, and the name had stuck.

Gallegher walked past the machine gun mount and over to one
side wall, looking out across the silent, dimly lighted
Vietnamese Army post. There was activity in the small fishing
village beyond, a bonfire of some sort in the central square, but
it was too distant for him to see clearly. The Vietnamese
fascinated him, and he had hoped to learn something of their culture
while he was stationed in Southeast Asia, but the Army
discouraged much contact with the locals, and the "hoochmaids",
hired from the village to do most of the cleaning, laundry, and
cooking duties, spoke very little English.

Michaelson emerged from the base of the tower and walked out
toward the beach, clearly visible in the cone of illumination
cast by one of the floodlights mounted along the perimeter. He
slipped through the fence and kept going across the sand. It was
against the rules to do so; guards were required to stay within
ten yards of their posts, and the beach was a free fire zone,
strictly off limits at all times. But Gallegher wasn't about to
point this out to the other man. A few seconds later, Michaelson
stopped, and Gallegher could soon hear the faint hiss as a stream
of urine sparkled in the floodlight. Embarassed, he looked away.

The reflection of the moon in the ocean, bordered by the
band of white sand, was unusually symmetrical this evening, and
Gallegher could not help noting the beauty and peacefulness of
the scene. It was hard to believe that he was in the middle of a
war. In the darkness, the hillside at the far end of the camp
was invisible and it was impossible to see the few blasted stumps
of trees that were all that remained for as far as the eye could
see. The area was kept defoliated so that no one could sneak up
under cover and infiltrate the base.

Michaelson had apparently finished, because when Gallegher looked back in his direction, the man was nowhere to be seen, and a few seconds later he had climbed back up into the guard post.

"Cold tonight," he muttered.

"Yeah," Gallegher agreed. It was funny, he thought. The temperature at night never dropped below seventy degrees, but that was such a change from the day that he still shivered unless wrapped in a blanket or sleeping bag. "Is it winter or summer here?"

"Who the fuck knows?" Michaelson slipped a transistor radio out of his pocket and turned it on. Tinny rock music filled the night. "Hey nubie," he said more loudly. "You're the one pissed on the side of the tower last time, aren't you?"

Gallegher nodded. "You don't have to tell me again."

"Well I'm telling you again anyway. You don't piss anywhere near the fucking tower, understand? Having to sleep in this stinking country is bad enough already without adding to it."

"All right. I know." Gallegher allowed himself to sound annoyed, unwilling to be further humiliated. "I'll walk up the road a ways if I have to."

Michaelson's face broke into an amused grin. "Might as well use the goddamned sacred beach. It's not worth shit else." Many of the enlisted men were particularly aggrieved that they were not allowed to swim from the beach during their off duty hours, and the only other section of usable coast in the area was that adjoining the village, where the fishermen had pulled their boats up onto shore for the night, and most of the camp personnel were not allowed in the village under any circumstances.

"It's not very private with all that light. Someone might report us for being out there. The Vietnamese do consider it forbidden ground, you know. You could have gotten us into a lot of trouble." Gallegher meant this as a gentle admonition, but Michaelson took immediate offense. He refrained from adding his personal opinion that any act of disrespect toward religion automatically provoked retribution. His strict Calvinist religious background portrayed the universe as a great clock, with balance coming to all things in their time.

"Don't pull that righteous crap on me, nubie! Who cares what the goddamned gooks think? They can't even run their own country, they have to have us come in and fight their fucking war for them, and then they tell us we can't even use their shitty beach! Well, piss on it, nubie, and piss on them, and piss on you too if you don't like it!"

Gallegher shrugged. So much for the social graces. He didn't feel the least bit sleepy, but there wasn't much else to do. He had brought a book for his shift even though he wasn't supposed to. No hostile action had ever taken place at Phu Hiep, and the four hour shift was lonely and endless with nothing to occupy his mind. Reading helped to make it more bearable, and he was willing to accept the risk. If the Sergeant of the Guard could sneak up on him before he had a chance to hide it, he probably deserved to be caught.

"I guess I'll turn in," he said, but Michaelson wasn't paying any attention. His head was jerking in small movements in time to the music, and he was tapping out some rhythm on the barrel of the M60. For one instant, Gallegher felt an overwhelming rush of rage at the man, but it passed quickly and he climbed down the ladder, shaking with reaction.

Stone had already curled up in his sleeping bag, apparently unconscious. Some of the long timers seemed to be able to drop off to sleep at will, an ability that Gallegher envied. He knew from experience that it would be at least an hour before sleep claimed him, and that every time a jeep passed on the nearby company road, he'd wake up for a few seconds, trying to identify the sound.

Gallegher was very close to unconsciousness forty five minutes later when there was a stirring beside him. In the darkness, he could not see clearly, but Stone was obviously up and active. "What's going on?" he asked sleepily.

"None of your fucking business. Go back to sleep." But there was a flash from Stone's cigarette lighter as he rummaged in the small pack he had brought with him. In the glow, Gallegher could make out the roll of toilet paper that Stone habitually carried with him. No one ever said anything in front of him, but it was well known that Stone had a case of the G.I.'s, chronic diarrhea, which had not responded at all to treatment. Rumor had it that on one occasion he had stuck his rear out past the doorgunner on a chopper, although Gallegher had never met anyone who claimed to have actually witnessed this particular feat. But he wouldn't have put it past the man.

The flame went out and the dim light that seeped in around the tower entrance was momentarily occluded as Stone exited. Gallegher was suddenly aware of a need to relieve his own bladder and, fully awake once more, there seemed no better time than the present. Pulling on his boots, he crouched and stepped through the doorway.

It was completely silent outside except for the faint breaking of surf on the beach. There was even less light from the ARVN camp, and the bonfire in the village seemed to have been extinguished as well. Gallegher walked several yards down the road, looking for an appropriate place to pee, glancing around curiously, wondering where Stone had gotten to. Almost immediately he spotted the other figure, out beyond the barbed wire, squatting on the beach. Shaking his head resignedly, Gallegher contented himself with urinating on one of the posts that held the wire in place. One of these days, he was sure, Stone or Michaelson were going to get caught. Knowing his luck, Gallegher would probably be blamed right along with them.

Three hours later, he was shaken awake by a hand on his shoulder. "Hey, nubie. You're on in ten minutes. Get yourself together."

Gallegher muttered something unintelligible in reply, but climbed awkwardly out of his sleeping bag and began to dress. Michaelson had disappeared back up into the loft. Gallegher tied his bootlaces in the darkness, slow, deliberate movements as he sought to dismiss the fogginess of sleep. Pausing only long enough to find the M16 and his book in the darkness, he grabbed the ladder and climbed up into the relatively lighted tower. The single dim bulb really wasn't adequate for reading, but he had learned to make do, squinting at the tiny letters, on his previous shifts.

"I'm on," he said unnecessarily. "See you in the morning."

But Michaelson wasn't paying attention, was staring intently out toward the ocean. Mildly alarmed, Gallegher became more alert and crossed to stand beside the other man.

"Something moved out there." There was a tension in the voice that Gallegher had never heard before.

"Where?"

"Don't know exactly. Caught it out of the corner of my eye. Can't see it now, but I know something moved."

"One of the village dogs?"

"Maybe. Maybe not." Michaelson picked up his M16 and removed the dust cover. "They don't usually let them out at night."

"What're you going to do?" Gallegher was worried that the man intended to shoot out into the darkness. The regulations said that no one fired from a guard post until they had checked in with the Sergeant of the Guard on the field phone for clearance, but he knew that Michaelson had a rather cavalier attitude toward the regs.

Before Michaelson could answer, another voice interrupted. "What's up?" Stone had climbed silently up to join them, his own weapon already uncovered. He had not waited to put on his boots and Gallegher noted incongruously that both of the man's socks had holes in them.

"Something moved. Out on the beach. Can't see it now."

Stone sniffed. "Maybe we should send the nubie out for a look see."

Michaelson turned and regarded Gallegher thoughtfully, and the younger man felt as though he were being evaluated for sale. "No. He'd piss his pants if he ran into a Cong. I'll go."

"You're covered." Stone moved to man the machine gun while Michaelson clambered down the ladder.

"What do you want me to do?" Gallegher still suspected that Michaelson had imagined the movement, but he wasn't about to say so.

"Nothing. Just stand there. I'll tell you when to do something." Stone hadn't even looked in his direction. For once, his eyes were in complete control and he moved the barrel of the machine gun as Michaelson appeared below, slipping through the barbed wire. Stone kept the M60 aimed at a spot leading Michaelson by several feet as he moved out into the brilliant light.

"Shouldn't we call in to the Sergeant?"

"And tell him what, nubie? We don't want him out here unless we have to. He's probably sleeping on his desk right now with some PFC manning the phone. You want to wake him up?"

Gallegher subsided with a sigh. But he removed his own dustcover and checked to make certain his ammunition magazine was securely locked in place. Just in case.

Michaelson was now about thirty yards in front of them, right at the crest of the beach. He stopped, looking from side to side, then turned back toward the tower and shrugged elaborately. Stone swore under his breath, but he kept his hold on the M60. Gallegher watched as Michaelson glanced around once more, then down toward his feet. A few seconds later he squatted, extended his free hand toward the ground while the other supported the barrel of his M16.

They could not see clearly what happened next from that distance. Michaelson seemed to be patting his feet, ankles, and calves. His movements became more rapid and more violent until finally he came erect once more and turned toward them. He yelled something incoherent as he broke into a run, or as close to one as he could manage wearing combat boots in the soft beach sand.

"Go down and find out what's going on," ordered Stone and Gallegher moved to obey without hesitation. He had just stepped out of the tower base when Michaelson ran into him, still looking back over his shoulder.

"What's the matter?" Michaelson's face was obscured by the darkness and Gallegher could not see his expression, but the man was obvious agitated.

"Help me get the damned things off," he answered hoarsely, leaning down to brush at his legs once more.

"Get what off?" Gallegher looked around. "Move out into the light so I can see."

Surprisingly, Michaelson did as he was told without protest, and in the faint light, Gallegher could see that several small white bodies clung to Michaelson's pants legs, none more than two inches in diameter. "Sand crabs," he said softly. "You must have walked into a nest of them."

"I know what they are," Michaelson's voice was shrill with tension. "Help me get the damned things off."

Amused, but careful not to show it, Gallegher crouched and began picking the small bodies off and tossing them aside. They held on with surprising tenacity, but it was only a matter of a few seconds to detach the remaining few creatures. Michaelson was breathing heavily when they finished, and he kept turning about, searching his clothing and the nearby ground for any surviving sandcrabs.

"Maggot!" It was Stone calling from above. "Get your ass up here!"

With a last glance to each side, Michaelson rushed to comply, Gallegher only a few steps behind. When they joined Stone in the loft, he was traversing the machinegun back and forth along the line of the beach.

It was not necessary to explain why he had called them. Out in the overlapping circles of light, the entire surface of the beach was in movement. Gallegher stood there stupidly, his mouth open, as he watched the landscape churn about. There must have been thousands, perhaps millions, of sand crabs moving out in the night. He knew nothing about the creatures, but perhaps they periodically spawned or mated in unison; that was the only explanation he could think of.

Even as they watched, the far end of the lighted area settled back down. The locus of furious activity began to shrink visibly, and the formless alarm he had been feeling started to disappear. Michaelson, however, soon raised the emotional ante by whispering raggedly, "They're coming this way."

Sure enough, when Gallegher leaned out and looked down, he could see that the leading edge of the swarm of sand crabs had moved out of the light into the shadows that shrouded the base of their tower. They stood directly in the path of this migration, or whatever it was.

"They can't get up here," said Stone. "Get the gear and bring it up."

"No way!" Michaelson moved away from Stone. "I'm not going back down there until daylight."

"I'll get it," volunteered Gallegher, delighted to be in a position to show up the other man. "I'll throw it to you."

Stone nodded and turned to look back down toward the beach while Michaelson crouched at the top of the ladder. Gallegher descended to ground level, picked up all of the gear, tossing each piece in turn up through the hole cut in the ceiling, where Michaelson easily caught them and set them aside. The last things to go up were the sleeping bags, and it was as the last of them disappeared through the hole that the swarm of sand crabs lapped over the entranceway.

It was too dark to see them clearly, but there was a soft clicking of hard bodies crawling over one another that he found irrationally frightening. Gallegher almost jumped to the ladder, climbing up with unusual alacrity.

"They're inside," he said softly, and Michaelson nodded, his eyes bright in the subdued light. Gallegher was amazed to see how frightened the man really was; his whole body seemed to shake as he knelt beside the hole in the floor, staring down into the darkness.

"Can't see anything," he complained.

Stone fished in his pocket, pulled out the lighter. "Here, " he tossed it over. Michaelson caught it, flicked it on, and lowered it into the darkness.

Gallegher looked outside, but whatever movement there might have been around the base of the tower was concealed by the darkness. "They'll pass us in a few minutes," he predicted, but without any confidence that he was correct.

"Shit!" Michaelson jerked back from the ladder. "They're coming up."

Stone left his post, crossed the floor and took the lighter from Michaelson's hand. Gallegher joined the other two as Stone lowered the light to illuminate the room below. At the foot of the ladder, thousands of sand crabs had piled up, one on another, building a tower out of their own bodies. Already it was past the first rung of the ladder, braced against it, and climbing steadily.

"What're we going to do?" There was panic in Michaelson's voice now, and Gallegher noted the withering glance that Stone cast in his direction.

"Give me a hand with this, Gallegher." It was the first time Stone had used his name, and the first hint that the man was frightened himself. Gallegher brushed past Michaelson to where Stone was trying to pull the top of the ladder free. "If we knock this loose so it'll fall, they won't be able to get up here."

Gallegher nodded in agreement, but their combined efforts could not pull the nails free. Stone ignited the lighter again, and by its wan light they could see that the sand crabs were above the second rung now, still climbing. It was Gallegher who sat down first, bracing his back against the machine gun mount. He began kicking at the top left corner of the ladder, short, powerful blows designed to jerk the nail free. Stone joined him, concentrating on the other corner. They seemed to have been kicking endlessly with no result when finally Gallegher's corner came loose and, two kicks later, Stone's broke free as well. The ladder dropped out of sight with a muffled clatter.

Stone turned and his mouth curved into what might almost have been a smile. "That'll take care of them fuckers."

Gallegher smiled back, then turned to see what had happened to Michaelson. Maggot was crouched against the far wall, staring in their direction, apparently unable to accept that they had succeeded. He was locked in that pose when a wave of white bodies clambered up over the outer wall and into the loft of the guard tower.

It was never clear in Gallegher's memory after that just what happened. There was a lot of shouting and running around, and he remembered seeing Stone twisting from side to side, covered with small white bodies, thrashing about with his arms. Then he remembered Michaelson blundering into him from one side, his face bleeding, one small crab dangling ludicrously from a lock of his hair, and then his footing went out from under him and he fell through the hole into the darkness. And that was all he knew until he woke up in the medical section with a bandaged head sometime the following day.

There was an inquiry into the disappearance of Stone and Michaelson, and Gallegher was required to testify. He was ordered beforehand, however, to make no mention of his "hallucinations" about the sand crabs. The investigating officer made it clear that he thought at best that Gallegher's concussion had made it impossible for him to remember what had actually happened, and that it was far more likely that the images he insisted on recalling were probably drug related. Gallegher initially argued stubbornly that his memories were true, but soon realized that the Army really didn't want to know what had happened. They just wanted to file the case in some pre-existing niche and forget it.

So the two men were eventually listed as AWOL even though
all of their gear had been recovered and Gallegher was returned first to limited, then to full duty, but transferred to another unit. No attempt was made to explain the large amount of blood which apparently had been splashed around the inside of the guard tower, so much in fact that it had been torn down and replaced. As far as the Army was concerned, the case was closed pending further developments.

As for Gallegher, he was never able to face walking on a beach again. And his dreams would ever after be troubled by visions of countless small scurrying white bodies returning to their sandy home.

And the tiny, soft burdens that must have been clutched in their pincers.

FARM ON THE DOWN

Even as a very young child, Alan Weld knew there was something strange about his grandfather's farm. The whole world was full of mysteries at the time, so he underestimated just how out of the ordinary it really was, and if he ever mentioned its odd aspects to his friends at school, they probably assumed that he was telling tall stories.

Alan was a fearful child, undoubtedly influenced by his mother's fragile nerves. She was always afraid someone would break into the house, that a neighbor's dog would suddenly become rabid, that rats would find a way into their basement, or that she'd find a snake in the shrubbery. Her husband was patient with her, less so with Alan, and his furious reaction whenever his son displayed irrational fears of his own led to their suppression rather than dispersion.

The farm was on the north side of Managansett bordering Metkis Downs, a golf course and country club that foundered during the 1990s. Alan's family didn't visit there very often. His father and his grandfather had never gotten along and they went primarily out of a sense of duty to Grandma Emma, who suffered from lung cancer and rarely left her bedroom during the years that Alan knew her. He was invariably uncomfortable in her presence – the rasping sound of her breathing was like the gasping of some inhuman creature – so his grandfather would take him outside and provide some form of entertainment while his parents paid their monthly visit. Alan's mother tried more than once to get her husband to patch things up with his dad, but without success. "We just live in two different worlds." Alan thought he was being metaphorical.

It wasn't a commercial farm, although Alan's grandparents supplemented their meager income by selling eggs and other produce to some of the neighbors and a couple of restaurants. There was a henhouse, wrapped in wire mesh to keep out the foxes, and a couple of acres of tilled land – corn, peas, cucumbers, rhubarb, squash, carrots, potatoes, radishes, lettuce and watermelons. There were two dairy cows and a handful of pigs but no other livestock unless you counted the reclusive tomcat that lived in the barn. The farm was bordered on either side by overgrown fairways and in the back by an extensive woodlot, land his grandfather owned but had never cleared.

"There's no such thing as a good neighbor," he told Alan on one occasion. "Just tolerable ones."

The earliest incident Alan actually remembered was on the day his grandfather taught him to make a corn cob pipe. First, he cut the bowl from a shucked and cleaned piece of cob, hollowing it out and punching a small hole in one side with a nail. He'd already dried some stiff reeds and he cut a length of one of these and wriggled it into the hole so that it was a tight fit and formed the stem. Then he filled the bowl with corn silk and set it alight and young Alan felt like a million dollars, puffing away and trying not to cough too much. He was only six years old.

They were sitting on a section of crumbling stone wall that separated a plot of corn from the neighboring trees, puffing away like old time locomotives, when a hint of motion at the edge of his field of vision made Alan glance that way. His grandfather turned to see what had caught his attention and the next thing Alan knew they were walking – actually his grandfather was walking and Alan was half running – back toward the house. The elderly man's gnarled fingers gripped his forearm painfully and not a word was spoken until they were back in the neatly tended yard.

"You saw it, didn't you?" The old man's voice was thick with emotions Alan couldn't interpret.

"There was something in the woods, but I didn't see what it was, Grandpa."

His grandfather was silent for a few seconds. "Your father never saw a thing, Alan, in all the years he lived with us. I suppose that's what kept him safe. They can't hurt you if you don't see them."

Alan tried to cajole his grandfather into telling him what lived in the woods. "You'll find out for yourself one day, like as not. Just remember to be careful." And then he insisted that Alan not tell his parents about what had happened, that it remain a secret between the two of them. "If you get your mother upset, they might not let you come to see us anymore."

Alan's mother was very sick the following summer. She was in and out of the hospital and his father – haunted by memories of his own mother's recent death – had trouble coping. Rather than allow Alan to see him in such a state, he bundled his son off to stay at the farm for a few days that ended up being the better part of a month.

It was kind of an adventure at first, but there was work to be done and his grandfather couldn't spend all of his time entertaining a mildly hyperactive ten year-old. There were few neighbors nearby and no kids Alan's age, so he indulged in elaborate, sometimes secretive games. He had been warned to stay close to the house at all times, but his definition of "close" had a certain amount of elasticity. By the end of the first week, it encompassed the nearby tilled fields, by the second, it stretched to the edges of the property in every direction and beyond in a few.

Alan hadn't planned to visit the woodlot; it just sort of happened. He was walking along the fieldstone wall that bordered the property when he realized where he was. Just ahead was the spot where they had smoked corncob pipes and where Alan had thought he had seen something move among the trees. This somewhat older version of himself dismissed the latter as imagination, but he was curious enough to continue forward and hop down on the far side of the wall between two bent trees, the only readily accessible break in the barrier presented by underbrush for a considerable distance in either direction. The property extended all the way to the abandoned golf course, which was no more than a hundred yards distant. There seemed no reason to worry about getting lost.

Alan was a city boy but he was already interested in plants – though mostly from illustrations in books. He recognized some of the leaves and flowers, but others were a complete mystery. What puzzled him was the amazing variation in color, shape, size, and configuration. Although there was no proper path, there was little serious underbrush once he was under the canopy of branches. The trees themselves were well dispersed, so Alan had no difficulty penetrating deeper into the woods. It was only when he tried to turn back that he encountered a problem. Although he didn't wear a watch, Alan had a pretty good sense of the passage of time and it occurred to him that he should have emerged from the far side of the trees by now. Instead, the foliage loomed thicker than ever, and there were thorn bearing brambles and vines ahead and to either side. He decided to retrace his steps, but when he turned he immediately became disoriented because of the equally impenetrable undergrowth to his rear. He had no idea which way he'd come. For the first time, he felt a tremor of anxiety.

Alan knew that the woodlot wasn't all that big, but that was from the outside. Now that he was deep within its borders, it seemed immense, a country unto itself. It was also peculiarly silent. The sounds of traffic on the nearby interstate had been audible everywhere on the farm, but he had heard nothing since jumping down from the wall – not even birds or insects. And then he heard a new sound.

A branch snapped somewhere out of his line of sight. Alan turned in time to see a patch of brush sway as though something very large had passed through it. He thought he might have glimpsed something like a heavy, muscular body, but it could have been the shifting of shadows. He'd been feeling very grown up, exploring on his own, but was suddenly just a kid again. He started back the way he thought he'd come, walking quickly at first, then breaking into a run that ended abruptly when it became obvious there was no negotiable gap in the brush.

It was as though someone had been moving things behind his back. Alan scouted to one side then the other without finding any place where he could easily advance. Even worse, he began to wonder if he was headed the right way. There were no real landmarks. Every direction looked the same. When the something moved through the brush again, it seemed closer.

Alan panicked. He turned and ran in the opposite direction, neither knowing nor caring where he would emerge from the trees, so long as he did reach the open. The branches overhead blotted out the sky and Alan couldn't tell where the sun was. It was the middle of the day but the shadows had thickened and seemed almost alive. His clothing was torn in a few places and his skin in a few more. He staggered to a stop, sat on a fallen tree, hugged his knees with his hands, and told himself he was being silly.

But a moment later he knew he was not alone in the woods.

He could almost feel the presence through the ground. This time the brush didn't just rustle. Stems – some of them substantial – snapped like matchsticks. In the shadows to one side, an even deeper darkness began to take shape in the distance; a thick, massive body was making its own path as it advanced, and it was headed directly toward him. Alan knew that he should run, or hide, or at least climb a tree but somehow he was certain that no action he took would be effective. He stayed where he was, awaiting his fate, and then screamed when something touched his shoulder from behind.

It was his grandfather.

He pulled Alan to his feet, fingers digging into his arm, and then they were running through the woods. Behind them, something followed in their wake, something that shook the ground as it passed. Neither boy nor man looked back to see what it was. They didn't want to know. Fortunately his grandfather had somehow found a path unencumbered by the brambles and briars that had thwarted Alan earlier and after a surprisingly short time there was daylight ahead and Alan saw the twisted trees where he had entered. The two of them stumbled through, leaped over the stone wall, and fell to their knees. His grandfather's voice was hoarse with emotion. "Didn't I tell you to stay away from the woods?"

Technically speaking he had not, but Alan wasn't about to argue the point. "Let's go back to the house and get you cleaned up."

Neither of them spoke on the way. Alan undressed, took a bath, and found fresh clothing, then joined his grandfather in the kitchen where he was making lemonade.

"What was it, grandpa? The thing that chased us."

His grandfather poured two glasses of lemonade and sat down at the table. "It might have been some kind of animal." He wouldn't meet the boy's eyes.

"What kind of animal?"

"A raccoon maybe. Or a wild dog. It's gone now, whatever it was."

Alan bit his lip, convinced that his grandfather wasn't going to tell him the truth. He started to turn away.

"Do you believe in monsters, boy?"

He stopped and considered his answer. "Dad says there's no such thing. That they're just imagination."

"Imagining is something your father never was very good at." Alan had no idea how to respond to that, so he didn't. "I suppose he's right in a way, but there used to be monsters, a long time ago."

Alan's confusion must have shown in his face. His grandfather smiled. "But that's a story for another day. Why don't you find the truck keys for me and we'll go find ourselves some ice cream."

Alan stayed clear of the woods for the remainder of his visit.

A week before his eleventh birthday, the monthly visits - which had become less regular after the death of his grandmother almost a year earlier - stopped almost completely. The following year they drove out to the farm at Christmas and once or twice over the summer, never staying long. Then Alan's father got a new job in Lansing, Michigan and the family moved. Alan talked to his grandfather on the telephone a few times after that, but never saw him again. He was almost sixteen when his grandfather died. The cause of death was listed as an animal attack. He'd been found lying in a field not far from the woods, bleeding from numerous wounds, and had never regained consciousness. Alan never considered the possibility that it had been the same animal that had chased the two of them years earlier. He was sure that he had imagined the whole thing.

The Welds flew east for the funeral, after which there was a meeting with a lawyer that Alan didn't attend. His father had planned to put the farm up for sale immediately, but the terms of the will had made that impossible. The entire estate had been placed in a trust in Alan's name, to be maintained by the proceeds of a surprisingly large insurance policy until he turned twenty-one. There was a prohibition against selling the property for the first twelve months after he came of age, but following that there were no strings attached.

His mother explained this to Alan at the time and they never spoke of it again. Alan was quite full of himself for a few days, but he was struggling with algebra, had recently discovered girls, and these distractions chased thoughts of the farm out of his mind pretty quickly.

Alan was halfway through his freshman year at Michigan State when both parents were killed in a plane crash, their first actual vacation since they'd married. The insurance would have paid for the remaining three years of college, but at the end of his sophomore year Alan decided that he didn't want to be a botanist after all and dropped out. He broke up with his long standing girlfriend a few months later, got laid off from the store where he clerked, and realized he was profoundly unhappy with his life.

When the letter came from the lawyer, informing Alan that he would soon be entitled to take over management of his inheritance, it was a godsend. He sold off most of what he owned, turned his not insignificant bank account into a cashier's check, packed what was left into a battered Volkswagen, and drove east.

Although Alan was still a few weeks shy of his majority, Perlmutter – the lawyer - saw no reason why he shouldn't have access to the property immediately and provided a key. Alan hardly recognized the house. The neatly kept yard was quite overgrown. The caretaker had cleared a path to the front door but had allowed the rest to grow wild. The interior of the house smelled musty, but a cursory inspection detected no signs of a leaky roof, visible mildew, or intrusions by animals. Someone had covered up the furniture, disposed of all of the leftover food, and turned off the electricity and water. Alan cleaned up one of the bedrooms – not the one where his grandmother had died – and the utility companies promised to resume service.

For the first few days, he lived under rather primitive conditions, but was happier than he'd been for some time. Paradoxically Alan felt as though he was simultaneously reclaiming something from his past and getting a fresh start. He explored the house systematically, found a drawer full of photographs of his father as a child and his grandparents as young adults, but everything else was prosaic. The discovery he prized above all others was his grandfather's oversized wristwatch, which still worked, and he took to wearing it even though the band was too large and it kept slipping down over his wrist. He sorted out the trash, hired a professional service to clean the interior of the house, a lawn service to restore the yard to respectability, and had the exterior repainted.

The fields were thick with weeds and brush, and what remained of the corn field, now gone wild, was infested with crows who noisily expressed their displeasure whenever he ventured there. Alan considered having them cleared as well, but feeling no desire to actually raise crops decided to leave them as they were. The cash residue from the insurance would be substantial. Combined with the remaining proceeds from his parents' estate, he would be able to live on the interest, so long as he remained frugal. Alan had no intention of retreating into indolence, but neither was he inclined to rush into a future he wouldn't enjoy.

Alan didn't approach the woodlot until he'd been there for almost two months. It was late spring by then and he had decided to scout the borders of the property. The stone wall was still in place, but parts of it had fallen and other parts were completely overgrown. He felt a mild foreboding when he caught sight of the woods, but shook it off. He had long since convinced himself that imagination and disorientation had magnified things in his memory. As his grandfather had suggested, it was probably just an ordinary animal exaggerated out of proportion.

At last he noticed the two distinctively warped trees and the gap they provided through the vines and saplings. Very deliberately Alan climbed over the wall and stepped into the musty half darkness, but he didn't go very far and felt a rush of relief when he turned back, telling himself there was nothing in the woods to interest him.

Although he kept to himself much of the time, Alan wasn't a complete recluse. He even met a local girl who surprised him with her almost aggressive sexuality. They spent several pleasurable afternoons in his bedroom and he'd have offered her a key except that he rarely bothered to lock the door. Julie injected a lively spontaneity into his life, appearing on his doorstep without warning, sometimes with elaborate plans for the day, sometimes just looking for sex or company.

On Alan's twenty-first birthday, he put on the only necktie he owned and went to see Perlmutter. The lawyer spoke in a near monotone as he described the terms of the behest, proffered the papers that required signatures, and then handed Alan a sealed, legal sized envelope. "Your grandfather left this for you."

"What is it?" He felt an odd reluctance to accept it.

"I have no idea. He added to it from time to time but always sealed the envelope before returning it to me."

Alan took the envelope and put it in the folder with the other documents, thanked Perlmutter for his time, and took his leave. Back at the farmhouse, he put the papers safely away, all except the envelope, which he placed on the narrow kitchen table. For some reason he felt uneasy about opening it. Instead, he made lunch, ate it, and tinkered with a window that kept sticking, then finally sat down and peeled back the flap. It was a letter, or more properly, a series of handwritten pages, all in his grandfather's hand, but obviously composed over a period of time. Alan picked up the first sheet and began to read.

"I am writing this note to you on your fourteenth birthday. I hope that I will have a chance to explain everything in person, but in case something should happen to me, I have decided to set down the important things you will need to know." The first two pages were of little interest. There was a description of his grandfather's financial situation, which told him nothing that Perlmutter hadn't already explained. There were a few sentences describing idiosyncrasies of the house and property – the location of an old well, a crude drawing showing where waste water ran to an underground cistern, a warning that squirrels liked to gnaw their way into the attic.

"I should tell you about the woods at the rear of the property, but it is hard to find the right words. I've mentioned that they are dangerous, but I haven't explained why. I'm not sure that I can even now. Most people will never see or experience anything out of the ordinary and they are perfectly safe there. A few people, like you and me, can see more than that. I can't tell you exactly what you'll find because different people see different things. My mother thought it was full of witches but my father and brothers never noticed anything at all. I saw, well, it doesn't matter what I saw because it'll be different for you. If you ever enter the woods, always leave the same way that you came, and never leave anything behind. That's very important. What is done must be undone. Every beginning must be complete in its ending."

The next page began a rambling account of his father's childhood. Alan skimmed through this, intending to return to it later. Although none of the pages were dated, they were clearly written at various times. Sometimes material was repeated, as though his grandfather had forgotten what he'd already written. There were more references to the woodlot, sometimes referring to it as a "thin spot" and they grew more frequent as Alan progressed through the document. Some of the last pages were nearly incomprehensible, sentences running together, their meaning not always clear. Apparently his grandfather had come to believe that some malevolent presence lay on the "other side" of the woods, waiting for an opportunity to cross over. When Alan's grandmother had died, the older Weld had seemed to age dramatically over the course of a very few days. It would not be too surprising if he had retreated into a kind of dark fantasy toward the end. Alan put the pages back in the envelope and told himself to forget about them.

But the next morning, he found himself walking toward the woodlot.

Although Alan was convinced that his childhood terror had been the product of an overactive imagination, abetted by his grandfather's strange behavior, he could not shake the feeling that he did not completely understand what had happened to him. He was better prepared for exploration this time, both physically and psychologically. He wore his grandfather's wristwatch to measure the time, was no longer an impressionable child, and had brought along a small compass to orient himself. Upon arriving at the twisted trees, he hesitated briefly, then plunged forward.

It seemed to be a perfectly ordinary stretch of woodland. Alan had learned enough botany to recognize many of the plants, and the unfamiliar ones were not extraordinary. The trees were more densely situated than he remembered and he had to detour around mounds of brush several times, but within a few minutes he could see the foliage thinning out ahead. There had been nothing to indicate he was not alone, not even the sound of birds.

Alan emerged onto the abandoned golf course, which had been rendered almost unrecognizable by more than twenty years of neglect. He had driven past it several times and had a rough idea what to expect, although it seemed even more overgrown from close at hand than it had from a distance. The remains of a sand trap were off to the right, and the general shape of the fairway was obvious. On the far side was a gentle slope that led up to the original clubhouse, which was now an eyesore with sagging roof and covered windows. It looked unusually foreboding, as though it was staring down at him with disapproval.

One oddity did catch his attention. It had been bright and sunny when he'd set out for this walk, and now it was overcast, the sky grey and seeming closer than usual. There was an acrid taste in the air and a wind had picked up. Alan knew that New England weather was very changeable but had had no idea that a storm front could move in so quickly.

He decided to head back and find shelter before it actually started to rain. It seemed quicker to walk around the edge of the woodlot rather than retrace the circuitous path through it, so he set off briskly. The sand trap was immediately ahead and he angled slightly to bypass it. As he did so, something moved under the sand.

It rippled like water disturbed by a pebble, concentric rings that expanded and weakened before they reached the edges. Alan thought it might be some freak of the wind at first, but the turbulence continued, became more agitated as he approached. By the time he was half a dozen paces away, it was seething violently, spurts of sand erupted into the air, and the ground seemed unsteady under his feet.

Alan didn't run. He could almost hear his father shouting at his mother that she shouldn't give in to fear. But he did walk away, very quickly. Snakes, he told himself. There must be a colony of snakes nesting under the loose sand.

The woodlot was a rough ellipse and he made his way without incident to the end farthest from the road. From that point, it was a fairly straightforward trip across the chaotic cornfield and a narrow brook, then through a small stand of apple trees to the house. Or at least it should have been straightforward.

Alan didn't like the look of the cornfield. He had never seen it from this angle before, of course, but it was more than just the altered perspective. The desiccated stalks were stick figures drawn in positions of agony and terror. Alan slowed his pace, reluctant to walk in among those contorted shapes. He chided himself for being silly, childish, but that didn't make the feeling go away. And then there were the crows.

They rose into the air like a cloud. There were more of them than he had ever seen before, and they seemed unusually large, as big as hawks. They flew to the edge of the cornfield and hovered there, as though guarding the borders of their kingdom against invasion. As Alan drew closer, one of them darted forward, sliding through the air with preternatural speed. He ducked out of its way just in time, staggered and almost fell.

"What the hell?" He retreated a few steps and watched as the lone bird banked and returned to the flock circling above the edge of the cornfield. When they began to drop toward the field, he resumed his advance. They rose as one and this time half a dozen darted toward him. There was no question about their malevolent intent and

Alan turned and ran, managing a couple of dozen steps before a twist of grass snagged his ankle and sent him sprawling.

He rolled over, arms raised to protect his face, and stared up into an empty, leaden sky. When he sat up, he saw that the crows had returned to their own territory once more.

"All right, I get the message." He stood up, brushed himself off, made a mental note to have the field cleared after all. He hadn't minded the crows until now, even when their raucous cries had been clearly audible at the house, but this was going too far.

Still loathe to return to the woods, he retraced his steps and started across the opposite end of the fairway, where a rusted hurricane fence lined the roadway. There was little traffic here and the pavement was broken by frost heaves and potholes, which looked even worse than he remembered. There were several gaps in the fence and he slipped through the first he encountered, jumped a narrow, clogged drainage ditch, and found himself standing on the sandy shoulder.

The rumble of a distant automobile engine was the only sound as he set out to walk back to the farm. It took less than ten minutes to bypass the woodlot. Just beyond lay the ruins of the henhouse. The roof had collapsed long since and the entire structure was covered with a blanket of wisteria and trumpet vine, while sumac and other young saplings had sprung up everywhere, as though the woodlot had sent an occupying army of its own young. From this angle, the semi-collapsed building looked almost like a crumbling European castle, the kind of place where Dracula would hang out.

On the opposite side, a stand of stunted apple trees marched up to the edge of the neatly tended yard. Alan caught a glimpse of his new home and frowned. It looked considerably less welcoming than it had in the past, almost as though it was watching him, waiting for him to drop his guard. Even the apple trees seemed to stretch their branches toward him, ready to grab him as he passed.

Without realizing that he had done so, Alan came to a stop. And then the distant automobile came into sight.

It seemed to be crawling along the road and the engine sounds resembled nothing so much as the growling of a wild beast. Although it was necessarily coming almost directly toward him, Alan fancied that this wasn't simply because that was the way the road led but rather that it was somehow aware of his presence and that he was its ultimate goal. After all, there was nothing beyond this point except abandoned farms, the barred entrance to the reservoir, and the old Boy Scout camp that had closed while his grandfather was still alive.

Alan kept moving forward along the side of the road, but his eyes strayed to the distant – and soon not so distant –automobile. His heart began to beat faster and he felt short of breath, sure signs of the anxiety attacks he had experienced as a child when his and his mother's fears of the world had reinforced each other. He told himself not to be foolish, but he could not look away.

The car would pass him before he reached the house. Alan felt an irrational desire to run, to shut himself up indoors, but his older self insisted he was being foolish. His fears ultimately triumphed, but by then it was too late. The car had crested the last rise and was bearing down on him.

Alan stopped, watching it approach. Time seemed oddly discordant; the car rushed toward him, but it closed the gap very slowly. He took a step backward, then another. There was a cool breeze but sweat dripped from his forehead and his clothes clung to his body. Although he told himself he was being silly, he looked back, searching for an escape route. Just in case, he told himself. It might be a car full of kids on drugs. Better to be safe.

He had retreated another ten steps before he realized what he was doing, then stepped off the sandy verge into the tall grass despite the poison ivy that proliferated here. The automobile was around the final curve and would reach him within a few seconds. He saw spurts of sand as the passenger side wheels veered onto the shoulder.

Alan started to run.

He could have darted into the woods immediately, but by the time he realized that he had reached the beginning of the hurricane fence. There was a gap ahead, but he wasn't sure if he could make it that far in time. The long grass seemed to be pulling at his ankles, impeding his progress. He staggered, regained his balance, then began to run even faster when the deep, throaty sound of a horn bellowed from behind. The gap was just ahead. He didn't dare look back but he knew it was going to be close. At the last minute a hidden vine tripped him up but he threw himself forward, banged one shoulder against the last upright, and rolled forward into the skirt of the fairway.

His body wanted to lie there and replenish the oxygen in his blood, but Alan turned over and half rose. The automobile was close, only a few meters away, a model he had never seen before with peculiar angles and a hunched, somehow unnatural shape. It had stopped on the side of the roadway just short of the gap, engine grumbling with frustration. There were four people inside, but he couldn't see their faces, didn't want to see their faces. Alan stood up and began to back away.

Almost immediately, the automobile moved off the roadway, its front end pressing against the ruptured fence. The gap was too small for it to pass. Alan suppressed an impulse to laugh, then caught his breath. The fence was beginning to lean toward him. They were forcing a way through. He turned and fled toward the fairway proper.

Alan decided that his best bet was to lose himself among the trees. They couldn't follow without leaving their vehicle behind and somehow he knew they wouldn't do that. He changed course, tore a sleeve on a thorny bush, and stumbled toward the safety of the woodlot. Behind him, he could hear the sound of metal tearing as the fence collapsed.

He barely made it. The horn blared piercingly just behind him as he sprinted between two large trees set closely enough that his pursuers would be unable to follow. Alan staggered a few more steps, short of breath, and finally stumbled and went down on all fours, banging his knee in the process. He glanced back over one shoulder and saw that the front end of the automobile was pressed right up against the trees. The passengers were still inside and as Alan rose unsteadily to his feet, anger overwhelmed most of his fear.

"What are you assholes playing at?" His shout was almost the only sound. Even the engine noises had become nearly inaudible. Still furious, he stood and moved toward them with some vague idea of memorizing their license plate. There was no license plate. There wasn't even a place for it. And as he drew closer, he could see the interior more clearly, could see that there was no clear line of demarcation between passengers and their seats, that the car and its occupants were a single, impossible unity.

He turned away and hobbled deeper into the woods.

Alan quickly became disoriented and lacked the presence of mind to consult his compass. He was quite sure that he had passed the same rotted stump more than once and that he'd been walking long enough to have crossed the woodlot lengthwise several times before he finally spotted a lessening of the foliage ahead that told him he was near the edge. He approached cautiously, afraid that he'd returned to the fairway, but he could see the shadow of the hen house off to his right and the cornfield to his left. Both appeared to have returned to normal.

Drawing a deep breath, he pushed through a mass of brambles and out into the open.

Just to his left, he spotted the gap between the two distinctive trees where he had first entered hours earlier and remembered his grandfather's admonition to always leave the same way he'd come. He felt foolish now but he wasn't about to tempt fate again. He re-entered the woods cautiously, edged along the perimeter, and exited the way he had come. Then he turned and ran for home.

Nothing accosted him on the way. A bird flew overhead, but it seemed normal and ignored him. The grass didn't encumber his feet and even the air seemed fresher. Best of all, the sun was high in a perfectly clear sky. He passed the edge of the cornfield and turned toward the house. And stopped abruptly.

There was a dark colored automobile parked in the driveway.

The flash of terror passed quickly. It was a perfectly ordinary Toyota. Julie's car. She must have dropped by to see him. He started forward again and as he did so, the front door opened and a figure emerged. It was Julie, who smiled broadly when she saw him.

"There you are! I thought I'd missed you."

Alan felt a physical wave of relief as normality was restored. He closed the gap between them and held his arms out. "You have no idea how glad I am to see you. What are you doing here? Did you get off work early?"

She shook her head. "No, same as always."

Alan realized that he must have lost an entire afternoon, raised his arm to check the time. His arm was bare; his grandfather's wristwatch must have fallen off wrist at some point. Alan remembered the second part of his grandfather's warning, about not leaving anything behind and wondered what the consequences might be.

Julie wrapped her arms around him and drew him close. "I've been looking forward to seeing you all day."

And then she tore his throat out with her teeth.

CITY GIRL

Ted didn't know exactly why he noticed the girl that morning, what it was about her appearance or demeanor that led him to abandon the plans he had made for his day off. If she had come by the bus stop five minutes later, or ten earlier, he might have remained ignorant of her existence. Even after it all had ended, he didn't know whether or not to lament the coincidence of timing which so altered his life.

It was the bus stop at the corner of Lassiter and Dolmen Streets, several blocks from his apartment but the only point nearby where he could pick up one of the cross town busses that ran out to Shore Park. Shore Park had an unsavory reputation and even the police have advised residents to use other facilities for recreation, but the north end was still quite heavily trafficked and other than an occasional purse snatching, he had never witnessed any real crime in that area, not did he personally know anyone who had been a victim. On his limited budget, and with just a single day off in the middle of the week, he had few options, and while the breeze off the river frequently bore olfactory reminders of the deteriorating state of the city's sewage treatment facility, it was nevertheless several degrees cooler than the stagnant air trapped in the canyons of the city during the summer months.

He was staring idly up Lassiter, watching for his bus, a canvas book bag slung over one shoulder, when the girl emerged from one of the shops on the right side of the street, took advantage of a gap in traffic to cross in the middle of the block, then turned and started in his direction.

At first, Ted's interest was entirely casual; from this distance, it was clear that she was short, fairly slender, and kept her straw colored hair long, almost descending to waist level, gathered together by a single bow at the nape of her neck. She wore a pale blue blouse, darker blue skirt, and carried a small black purse in her right hand. Although he was still primarily interested in spotting his bus, he followed her progress out of the corner of one eye, wondering if he would be afforded a brief, vicarious glimpse of a beautiful woman.

In that, he was to be disappointed. By the time she reached Dolmen, directly across from where he stood, it was clear that her face was aggressively ordinary. Each feature individually was unremarkable, and assembled into a whole they were slightly out of proportion, the nose a fraction of an inch too wide, the chin slightly too shallow. Although not quite as petite as he had originally guessed, she could not have weighed more than 110 pounds, and was half a foot shorter than his own five foot ten. Her complexion was clear, heavily tanned, and he wondered idly if she had obtained it naturally or from one of the tanning salons that had replaced the video game parlors on Front Street.

The traffic light had stopped working weeks earlier and the overworked city maintenance department had yet to make an appearance, so the girl was forced to wait on the far side of the street until a gap opened in the stream of taxicabs, delivery trucks, and private vehicles traveling east on Dolmen toward the express route to downtown. This allowed Ted ample opportunity to check her out, with what he thought was considerable discretion. He carefully averted his eyes when she finally started across the street, turning away briefly and slowly swinging his head back so that it would appear accidental when she came into his field of view from close at hand.

She was no more attractive from a meter away than she had been from the opposite side of the street. If anything, her nose seemed slightly broader, and she had the faintest hint of a moustache. Her figure was slightly better than he had expected, but her clothing had seen better days. There was a small rip in the hem of her skirt, just above the knee, and a pale yellow stain the size of a quarter on the back of her blouse.

Ted had planned to check her out as she passed, but she paused, one foot extended for the next step, her forehead suddenly creasing, lips pursed, as though she had just remembered something. Against his better judgment, almost against his will, he allowed his gaze to linger, even to descend. From this angle, he could see partway down inside the blouse, all the way to the thin white line where her freckled chest was concealed by a white bra. Ted shifted his weight nervously from one foot to another, afraid to be caught with guilty eyes, but also reluctant to let the moment escape. At the same time, he was amused and a bit puzzled by this mini-obsession with its patently unremarkable object.

Time seemed to freeze and rush by simultaneously. For long seconds, neither of them moved; Ted continued his clandestine examination while she remained deep in thought, undecided whether to proceed or remain where she was. He was terrified of being caught with trespassing eyes but unwilling to relinquish the view. When she finally resolved whatever internal conflict had caused her to pause and moved on, it was as though someone had clenched a fist around his heart. The pain was so intense it was quite literally physical.

He turned and followed her.

Ted truly hated the city sometimes. There was the crime, the muggings, rapes, murders, and assaults that fill the newspapers nearly every evening. And the filth. Sometimes the trash collectors skipped his street and the landlords left it piled on the sidewalk until the following week. And when they did pick it up, they spilled nearly as much as they loaded into the trucks, or at least so it seemed. Corruption in the highest places was almost a job requirement and the degree of apathy may be gauged by the twelve percent average turnout for the last four municipal elections. At times he thought the entire city was sliding rapidly toward chaos and that he was the only one with the good sense to panic. There were days when he struggled to find any good reason to remain, but in the end his lethargy was so pervasive that he never mustered the energy to relocate, or even to look for employment elsewhere.

Perhaps that explained why he compulsively followed her that day, through the downtown, past street vendors and beggars, serious buyers and window shoppers, businessmen and infrequent tourists, finally losing her when she hailed at taxi. Her looks were unremarkable, she had given no indication of even noticing his existence, but he was somehow drawn to her like an asteroid plummeting toward a black hole.

Once she was gone, the pain of loss, surprising in its intensity, quickly changed to a sense of embarrassment, and relief that there were no witnesses to his foolishness. He oriented himself and returned home, the excursion to Shore Park forgotten, his mind chaotically troubled.

That might have been the end of it, except that Ted encountered the same girl again two days later. It was during the early evening; he had decided to eat at a diner near the office and return home on a later bus rather than deal with the press of five o'clock commuters. He had actually managed to get an aisle seat on the bus, an unusual situation this past year, about two thirds of the way back, and fully a third of the other seats were empty.

Two stops later, she got onto the bus.

Ted recognized the new passenger instantly, almost locked eyes with her before realizing that he was staring, then quickly turned his head. She took a seat three forward of him and on the opposite side of the aisle. Ted picked up a discarded newspaper from the seat and pretended to read it, holding it just high enough that he could look past the edge and examine her profile.

She was quite attractive from this angle, he realized. It was a genuine pleasure to watch her, the curve of her cheek, the way her throat moved as she breathed. So attractive that he missed his stop and never even noticed until she left the bus at Tulford Park. By the time he had gathered my wits and followed, she was lost in the crowd and he was left to walk seventeen blocks back to his apartment.

The second encounter was tantalizing enough that he began to watch for her, and a week later he spotted her coming out of one of the hairdressing salons on Lassiter. Ted had been on his way to Dr. Brodsky's office for his annual physical, but opted to arbitrarily cancel that appointment without notice in favor of following her once more.

They spent most of the day in Shore Park. Ted hadn't been there in years, and despite the refuse that littered the shore, it was still clearly the best stretch of beach in the city. His quarry appeared to be restless; she would sit on a dune overlooking the water for a while, then walk the beach, or wander along the meandering paths through the largely overgrown gardens, then back to the dunes, ignoring the inquisitive looks from passersby. They were for the most part an unsavory lot, but she had an air of authority that seemed to warn them off. On more than one occasion, snickered laughter and unveiled stares proved she'd aroused presumably unwanted attention, but no one approached her and their snide remarks and suggestions were surprisingly guarded.

Ted wasn't so lucky. Two or three times he avoided unpleasantness by looking sheepish and unthreatening, twice parted with cash in response to ambiguous requests/demands that hovered above the line between importunity and extortion. On one of those occasions, he lost sight of her momentarily, but luckily spotted her minutes later, making another circuit of the woodland.

She left shortly before dark, and in the fading light, Ted chanced getting closer to her once they had rejoined the heavier pedestrian traffic on Mallway. It was an unusually pleasant evening, the height of summer, warm, but with a dry, cool breeze coming in off the water. It was so comfortable that she apparently decided to walk the entire distance back to her apartment, which was how he discovered where she lived.

Ted was not a complete stranger to sexual encounters, although it had been over a year since he had so much as bought a drink for a woman. Although not unattractive and fairly entertaining company, he had always been a rather private person, making friends infrequently but rarely with any real difficulty. His reticence in this particular case was uncharacteristic.

He just didn't want the vision to fade.

She appealed to him because the only faults he knew about her were ones he could forgive, the slight misalignment of her face, the fact that she smoked, although infrequently. She presented a bit of a mystery, and he looked forward to unraveling her secrets gradually, over an extended period of time, as though opening an onion layer by layer. Most of all, so long as he concealed his interest, he was in near total control of the situation; she could not terminate a relationship she did not even suspect existed.

Knowing where she lived, Ted was able to follow her with more frequency in the days that followed. Since he was working five days a week and most Saturday mornings, there were few opportunities during the day, but fortunately she seemed to be a night person. He began eating in the small coffee shop across the street from her apartment house, dragging the meal out as long as possible, watching the front doorway. He learned to spot her profile from a great distance, from many angles, and could even pick out her particular stride in a forest of legs.

On one of these occasions, she discarded an envelope into a public trash bin, and that's how he finally learned her name.

Christine Eblis. There was no return address.

Ted also began to carry his handgun again.

It had been a long time since the mugging which had left him with a jaw broken in three places, and the small .38 calibre pistol he had purchased on the following day was filthy with oil and dust when he retrieved it from the kitchen drawer where it was stored. There had been no specific incident that caused him to arm himself again, but Christine had another minor fault that demanded it.

She spent a great deal of time walking through the more unsavory parts of the city.

Briefly, Ted thought she might be a hooker. He had no idea how she supported herself. On three occasions now he had managed to follow her on a week day, but these trips had never resulted in any evidence of gainful employment. In fact, every time she left her apartment, it seemed to be for recreation only. She wandered through stores, but never made purchases, drank coffee in diners but never ordered a meal, rode buses and taxicabs, but always set off walking to no evident purpose when the trips were over.

But she didn't dress like a hooker. Ted thought she probably wore makeup but it was always understated, and her clothing was...well, wholesome, certainly not seductive. Although he found her immensely attractive, it was in a subtle, understated fashion; she was appealing rather than sexy, vulnerable rather than challenging.

Even more significantly, he had followed her around at night for hours at a time, sometimes as often as five nights a week. A few times there had been brief conversations with passing men, but if these had been approaches, they had been universally rebuffed.

She seemed to be extraordinarily lucky. Despite the fact that she prowled nightly through neighborhoods Ted distrusted during the daylight, she was never seriously accosted, her purse was never snatched, and the closest she came to physical harassment was a pair of noisy teenagers who hassled her one evening for a few seconds, then moved on, oddly subdued.

Ted began to fantasize scenarios in which she was attacked by muggers, sometimes those same muggers who had broken his jaw, affording him the opportunity to spring heroically to her rescue. Shaken but grateful, she allowed him to escort her back to her apartment, then invited him up for coffee, and then...

So he kept his gun loaded and concealed by his jacket. Ted was five foot eight, 160 pounds, and hadn't won a fistfight since sixth grade. He hadn't managed to land a single punch in his encounter with the muggers.

It almost worked out the way he had imagined.

It was a Friday night and he had been following Christine for almost three hours. Her stamina was a source of constant amazement to him. During the first few weeks of their one-sided relationship, his feet had hurt constantly. Clerical duties confined him to his data terminal most of the time, and these extended walks had required the toughening of calf muscles and the soles of his feet. Christine never seemed to falter.

They were in the warehouse district just west of the commercial docks. Most of the streetlights in this part of the city were no longer working, and the only businesses operating were seedy bars, some of which also claimed to be restaurants, an occasional pawn shop or video parlor, and several houses of ill repute, most thinly disguised as hotels. Christine had just started down one of those theatrically narrow alleys between two multi-story buildings and Ted was hovering in a doorway on the street opposite, anxious not to lose her, but unwilling to enter the alley until she was out of sight, lest he betray myself.

Three figures slid from behind a dumpster and moved after her.

Ted knew immediately that their intentions were evil. Their silence, the way the shadows sort of glided along the far wall, everything about the situation cried "Menace".

His hand slid down to touch the pistol, but even though its presence was reassuring, Ted was still paralyzed by doubt. Would he be able to handle the situation or would he blow it and, perhaps, endanger both their lives? Should he proceed, or turn the other way, look for a working telephone, call the police? The last idea was patently absurd; there wasn't a functioning public telephone within twenty blocks.

So he followed them into the alley.

They had already caught up to her by the time he reached them. The tallest was a powerfully built man, and if acne had not scarred his face so badly, he would have been handsome. One of his companions was thin, reedy almost, probably weighed less than Ted, with a dark complexion and a broad moustache that looked too large for his face. The third man was of average build, had shaved his head, and bore a large, dark tattoo on each arm.

Ted concealed himself by crouching behind some decaying wooden crates that had apparently been abandoned in the alley. Even in that dim light, they didn't provide much cover, and had any of the three glanced in his direction, Ted's presence would have been discovered immediately. But they were preoccupied with their intended victim, Christine.

She stood with her back to the wall, head up, arms on her hips. The acne covered man faced her directly, speaking in a voice so low that Ted could not make out the individual words, although the tone dripped with amused venom. Skinhead and Moustache were sliding their feet aimlessly back and forth, slowing working their way to each side, one cutting off any retreat further into the alley, the other prepared to stop her if she bolted for the main road.

Ted slipped the pistol out of his pocket. It took three tries; his hands shook and his fingers felt so numb he could hardly grasp the weapon.

She was wearing a white blouse and a short, gray tweed skirt that evening, and in the dim light that penetrated the alley, she seemed almost radiant. Ted became so preoccupied with her appearance that momentary disorientation set in, and when the tableau changed abruptly, it took several seconds for his mind to process what he was seeing.

That's all the time that was required.

Perhaps on his own initiative, perhaps in response to some subliminal command from his partners, Skinhead lunged forward, reaching out to grab Christine's arm. Moustache hastened to follow suit, but the footing was uncertain and he staggered to one side as he attempted to leap forward. Christine turned to face her attacker, raised one arm in an apparently defensive gesture.

Something about her hand seemed distorted, disproportionate, although the light was so bad that Ted could never be certain. Skinhead didn't cry out, but his body altered course in mid-air, slammed against the far wall, slid slowly to the ground without moving. Ted's eyes refused to track away from that motionless shape for a second or two, so he never did see how she dispatched Moustache; when he turned my eyes back toward

Chrstine, the second thug was lying on his back, one knee crooked upward, completely motionless.

Acne stepped back, confused rather than fearful; there hadn't been time for fear. Christine took one step forward, actually smiled, the curve of her mouth illuminated quite distinctly despite the general gloom, and spoke a few words in a calm voice. They were both insulting and obscene.

With an inarticulate cry of rage, Acne raised both arms and lunged forward.

She seemed to be slapping at him, struck only twice, once in the body, once alongside the head. His bellowed cry cut off instantly and he stood motionless for several breaths, then fell silently to the ground. He never moved again.

The pistol was in Ted's hand but forgotten now. He watched in mingled confusion and alarm as Christine crouched over each body in turn, pausing for a few seconds, then moving on, finally rising and walking off into the darkness as though nothing had happened at all.

He discovered two further things before leaving that alley. Drawn forward despite an inner voice that advised immediate flight, he examined the three would-be muggers, each of whom was quite thoroughly dead, without touching them. Skinhead's jugular had been severed completely; in fact the entire front half of his throat was gone. Moustache had been disemboweled, deep incisions extending up his abdomen to the middle of his chest. Acne had lacerations across one side that exposed the white arcs of his ribs, and the left side of his face was smashed in, chunks of bone having penetrated up into the skull casing. But the most frightening thing was that even though no more than a minute or two had passed since these men had lived and breathed, even though their blood was still slick and wet on the wall, the ground, seeping through their clothing and what remained of their flesh, all three of the bodies were stone cold.

So cold that you'd have thought every bit of heat and energy which had powered their bodies had been drawn out in an instant.

The second thing Ted found was Christine's purse.

He never thought about returning it, anonymously or otherwise. Any such action would have revealed at his presence, shadowing her excursions, and now more than ever he wished that secret kept. But despite the fact that he had just watched Christine kill three human beings, he was already making excuses for her actions. After all, they had clearly been threatening harm and she had merely acted in her own defense.

He still found her as fascinating as before. Perhaps even more so.

Concealing the purse inside the flap of his jacket, Ted brought it back to his apartment.

Its contents were absolutely ordinary -- lipstick, a compact, a bottle of aspirin, a douche, a small box of tampons, two packages of tissue, nail polish, hairspray, cold medicine, a roll of dimes, two packages of lifesavers, a card of needles, three rolls of thread, a comb, a small pad of paper, two pens. They were exactly what he would have expected to find in a woman's purse, except for two things. None of the items had been opened and there were no keys, not even to her apartment.

Later he would wonder if she even had an apartment. Perhaps she just lurked in a corner of the apartment building periodically.

That's when Ted began to wonder if Christine Eblis was a real woman at all. Real, of course, but not a woman. Not even a human being.

He stopped following her, in fact began avoiding areas he knew to be her usual haunts, even walked an extra six blocks to pick up a bus that went nowhere near the Lassiter Street area. Despite his infatuation, a growing sense of wrongness had matured into fear for his own safety, and he consciously suppressed any lingering romantic inclinations, refusing even to indulge in his customary fantasies involving her.

That might have been the end of it, as least insofar as Ted was concerned. But somehow he must have slipped up, given her some hint of his existence.

She was on his bus one night two weeks after the incident in the alley, even though it was a route he had never seen her take before. Although she didn't look in his direction, in fact brushed past without a glance, he was convinced the encounter had not been coincidental.

Two days later, Ted glanced out of his apartment window and saw Christine cross the street and get into a cab. The angle was bad and he never saw her face, but he had studied her every move for so long that he could identify her instantly.

The doorman told him the following day that "some woman" had come by looking for him but had declined to leave a message. That evening, he was watching the local news on Channel 13, live coverage of a drive-by shooting in the south end, and one of the bystanders turned and looked directly into the camera as it panned past, seemed to stare right out through the screen at him.

It was Christine.

He began to develop theories about her nature. Perhaps somehow the corruption in the city had given rise to a manifestation of its own putrid heart, or perhaps it was a counterbalancing force preying only on those who acted as parasites in the body politic. She might be the equivalent of a white blood cell. If that was true, he thought himself safe, a contributor rather than a destroyer, healthy tissue.

Ted certainly hoped that was the case, more fervently when someone started pressing his door buzzer late that evening. He wanted to pretend that he hadn't heard it and just take a shower and go to bed, but as he sat in the darkness, he knew that sooner or later he would stand up, cross to the door, and open it.

And he knew whom he will find there.

THE SPLICER

In retrospect, Scott suspected that the first tampering with the film program had occurred during the Godzilla Festival.

Saturday was always science fiction night at the Managansett Cinema, just as Fridays were reserved for horror films, Mondays for swashbucklers, and so on. Old Man Bradford couldn't afford to show first-run movies in the town's only theater, but he made up for it with sheer volume. Every show was a double feature on week nights, triples on weekends.

The same economy was reflected in the staffing. Candy Carter sold tickets from one side of the booth, popcorn and candy from the other. Scott collected the tickets at the entrance to the theater, did a brief stint as an usher, then climbed the narrow stairway to the projection booth. No digital equipment there, of course. It was a real struggle on Friday nights, the only time they were actually busy and played to a nearly full house. Generally there were less than two dozen customers, generally teenage couples so preoccupied with each other that he could have shown three hours of blank tape without their noticing anything. Scott would never have lasted three years on this job if it required any real initiative or brainpower; he operated the projector mechanically and possessed no understanding at all of the means by which celluloid images were transferred to the screen. His boss occasionally made disapproving sounds about his shoulder-length blond hair, of which Scott was inordinately proud, but had never pressed the issue, perhaps because Scott was willing to work for such low wages.

Scott had long since stopped paying attention to the movies, almost all of which he had seen several times before, preferring to spend the time lost in one daydream or another, usually involving the dispensation of large sums of cash or the resolution of dramatic political crises for which only Scott Barkin had the necessary personal qualities. Infrequently, there were sexual overtones, but carnal acts or nudity made him uncomfortable, on the screen or off it, and he was still a virgin in his mid-twenties.

Which is probably why he noticed the girl in the torn dress during *Godzilla vs the Smog Monster*.

It was the third of three Godzilla movies that night, and Scott was anxious for it to end so that he could rewind the film, check to be certain the theater was empty, and lock up for the night. The smog monster had just taken to the air on its latest rampage when the camera shifted to a crowd shot, the usual aggregation of frightened figures running for whatever ineffective shelter they could find. At the forefront of the crowd, a slender Japanese woman fell to the ground, her blouse slipping from one shoulder. As she struggled to rise, someone stepped on the hem of her dress, which tore all the way to her waistline, briefly revealing a swath of white thigh before she was swallowed up by the crowd.

Scott only noticed it because even that faint hint of sexuality seemed anachronistic in a Japanese monster movie of the 1970s.

A week or two later, while the original *King Kong* was playing on the screen, Scott was started by the giant ape's rather revealing exploration of Fay Wray's clothing, at one point exposing a clearly naked breast for a split second. He vaguely recalled that some censored footage from the original print had been restored, so he just shook his head and chuckled.

It was the torrid love scene between Anne Francis and Leslie Nielsen in *Forbidden Planet* that finally led him to suspect that something was wrong. It was part of a double feature, opening with the classic *The Thing*. Margaret Sheridan had seemed a bit lightly clad for a posting in Antarctica and she displayed rather a fuller figure than Scott remembered, but otherwise there had been no obvious incongruity in that film. But when Nielsen and Francis began clutching at one another in evident passion during the second feature, Scott knew something was up.

"What the hell?" He rose from his chair and moved forward, peering out through the small window at the screen shimmering below. Nielsen had one hand closed quite obviously over a breast while his free hands worked at the fastenings of her blouse. The ultimate revelation was only prevented when Dr. Morbius, portrayed by Walter Pidgeon, put in an untimely appearance.

When the theater had emptied some time later, Scott stood staring at the coiled film. There had been no discernible reaction from the audience; could he have imagined the entire sequence?

"Hey, can I go now?"

Startled, Scott turned to see Candy standing nonchalantly in the projection room doorway.

"Yeah, I suppose so. Everything all set downstairs?"

She nodded, chewing gum energetically. "Of course. I'll deposit the box office take on the way home. You okay? You look kind of funny."

"Me? I'm fine. See you tomorrow." He was aware that he sounded distracted but he couldn't help it. Absentmindedly, he followed her downstairs to the lobby.

"Okay. Sure. See you." She watched him for another second, then turned and left.

That's when he noticed the kid with the thick rimmed glasses standing at one side of the lobby.

"Excuse me, mister." The kid stepped out of the shadows as Scott silently cursed Candy for not making sure everyone was gone. Scott estimated the kid was barely into his teens. "Was that some special cut of *Forbidden Planet* or something?"

So he hadn't imagined it. But he didn't want to give anything away to this kid. Not until he had a chance to think. Scott kept his expression neutral. "What do you mean? It looked fine to me."

The boy seemed confused. "Some of that stuff wasn't in the original movie. I thought maybe it was a restored version, like they did with *King Kong*, you know."

Scott shrugged. "I don't know, kid; I just show 'em. Sometimes we get the old ones spliced together wrong. Come on, let's go. I have to lock up."

Later that night, somewhere deep in his brain, Scott conceived the idea that this variant of the original film might be valuable, but try as he might, he could think of no way to take advantage of the situation. It would have to be sent back to the distributor in the morning; even if he had the facilities to copy it first, he had no idea how to make use of his discovery. The thought that he was missing a chance to make money, possibly quite a lot of money, was disturbing.

The very next weekend, Scott realized that he had misjudged the situation.

It was a triple feature this time, starting with Gene Barry in *The War of the Worlds*. Scott paid little attention until the final moments, then moved his chair to a better vantage point. Next up was *Silent Running,* one of the few movies he still enjoyed watching, primarily because of the cleverly conceived robot characters. He had heard somewhere that they had actually hired amputees to play the parts, standing on their hands inside the confining costumes, and he never tired of trying to imagine how each shot had been constructed.

Within minutes, Scott knew that something was wrong. He knew without question that the crew member named Wolf was not a tall, slender, redheaded female. At least not until now. He was so stunned that he never even noticed later when, during the fight scene between Raquel Welch and Martine Beswicke in *One Million Years B.C.,* the former's furry bra was completely removed.

He waited impatiently for the last disheveled couple to fix their clothing and leave the auditorium, then descended to the lobby and helped Candy finish her cleaning up. She looked at him suspiciously - he had never offered any kind of assistance before – but made no comment.

"Walk me to the bank?" There had been two muggings in downtown Managansett that week and Candy had expressed concern about her own safety.

"Sorry." He shook his head. "I still have things to do before I leave."

She bit her lip. "I can wait, I guess. I'd feel better if I had some company while I'm carrying all that money."

Scott made an impatient noise. "It's not even a hundred dollars, Candy, for Christ's sake!"

"The muggers don't know that."

He shifted his weight from one foot to the other. "Look, just leave it for me. I'll make the deposit myself on the way home, all right?"

She looked dubious. "I don't know. I'm really supposed to do that myself."

"Then do it and stop whining at me!" he exploded. "I'm not paid to be your bodyguard or your nursemaid."

Candy's eyes widened and her mouth opened as though she were about to respond in kind. But then her features twisted angrily and she snatched up the deposit bag, whirled, and stormed out of the theater.

Scott carefully remounted the film on the projector and restarted it, convinced that his fortune was made if he could figure out how to take advantage of his luck. The credits played through and the story began.

Wolf was once again an actor named Cliff Potts.

That evening, lying awake in bed, Scott Barkin reviewed the possibilities. There had been an opportunity for someone to switch copies while he was downstairs arguing with Candy, but that seemed wildly improbable. He might be going crazy, having hallucinated the entire thing, but he dismissed that immediately because clearly the kid had noticed the same variation in Forbidden Planet. The only other alternatives that occurred to him were that either there was some way to modify the images before they reached the screen, or there was some way to make multiple people share the same hallucination. He had no idea how this could be achieved, but perhaps some brilliant and reclusive inventor had developed such a device and was testing it secretly. Certainly Managansett, Rhode Island, was pretty remote, intellectually as well as physically. The entire town seemed to lag a decade or so behind the rest of the world.

There still might be some way he could take advantage of the situation, but to do so he would have to identify the source of the alterations. The next day was comedy night, *Arsenic and Old Lace* and *A Funny Thing Happened on the Way to the Forum*. He was familiar with both movies and ought to be able to spot any variations. Somehow he would have to figure out a way to trace them back to their source. He passed the night restlessly, trying to come up with plausible contingency plans.

Disappointingly, Sunday's screen passed without event, as did those throughout the week. Scott was ready to chalk everything up to fatigue and tension when he showed up for work on Saturday.

The Blob passed uneventfully enough, Steve McQueen saving the day in the final moments. The classic was followed by the darkly humorous sequel, *Beware the Blob*, one of the few Scott hadn't seen before. His unfamiliarity caused him to miss some subtle divergences from the original, the highly revealing dress Carol Lynley wore during the party sequence, the dissolving of Cindy Williams' clothing during her death scene. The third feature, however, was another of his favorites.

Originally, Bradford had ordered *The Stuff*, another bloblike film to complete the triple feature. The distributor had accidentally substituted *Close Encounters of the Third Kind* which, while mismatched, was to Scott's thinking a much better movie.

His enjoyment turned to excitement during the scene in which Richard Dreyfuss and Terri Garr have an hysterical fight in their bedroom. Frustrated, confused, even frightened, Dreyfuss/Roy struck out at his wife. Garr/Ronnie fell back against the wall in astonishment, then began to struggle as her distraught husband tore at her bathrobe and began making violent love to her. They were both naked when their children arrived to investigate the disturbance.

Scott rushed downstairs as the film was ending to ensure that he could surreptitiously watch the patrons on their way out. To his disappointment everyone looked perfectly ordinary. There were several young couples who came regularly to neck in the back rows, two young males who seemed to have arrived separately and whose faces were familiar, a couple of elderly men, one distracted woman who constantly sub vocalized to herself, and the kid with the glasses.

Scott crossed to intercept the kid, trying to make it look casual. "How'd you like the show?"

The kid peered up at him dubiously. "I don't know where you get these cuts, mister, but if my mom finds out what you're showing here, she'll never let me come again."

"Let's not tell her then, right?"

When the theater was empty, Candy locked the door from the inside. She hadn't forgiven him his churlishness.

"Don't you have things to do?" She glared at him until he turned away, but he hadn't even noticed. His mind was racing at top speed.

Just to be certain, he rechecked the tape before leaving for the night. The screen now showed the original, unaltered version.

Obviously whatever device was being used was quite small, virtually undetectable. Even if it was some kind of hallucinatory gas, it would have to be contained in something. Perhaps he could at least identify who was carrying it into the theater. Scott began paying more attention to the movies as he showed them, but as he had expected, nothing happened during the next few days. He had concluded by now that whoever was responsible came on Saturday nights only, for the science fiction program.

The following Saturday, a notebook and pen were at hand. Scott knew few of the customers by name, but most of them were familiar enough that he could mark down some significant characteristic by which to differentiate one from another. He made twenty-seven entries in all, either while taking tickets or later, during a leisurely stroll through the theater before bringing down the house lights.

The Creature from the Black Lagoon passed uneventfully except that the female lead wore a bikini instead of her former one piece bathing suit. *Barbarella*, however, was transformed.

Scott knew something was up right from the opening sequence when the nude Jane Fonda received her assignment. He couldn't remember precisely how explicit the original scene had been, but this screening was downright lewd. Judging by the murmuring from various parts of the audience, the movie had even captured the attention of some of those in the back rows. And it didn't end with just the one change. Almost every encounter was altered in some fashion, always designed to provide longer and more revealing glimpses of Barbarella's body. The sequence involving the now transparent pleasure machine was so erotic that it evoked a sharp outcry froms someone in the audience.

The kid with the glasses gave him a strange look when he came out, but he rushed out of the lobby without speaking.

The next several weeks encompassed a painful process of elimination. Scott had decided to drop from his original list of suspects anyone who was absent during a subsequent incident. David Warner's rape of Mary Steenburgen in *Time After Time* eliminated seven people the very next weekend, but it took two more nights to eliminate the next five, which still left eleven contenders. Confusing the issue was an influx of new customers, primarily high school kids who had heard rumors of X-rated movies. Scott's quarry must have noticed that something was amiss or that his or her presence was suspected because there were no more revised scenes for almost a month, long enough that attendance dropped back to its usual levels.

Scott was on the verge of giving up when the changes resumed. They had been growing increasingly daring all along, and the single minded sexual nature of the alterations continued. But now the sex was frequently distorted, even violent. The mute girl, Nova, was subjected to some sort of painful electrical stimulation in *Planet of the Apes*, and the Morlocks tied Weena over an open fire for a prolonged sequence in *The Time Machine*.

For three straight weeks Scott was unable to eliminate anyone from his remaining list of suspects, which included two teenagers, the woman who talked to herself, an old man who seemed to fall asleep frequently, a man in his mid-twenties who suffered from the worst case of acne Scott had ever seen, and an overweight middle-aged man whom Scott had chosen for no particular reason as the most likely person to be the culprit. The kid with the glasses had stopped coming after Dian the Beautiful was savagely ravished in *At the Earth's Core*.

On the last Saturday in November, Scott got lucky.

For one thing, it was sleeting and the weather threatened to get even worse. Candy had been glancing nervously outdoors ever since she had arrived, even though she lived only six blocks away. Only seven people bought tickets and two of them were among those Scott had already eliminated. There was also an older couple he had never seen before. That left the acne case, the middle-aged man, and one teenage boy, the one who always sat by himself. He was Scott's second choice.

The first feature was Night of the Comet. For a long time Scott was afraid that there would be no change in the script, that this would be another wasted night in which he could eliminate no one. But when the insane stock boys stripped and spanked the two sisters before tying them up, he knew his quarry was in the theater.

There were only three possibilities.

Then the middle-aged man rose and walked up the aisle to the door, zipping up his coat on the way. Scott ran quickly downstairs and confirmed that the man had indeed left the theater. Two suspects remained – acne face and the quiet boy.

The second feature was Wavelength, a relatively low key story about a young couple who stumble upon a secret military base where three extraterrestrials are imprisoned. Scott watched intently but with growing unease. If nothing changed, did that mean the older man was his quarry? The brief nude scene early in the movie passed without being changed and Scott settled back in his chair thoughtfully, trying to decide how best to proceed.

The story unrolled before him but Scott's mind was elsewhere as Robert Carradine and Cherie Currie made their way through a series of tunnels, eventually to be discovered and captured. He was so preoccupied, in fact, that he never did see how the girl's sweater was lost during the fight with the guard, and only the brutality of the beating that followed was enough to startle him from his thoughts.

Scott was downstairs waiting even before the closing credits began to scroll across the screen. Just possibly something in the demeanor of one of the two remaining suspects would tip him off. Acne Face walked by, eyes downcast, hands tucked into coat pockets, and never even looked in Scott's direction.

The quiet boy never came out at all.

Scott checked the theater thoroughly but there was no sign of him. Some of his perplexity must have shown because Candy asked him if anything was wrong.

"One of the customers never came out," he explained. "That mousy kid with the buzz cut who's in here all the time. Maybe I ought to check the restrooms."

"Don't bother." She sighed. "He took right after the second picture started. I heard him call for a ride. I guess the weather made him nervous."

The world seemed to freeze for a moment. "Are you sure? He left right after the intermission?"

She shrugged. "About then, yeah. It was just after that old guy who comes here a lot walked out. What difference does it make?"

Scott never answered her question, never even heard it, and a few seconds later Candy turned away, shaking her head.

The following Saturday Scott was waiting for Acne Face, having decided upon his strategy the night before.

"I know what you've been doing," he whispered as he accepted the ticket. Startled eyes met his own, then darted away.

"I don't..." his voice drifted off.

"Wait for me outside, half an hour after the show ends." Scott spoke more firmly now that he'd started. "I won't tell anyone so long as you do what I say."

There was no reply but the look of guilt that passed over the acne-scarred features was as good as a confession.

There were no changes in that evening's double feature.

"I'm Scott." He offered his gloved hand in the darkness outside the theater. The slouched figure standing in the shadow made no effort to respond. "What's your name?"

"Chuck. Chuck Scusset."

"Please to meet you, Chuck. Look, it's freezing out here. Why don't we go some place quiet and talk about this, somewhere warm?"

And so it was that they ended up in Chuck Scusset's apartment only eight blocks from the theater.

Scott was no fanatic about neatness, but he was appalled by his surroundings. Chuck lived in what amounted to a bed-sitting room with an adjoining half bath on the third floor of Managansett's seediest apartment building. Other than the bed there was a single folding chair and a card table, no other furnishings. Chuck's clothing was apparently stored in two cheap suitcases and a half dozen cardboard boxes he had retrieved from behind one of the local markets. Chuck had taken the chair so Scott was forced to sit on the bed, the only relatively uncluttered area available.

It was evident that Chuck was a science fiction fan. There were piles of genre paperbacks and digest sized magazines filling shelves on the walls and piled on the floor. A model of the starship Enterprise stood in one corner of the room, surrounded by figures of monsters, aliens, and space-suited humans. There was no other indication whatsoever of human habitation except for an occasional candy wrapper or empty potato chip bag.

"So how do you do it?" Scott asked.

"I didn't do anything," came the sullen reply.

"No shit? The movies just changed themselves and you let me come up here just because you're a friendly guy."

No response.

Scott leaned forward, hands on knees. "Listen, Chuck. You're messing with copyrighted material here. You could get into a lot of trouble doing that."

"I don't hurt anything,"

Scott sat back, sighing with satisfaction. "Ah, but you do change things, don't you?"

For a few short seconds, it seemed as if Chuck was going to retreat into denial once more, but at last he nodded.

"All right, then. We can work out a deal, can't we?" Scott didn't wait for an answer. "Show me how you do it."

Chuck glanced away, apparently examining a water stain on the wall. "Can't."

Scott made an impatient noise. "Cut the crap, Chuck. You already admitted you're doing it, now show me the goddamn thing, whatever it is."

Chuck's eyes snapped back to look at him and his lips pressed firmly together. "I can't. I do it with, you know, my head. Like, I imagine how I want the story to go and it just changes."

This wasn't at all what Scott had expected and he wasn't sure how he liked it.

"You mean, there's no machine or anything like that? It's just something you can do but not anyone else?"

Chuck nodded.

Visions of a vanishing fortune raced through his head. But perhaps not everything was lost. He could arrange private showings, charge hundreds, maybe even thousands, of dollars for the privilege of viewing a previously unseen version of a famous movie. Maybe Chuck could do things like substitute Cary Grant for Clark Gable in *Gone With the Wind* or something. But wouldn't the studios want a big cut if he did that, or maybe file an injunction or lawsuit to make him stop?

"Listen, Chuck, there might be a lot of money in this for us."

"What do you mean?"

Scott provided a general summary of his ideas, not being too specific in part because he didn't want Chuck to suspect how hazy his planning was and partly because he wanted to suggest that he possessed arcane knowledge that would be necessary to make the plan work. It would never to have Chuck think that he might be able to work this all on his own.

"How much can you change things anyway? Could you maybe to a whole movie from nothing?"

Chuck shook his head and almost smiled. He'd begun to relax a bit, Scott noticed, but the set of his shoulders and neck was still alert, intent. "No, I can only, you know, kind of guide things as they go along. If I try to change too much, I lose control. I have to stay close to the structure underneath. Otherwise there's too much to keep track of."

Scott nodded. "Too bad, but I kind of thought that might be the case. That's why you only changed some of the movies, right?"

"I guess." With another of the sudden mood swings that Scott had already begun to recognize, Chuck had turned taciturn again.

"How come all the sex anyway? That's what gave you away, you know."

Chuck looked away, hands twisting in his lap, unspeaking.

"Come on, we're going to be friends, you and me. We don't need to have any secrets. If we're going to get rich, I have to understand how this works, how you make it happen, how much you can do."

Without turning away from his contemplation of the wall, Chuck shook his head.

Exasperated, Scott slapped his knees with his palms. "Listen, Chuck. I'm trying to be nice about this. Remember, I know about you. I can tell people what you've been doing."

Chuck didn't speak but he began rocking back and forth on the chair and his head jerked nervously, like a bird searching for insects in the grass. Scott thought he had the situation sized up pretty well but decided he didn't to push his point now, establish his claim before Chuck had time to think things through on his own.

"How would you like it if I told people you were a sexual pervert, Chuck? What do you think would happen then?"

Chuck's head twisted around, eyes wide, mouth moving as though he was speaking although he didn't say a word at first. His hands were so tightly clenched that his knuckles were white. "I wasn't hurting anybody! It was all just pretend!"

"Sure, just pretend sex. And pretty rough sex too. Rape and beatings and pain, right? That's what turns you on, isn't it?"

Head twisting desperately from side to side, Chuck seemed to be searching for an escape route. Convinced that he had the other man securely trapped by his own guilt, Scott leaned back and lay full length on the bed.

"But that's okay, Chuck. I won't tell anyone that you're a sicko whose only value to anyone, including himself, is that he has this trick inside his head that lets him change the way movies appear on the screen. As long as you play ball, your secret is safe."

"No! No one's gonna tell on me again. Not ever."

At first the words and the tone were so different that Scott didn't actually understand them. He raised his upper torso, balanced on his elbows, and saw that Chuck's posture had changed dramatically. He was leaning forward, both hands raised and clenched into fists. His eyes met Scott' squarely and didn't flinch away.

"I'll do you just like I did my old man." And suddenly, inappropriately, Chuck began to smile.

Scott felt the change first in his chest, a funny, itching sensation that fell just short of pain. For a few seconds he thought he might be having a heart attack and he glanced down the length of his body. Slowly but perceptibly his chest was bulging outward, forming a recognizable if somewhat exaggerated shape. The buttons on his shirt popped and the material peeled back revealing not his familiar, slightly hairy chest but instead a creamy, abundant female bosom.

When he felt the itching start between his legs, Scott panicked and tried to rise from the bed, only to discover that the blankets had somehow become twisted around his wrists and ankles, holding him firmly in place. Chuck Scusset rose, smiling broadly now, eyes preternaturally bright. The itching sensation grew more intense and Scott felt the muscle in his thighs and calves shifting, assuming different contours. Even his bones felt different. There was an odd pull at the base of his back, as though his pelvis had assumed a different shape, and his buttocks were swelling.

"What the fuck are you doing to me?" He tried to put strength into his voice but they sounded desperate even to him. And the pitch wasn't quite right. It sounded softer, more feminine.

"You've got good hair." Chuck spoke quietly, standing over him now. "I won't even have to change it." Scott's bonds pulled him back down onto the bend, pulling all four limbs taut.

Chuck had a knife now, held it in one hand while he used the other to undo the belt of Scott's pants. "It's not just movies I can change, you know. It's just that they're a lot easier."

Scott was stunned by what he saw as Chuck pulled down his jeans and underwear. There was far less of him than he was used to seeing. A part of him had disappeared completely. The blade flashed through the air in front of his face.

"But this is much more fun," said Chuck as the knife dropped. For the first time.

PRESENT IN SPIRIT

They watch me all the time.

I can't see them, exactly, but I can feel them, feel their eyes moving over my body even in my most private moments, in the shower, sleeping semi-naked in the humid August air, sitting on the can. The sensation is unmistakable, like a low electric charge passing over my skin, stirring the tiny black hairs on my forearms. Then I begin to sweat, not the honest sweat of summertime or hard work but almost a secretion, my body reacting to those violating eyes. And I know then that I'm not alone.

I think I'm haunted.

At first, I dismissed it all as nerves. I'm a rational person; my life has been structured on a framework of logic and common sense. What works I keep; what doesn't work deserves to be discarded, whether it's a broken tool, an outmoded concept, or an inadequate subordinate. Those principles guide me at home or at work, allow me to take a commanding position in both environments.

The purpose of business, for example, is to maximize profits, for the company and for the individual. This crap about participatory management is a ploy, a way for the sheep to exert control over the wolves. Wolves are survivors because they earn that right; if you're content to remain within the herd, don't expect any sympathy from me. I earned the top spot at Eblis Manufacturing and I apologize to no one for what I had to do to get there.

You'd have done the same in my position, if you had the guts.

The first time was at a company picnic. You know, one of those misguided attempts to foster a sense of family. Business and family are two separate entities, and the tendency to blur that distinction has been responsible for more bankruptcies and broken careers than I care to contemplate. I almost welcomed the faltering sales that led to its discontinuance some years back.

I was fairly low on the corporate totem pole that day, Inventory Control Manager, not a particularly powerful position given the simpleminded predisposition of President Bowes to give manufacturing whatever it wanted regardless of the economics of the situation. But back then, we could sell just about anything we made, the market seemed a bottomless pit waiting to be filled with giftware, and it was hard to rein in shortsighted enthusiasms.

"Can I sign you up for the bag races, Mr. Nicholson?"

It was Penny Redfern from the typing pool, called Penny Dreadful behind her back because of her horrible complexion problem. "I'm really not the athletic type, Penny. Why don't you try Joe Forester?" It was an effort to be polite; this entire day was a waste of time, but attendance was unofficially mandatory for managers.

"But we heard you play racquetball. Come on, it'll be fun." Penny's companion and roommate, Jennifer Sears, was almost strikingly attractive in a cheap sort of way. Rumor had it she was sleeping with the shipping supervisor, and the stockroom clerk, and a few others.

I played racquetball because it enjoyed considerable popularity within the layer of management directly above me and for no other reason. It happened that I had a natural talent for the game, and I derived a certain perverse satisfaction from seeing how close I could drive Nelson or Boggs or Garabedian to exhaustion before missing an easy shot and forfeiting a match.

I suppressed the urge to suggest that Penny adopt the sack as a way of concealing her raspberry complexion. "Then you've probably also heard that I play badly."

"That doesn't matter, Mr. Nicholson," Jennifer pre-empted her companion. "This is just for fun. Come on, get out of that stuffed shirt for a couple of hours."

Insolence reaps its own reward. "Some of us prefer to keep our clothes on, Miss Sears, metaphorical or otherwise."

She stood there blinking for a few seconds, apparently needing the time to break down the meaning of my words, leech out the implications. Then her face turned pasty white and she bolted. Penny seemed honestly puzzled, gave a tentative parting gesture and hastened after her friend.

"Oh, there you are, James."

Just when I thought I could finally slip off by myself, Bowes showed up, with his inevitable Alan Crandall shadow.

"Hello, Mr. Bowes. Couldn't ask for better weather, could we?" Actually I'd have preferred a violent thunderstorm to these bright, cloudless skies. It would have brought a welcome end to these insipid mock festivities.

"We've been very lucky. James, Alan here has just been telling me about your reorganization plan."

"Oh?" I hadn't expected my proposal to pass through so many levels so quickly, but I wasn't about to miss an opportunity to advance my position. "I think you'll find it will speed things up considerably, and save a few salaries as well."

"Yes, well, that's what I meant to talk to you about. Economies are all well and good, of course, and I commend your efforts, but as I understand it, you plan to let go your three most senior people and replace them with clerical workers."

"In a manner of speaking. We'll have to rewrite the job descriptions, of course, to avoid the possibility of legal action, but frankly the more complex aspects of their jobs have been automated, and they haven't really earned their paychecks in over a year."

Bowes was plainly uncomfortable, wouldn't meet my eyes. How could this man ever have ascended to the presidency of Eblis, I wondered. He can't even face one of his junior executives.

"But Ted Barnwell has over twenty years with the company, and Simone Moran has been with us even longer."

"Excuse me, sir, but the Dennison press you had us scrap last month was forty years old."

"But it was obsolete, James. It couldn't accommodate our new die sets."

I didn't answer, just kept my eyes level, letting Bowes interpolate from his own words. To his credit, it didn't take long. "We'll talk about this further, James, at another time."

And he was gone, and Crandall with him, leaving me mercifully alone. Or so I thought.

It wasn't a specific feeling at first, more an undercurrent of uneasiness. The crowd was moving toward the athletic field, except for a few diehards congregating around the beer kegs and the sizzling grills. With Bowes' departure, I had slipped back into the woods surrounding the picnic area, wondering if I could make it across to the parking area without anyone noticing that I was leaving.

Someone was watching me.

I told you my life was based on logic, but that doesn't mean I'm not open to the possibility that my understanding of the world might have its flaws, that there might be things lurking just beyond the limits of my understanding.

Someone was standing in among the vine covered trees a dozen meters away. I couldn't see him very well, but it was clearly a child in his early teens. My first reaction was to move away, but there was something familiar about the boy, something that tickled the edges of my memory. I took a tentative step forward.

"You'd better not go too far from the clearing," I said quietly. "These woods go back for miles and you could get lost."

No answer, no movement, but I knew he'd heard me.

That's when the tactile sensations began, the creeping itchiness on my arms and legs. I shivered a little, wondering if I was coming down with a summer cold, not yet connecting the discomfort to the apparition. Because that's what it was, an apparition, make no mistake about it.

The boy abruptly stepped out into a puddle of light that dripped down through a hole in the foliage and I recognized George Shackleton.

If I was the kind of person whose perspective was locked onto the past, I would've spent a great deal of time thinking about my childhood friendship with George. We were an unlikely pair, him the bookworm, me the secret hell raiser. Both of us were caricatures of sorts, lacking the depth that comes with maturity. Even then, George was a professional victim, took the blame for more than a few of my pranks, the soaping of Mrs. Beck's windshield, the bag of sugar dumped in Old Man Grayson's gas tank. It never seemed to bother him that he was being punished for things I'd done.

George suffered from an excess of contentment, as far as I could see. He was happy to accept what life offered and never made the extra effort necessary to achieve something better. The last I had heard of him, he was still stuck in a no-future job, devouring trashy science fiction novels when he should have been developing his career skills.

The youngster who emerged from the trees was unmistakably George, probably twelve or thirteen years old. He had a crew cut and a Mickey Mouse Club t-shirt and there was a paperback book stuck in his side pocket. I shivered and turned away, more disturbed than I care to remember, and when I looked back, he was gone.

The following week, I checked the phone book. George was still alive. I called, found out he was working as a data entry clerk in Providence, single, overweight, and with no prospects. Rather sad. He suggested we get together, talk over old times, and I reluctantly agreed. "My schedule is pretty tight though. You know how it is, if you want to make something of yourself, you have to eat, sleep, and breathe your job."

He took the hint and never called back.

It was Dolly the next time. Dolly's my wife, a role for which she is well suited, most of the time. Some adjustment was involved, mostly on her part, before we settled into the proper relationship. Dolly is bright, enthusiastic, and even witty in a superficial way, the perfect corporate wife. Her enthusiasms are sometimes misguided, but her intentions are good. When she suggested that she find a job to supplement my inadequate pay as a management trainee, her motives were undoubtedly just as she'd stated them. But I knew where that path would lead, to a split in the definition of family head, and the turmoil that would inevitably follow. I forbade it, but as gently as possible, and truthfully I think she welcomed my decision because it gave her more time to spend with young Eric.

It was Thanksgiving weekend, the year Eric started school. Dolly wanted us all to spend the holiday with her parents in Vermont, but I had planned the time off to work on the following year's budget. Nor was I particularly willing to visit my in-laws. Fred had never liked me, made no secret of the fact, and I think Ernestine's overt friendliness was a mask she wore for her daughter's sake. She was clearly the stronger of the two personalities, though, and Fred's ineffectual job performance had left them with a barely adequate income for their retirement.

In any case, Dolly and Eric were gone for the weekend; her pregnancy wasn't advanced so far that she couldn't safely drive. The house was blissfully free of both Eric's constant caterwauling and Dolly's domestic soundtrack, so I hoped to get considerable work done.

Someone was crying.

I straightened up from my desk, startled and outraged, startled because I had become so absorbed in my work that any outside stimulus was disorienting, outraged because the desolate sobbing clearly originated inside the house. Someone had invaded my home.

Cautiously, I stepped out into the hall, trying to identify the source. It was from the rear of the house, one of the bedrooms. The sound was not at all menacing, but I slipped into the living room, quietly lifted one of the irons from the rack by the fireplace, and made my way to the rear.

The source was the master bedroom. The outrageousness of the intrusion overcame my nervousness and I advanced quickly, the iron at port arms, ready for action.

A half naked woman was sitting on my bed, our bed, facing away from me.

"Who the hell are you and what are you doing here?"

I had a forewarning of what was to come, although I didn't realize it until later. My skin felt as though it were trying to crawl off and every hair on my body was standing at attention.

The strange woman turned at the sound of my voice, revealing a familiar but disturbing face. It was Dolly, my wife, but not the Dolly I'd seen off early that morning. This was a younger version, her hair as long as it had been when we were first married, the face softer, more innocent. Her left eye was darkly discolored and a thin line of dried blood ran from the side of her mouth down to the point of her chin.

"Why, James? Why? I was just trying to help. You told me how important it was to be nice to people."

I reeled back into the corridor, so disoriented that my stomach lurched threateningly and I had to brace myself by leaning against a wall. It was an exact replay of an incident from my past, one that I admit is not a moment of which I am proud. It was the first company Christmas party since I'd become an assistant supervisor at Eblis, in charge of material handling. I'd stressed to Dolly the importance of making a good impression and she'd cooperated enthusiastically. A bit too enthusiastically, I'd thought at the time, my judgment distorted by an atypical overindulgence. It was the only time I'd ever struck Dolly, and in retrospect it was almost certainly an overreaction. On the other hand, she'd never challenged my authority again, not even the gentle chiding she'd employed throughout our courtship.

When I regained my self control and returned to the bedroom, it was empty, of course. I decided I'd been working too hard and went for a lengthy, soothing walk. Retrospectively, I wonder if I truly fooled myself even then, if I had not already realized in some crude fashion what was happening to me.

I was being haunted by the living.

Any doubts I might have had were adequately disposed of a few days later. It was a dark December night, threatening snow although none had fallen. Sales for the past three months had been twenty percent below projections, a foretaste of the general market softness that would plague us for the next two years. Most of my fellow vice-presidents chose to characterize it as an anomaly, a combination of dumping by our foreign competitors, uneasiness and underbuying by the major retail chains, and general consumer uncertainty, unfounded but devastating in its effect.

The actual yearend figures weren't out yet, but Jamieson, the comptroller, was under certain obligations to me and I knew roughly what they were going to be. Bad, across the line and under the double line, the first operating loss in the company's history.

Spring would see major upheavals at Eblis, careers ended. I was determined that mine would not be one of them.

The position of Vice President of Production and Inventory Planning was newly created and therefore even less secure than usual. My strategy was to present a plan to integrate labor reporting and material handling within that function, eliminating two supervisory positions and at least one laborer. The savings would be significant, and it would also deal a blow to the powerbase of my most serious rival, Sandy Bennett, who headed Production Administration. Sandy was methodical and inventive, but like most of her sex, overly preoccupied with details and lacking the killer instinct. If I worked things right, she'd be put into a position where she wouldn't even be able to argue against the merits of the change without appearing to be self serving.

I had worked out the personnel realignment, but there were problems with the reporting structure, conflicts of interest that Bennett would jump on in an attempt to discredit the entire proposal.

A way around them would have to be found before I could make the presentation, but my mind seemed to have locked up. I decided to take a walk through the factory to clear the fog.

It was dark and quiet on the production floor, the few security lights barely illuminating the walkways. I made my way through the pressroom, nodded to the security guard as he logged in at the key station, then headed for the polishing area, climbed to the catwalk and started toward the east end of the building.

I think I knew I was no longer alone even before Larisa called my name. The familiar agitation of my nerves, the clamminess of my skin, the hyper acuity of my senses, all the signs were there.

"Why'd you do it, Nicholson?"

I spun on one foot, searching the shadows, already recognizing the voice. He stepped out into the light, perhaps ten meters away. If it was an hallucination, it was a damned effective one; I even heard the catwalk creak under his weight.

"Joe! What are you doing here?"

"I came to see you, James. We're friends after all. Isn't that what you always told me? Allies against the bumblers at the top."

Larisa had been production scheduler when I was running inventory control and we'd worked out of the same plywood sided office on the manufacturing floor. Neither of us had many secrets, but I'd held onto mine. Joe, foolishly, had been forthright about his difficulties.

"Alliances change, Joe. It's all part of the game. What can I do for you?"

The conversation was surreal, a warped version of reality. On the day of his dismissal, Joe had come to see me all right, cornered me in the plating room. But he hadn't said anything specific, just stared and nodded and turned away, as though he'd read everything he needed to know from my face, my posture, my silence.

"Nothing at all, James. It's my turn to do something for you, as a matter of fact. Call it an installment on an old debt."

"What are you talking about?"

But Joe didn't answer, just reached out and dropped a folder onto the catwalk. "With my compliments." He stepped back into the shadows, and when I looked for him, there was no indication that he'd ever been there physically at all. Which wasn't surprising, since he'd made an abortive attempt on his own life five years earlier and was still paralyzed from the neck down, as I confirmed the next day.

But the folder of papers seemed very solid when I retrieved it, and it contained a detailed plan for the elimination of Sandra Bennett's entire department. The next morning, I couldn't find any trace of those documents, but the knowledge remained, imbedded in my brain, and I worked all night to incorporate them into my own master plan.

It was a solid proposal. Admittedly it was self serving, but the logic was unassailable, the savings substantial and real, and the elimination of a layer of management would have made the production process more responsive to actual demand. I was really quite proud of it, and under any other circumstances, it would have established me as a force to be reckoned with.

How was I supposed to know that Bennett was fucking Bowes?

The manifestations came with increasing frequency after that, and I quickly came to recognize the forewarnings, the physiological changes triggered by their appearance. Ted Nazarian accosted me one evening while I was walking back from the corner store, berating me for having complained to my parents that he kept putting his hands on me, often in indelicate places. It wasn't entirely a lie; he had taken me out behind the school and spanked me soundly, a clear violation of policy, when he caught me rummaging through Violet MacLennon's locker. If I'd bothered to think about him at all during the previous ten years, I'd have assumed he was dead, but now I think he must still be alive.

Lucy Deacon was sitting in my car one evening, still seventeen years old, belly swollen by an unplanned pregnancy. "You could at least have admitted you were the father, Jimmy. Do you have any idea what I had to go through afterwards, when no one believed me and everyone thought I'd just named you because you were good looking and your parents had money?"

"It wouldn't have worked out," I answered lamely. "Besides, it's not as if I raped you or anything. You practically seduced me, Lucy."

I blinked when she slapped me, and when my eyes opened, she was gone. But my cheek stung anyway.

And so it continued, a parade of people who'd crossed my path to their detriment, all of them still alive insofar as I could tell. I gave up checking after a while. Usually they accused me of past sins, occasionally they offered advice, which I carefully ignored. The encounter with Joe Larisa told me how reliable their council might be.

Had I lost my mind? Was this all guilt spawned delusion? I have to admit that possibility occurred to me more than once. There was no independent confirmation of any of the early manifestations, and my suspicion that I was the target of an elaborate hoax wouldn't stand up under close examination. For whatever reason, by whatever means, I was experiencing visitations from my past, either figments of my own imagination or the product of some natural process outside of everyday logic.

But they weren't delusions. Any doubt I might have entertained on that account was swept away by Scott Talbot.

Scott was one of my few overt enemies. I've had rivals by the score, contenders for this position or that achievement or the girl standing at the bar or the empty space right in front of the barber shop. But only one true enemy. We graduated from Managansett High together; he was the star of the basketball and baseball teams, I was class president. I'd lured Helen Tremblay away from him during our junior year, and he stole Peg Mahaffey when we were seniors.

Through happenstance, we drew adjoining rooms at the University of Rhode Island, and the proximity sharpened our antagonisms. I ran for floor president and Scott quietly but effectively campaigned for my opponent, an out of state student whose name I don't even remember. Fortunately, I pledged a fraternity early and moved out of the dorm, but I didn't forget about Scott. Unpaid debts always come back to haunt you; if I let him strike the final blow, he'd consider me fair game ever after.

A year passed, and then another. Juniors now, I was a member of the student government and Scott was likely to bring the basketball team to national attention for the first time in a decade. We'd met briefly on a few occasions during the previous two years, polite but mutually distant encounters at first, more amicable later. Scott either forgot about our earlier animosity or decided it was history, not worth worrying about.

History has a way of striking back at the disloyal.

It wasn't hard to get the drugs; you could buy anything you wanted right on campus with a minimum of hassle. And since Scott didn't lock his door, planting them in his closet wasn't all that difficult either. But the campus police ignored two anonymous calls and a letter, and I was finally compelled to call the state police and pose as one of Scott's "customers" before anyone actually checked it out.

Scott never knew that I was responsible for his expulsion, of course, but I guess he must have suspected.

The envelope was addressed to me and contained a thick packet of photographs. Dolly and Scott at the beach, in a restaurant, in bed together, Dolly performing services that she rarely if ever agreed to unless I insisted.

"It's all over with," she told me tearfully when I confronted her. "It lasted a week or two. You were so tied up at work that I was lonely and Scott came along at the right time I guess." And then she collapsed into tears.

I went looking for him, of course, found him eventually. After a fashion anyway. Scott Talbot was serving a life sentence in a Pennsylvania prison and had been there for nearly ten years. Impulsively I'd asked to see him, found a withered husk of the young man I'd known, nothing at all like the person in the pictures.

I'm not certain he even recognized me.

The encounters came with increasing frequency after that, sometimes overlapping, until I no longer ever felt that I was truly alone. Crowds were the worst; there was always the feeling that someone was staring out at me, accusing me of some imagined crime, threatening retribution or demanding an explanation. Occasionally I was fooled into confronting someone, only to discover it was an innocent bystander with a chance resemblance to a memory from my past. I cultivated calmness, struggled to ignore these interlopers.

I became President of Eblis when Bowes finally lost his battle with cancer. The bastard had refused to resign even when his kidneys were turning to mush and he had to be driven to and from the office.

My tenure lasted exactly one month, to the day, and I resigned only because the alternative was public dismissal. At least by tendering my resignation for "personal reasons", I could hope to find an acceptable position elsewhere.

It was the letters that did me in.

The Board of Trustees was deluged with them, apparently, letters questioning my character, my honesty, my loyalty to the company, even my competence as a manager. They came from people I had known, some I still knew, others I had forgotten entirely. Scott Talbot wrote from prison, claiming I'd been his partner in a drug distribution scheme. Lucy Deacon insisted I was the father of her illegitimate, now teenaged son. Violet MacLennon accused me of theft and Ted Nazarian insinuated that my sexual orientation was not what it seemed. There were similar accusatory letters from George Shackleton, Jennifer Sears, Penny Redfern, Joe Forester, Alan Crandall, Ted Barnwell, Simone Moran, Joe Larisa, and dozens of others, so many their names tend to blur when I try to remember them.

But one was worse than all the others.

I only found out about it by applying pressure on Jamieson, whose gambling IOU's were still locked in my wall safe. Dolly had written to the Board, Dolly, my wife, insisting that I was on the brink of a nervous collapse and that taking on this additional responsibility would certainly kill me.

"I was just trying to do what was best for us," she insisted tearfully. "I love you, James, don't you realize that? And seeing you jumping at shadows, talking to yourself, working yourself to death for no reason...I just couldn't let you continue that way without trying to help."

I was past anger, my rage so intense that even violence couldn't have provided an adequate outlet. Speechless, I turned away, meaning to walk out of the house, never to return. And then Dolly stopped me dead in my tracks.

"He said it would be for the best." She didn't even seem to be talking to me.

"Who said, Dolly?"

"What?" Her voice was distant, her eyes focused somewhere else.

"Who said it would be for the best?"

"Why, Joe Larisa, of course. Your best friend. He stopped by the house the other day and told me you'd been hallucinating and that he thought the workload was going to kill you."

"Dolly, Joe Larisa is paralyzed. He's been confined to a nursing home in Johnston for almost ten years."

"Well, he must have recovered then, because he seemed quite well when he stopped by here. He told me you have a lot more friends than you realize, James, and that I shouldn't worry anymore because they were all going to be watching out for you from now on."

And I guess they are.

THE DEAD BEAT SOCIETY

Jason saw the dead boy's face during his third viewing of the rock video.

He leaned forward, staring into the television screen, but the familiar face disappeared almost immediately into the manufactured mist that obscured most of the set. One finger brushed the surface of the tube, and a faint electric charge made his skin tingle. Even after the flaming finale, as the last strains of the Dead Beat Society's hit single *Payback* faded away, he sat dumbly, waiting for some explanation of what he had seen, or perhaps for the inevitable recovery of his sense of proportion, reassurance that he had fooled himself with a chance resemblance. But ten minutes later, he remained convinced that Mark Walton, or the image of Mark Walton, had been present in the video, one of the lost souls drifting through the mist of the void in which, according to the lyrics, they searched for salvation, consolation, or retribution. It was a transitory moment, obliterated by the fiery denouement, but no less powerful for its brevity.

It was impossible, of course. Mark had been enamored of rock music to a degree that even disconcerted his teenage friends, but the closest he had ever come to interacting with a genuine rock star was helping Jason sweep out their dressing rooms at the Sheffield Concert Hall in Providence. There was certainly no possibility that he had been involved in the production of a rock video prior to his death, almost exactly one year earlier, only three weeks before the two of them would have graduated from Managansett High School. That would have been a coup too marvelous to keep to himself. Neither was there any possibility that Mark had not really died, that the body recovered from the burning car on Breakneck Hill had been anyone else. Jason knew this with absolute certainty, because he had been there, had in fact been responsible for Walton's death.

"Goddamn," he whispered softly, sitting back in the overstuffed but leaking chair he had picked up from the Salvation Army thrift store while furnishing the dingy, dirty, overpriced apartment he had taken in Providence following graduation. His mother had offered to let him stay on at home, but his father's overt silence had been eloquent enough to dispel any lingering illusions he might have entertained about his welcome there. Besides, now that he was out of school, he needed his own place, room to stretch out and enjoy life.

"This shit's more powerful than I thought," he reflected, staring down at the home made joint that was slowly turning into ash on a plate littered with the remnants of last night's pizza. "Better go easy, Jason, or you'll be seeing vampires and werewolves next." He giggled inanely, without humor.

But the incident was disturbing enough that he watched all through the evening, waiting for the discordant, atonal strains of the Dead Beat Society to return, hoping to watch more closely this time. To no avail, as it happened; the video was not shown again that evening.

The incident had almost passed from his mind before it was repeated. He was in the kitchen, one day later, retrieving a cold beer from the small icebox to wash down a meatball sub, when he heard the opening guitar riff. He banged his thigh against a chair rushing into the other room, arrived as the guitars were fading back to give room to the electronic drums, an almost disturbing beat building with each recursion of the opening theme, understated at first, then progressively louder, more complex, pulling the listener into the monotonous but compelling pattern.

He waited patiently while the instrumental section receded, not even listening to the lyrics. A few seconds into the final verse, when the fog makers had concealed most of the set with billowing clouds, the Dead Beat Society visible above on their elevated stage, the "restless souls" moving below, appearing and disappearing in the mist, Mark Walton stepped out into clear view, head tracking from his own left toward the center of the screen, locking onto Jason's eyes for just a split second before fading away as an animated human figure enshrouded in flames rushed out to fill the entire screen, "the hell-born vengeance" of the final refrain.

And that was even more peculiar, because he was quite sure that, on the first occasion, the familiar face had appeared at the opposite side of the screen, and had moved slowly from left to right. This time "Walton" had remained relatively motionless, his features obscured only when the burning caricature rushed forward to fill the screen.

Could they have shot two different versions of the same video? It seemed unlikely.

Jason had some really good dope hidden unimaginatively in his refrigerator; the janitorial job at the Hall normally didn't pay that well, but his uncle was the manager, and nepotism was certainly numbered among his vices, even if he didn't think of Jason with any particular familial fondness. He'd been saving it for a special occasion, and currently his senses were distorted by nothing stronger than the single beer he'd downed immediately upon arriving home from work. So he was pretty certain that what he had seen was what had really been there.

So how had Mark Walton become part of a rock video that only appeared twelve months following his death?

Reluctantly, Jason allowed his mind to revert to the night when he and Mark had met for the last time.

Jason had been dealing in those days, low grade stuff he picked up from equally unreliable suppliers, cutting it himself out in the back of his garage when his old man wasn't around, repackaging it and selling primarily to younger kids who didn't know any better. Some of the little assholes could get high on just the idea of holding, didn't have to light up at all. He figured he was doing them a favor, keeping them away from the stronger stuff.

His mistake had been in telling Mark what he was doing, and providing a little cosmetic enhancement of the quality of his merchandise.

"How soon can you get me some of the good stuff? I need it for this weekend."

At first, Jason hadn't understood what Walton was talking about. The two were casual friends, after a fashion, united primarily in their interest in rock music and disdain for the faculty, staff, and most of the students at Managansett High.

Something of his confusion must have shown, because Walton moved forward, pressing him up against the hall locker. Voice lowered, he spoke rapidly, eyes alert for potential eavesdroppers.

"I got a hot date coming up Saturday night, you know? I think I can get in this bitch's pants if I loosen her up, you know, but I need to loosen her up."

Jason blinked with realization. "Oh, sure." He made a point of glancing around conspiratorially. "Look, meet me down at the cemetery tonight, around seven. It's gonna cost you, though."

"Yeah," Walton didn't seem distressed. "How much?"

Jason quoted a price that raised the other boy's eyebrows, but he didn't back off. "All right, but this better be some good shit."

"Oh, it is, Mark. It's the best."

It hadn't been. As a matter of fact, it wasn't even up to his own rather dismal standards. He had run through most of his supposedly uncut stock recently, and he suspected that his sources were heavily adulterating their wares even before he compounded the process. What remained would not accommodate Walton's demands and another delivery he had promised for the following day unless he became very creative.

"What the fuck," he said aloud, "he'll be so interested in getting laid, he'll never notice. Probably never had any good shit himself anyway."

Walton unfortunately had more experience with drugs than Jason had suspected, and had not been pleased. Sunday afternoon, the two stood next to Walton's car, parked off the road in Lincoln Woods State Park. Jason was trying to smooth things over, while Walton grew angrier with every passing moment. When Walton finally struck out angrily, slapping him along the side of the head, Jason had reacted without thinking, backing away, crouching down, and picking up the first thing that came to hand, a fist sized stone. Walton was, after all, three inches taller and thirty pounds heavier.

Perhaps confusing Jason's crouch for a cower, Walton had advanced again. "You'll never fuck me over again, you asshole!" Fury clouded Jason's vision as he rose, swinging his makeshift weapon up from the waist, aiming at Walton's jaw. But the larger boy ducked partially away and was struck instead squarely on his left eye socket. He dropped as though shot, unconscious, blood streaming from lacerated skin and what Jason realized was a burst eyeball.

Loading him back into the car wasn't so bad, nor did he feel any great remorse when he reached through the open window minutes later and shifted into drive, sending the car and its unaware passenger hurtling of the side of Breakneck Hill. To his disappointment, the vehicle did not burst into flames during its descent, and he was forced to climb down the wooded hillside and use his lighter to ignite a pool of spilled gasoline, then escape through the woods before anyone showed up to investigate.

He never did know whether Walton had survived the crash only to be burned to death. It didn't really seem to matter.

The night he first saw Walton in the video, he dreamed that he was attending a concert performed by the Dead Beat Society, and the audience had been filled with thousands of clones of Mark Walton. They had all been watching him, Jason Van Oort, not the performers, impaling him with their eyes. Transfixed by their stares, he was unable to react when the room erupted into flames, flames which quickly engulfed the seated figures, melting their features to reveal the naked skulls beneath the flesh.

He woke with a start, blinking, then scrambled to extinguish a small, smoldering flame in his blankets. Although he couldn't remember doing so, he must have lit a final cigarette before going to bed. He never did find it though and assumed it had been completely consumed by the fire.

Jason didn't have a rational explanation, and wasn't ready to accept a supernatural one, but without consciously deciding to do so, he stopped watching videos. He was taking in enough money from his job now that he could afford a really good CD player and a stack of discs, and there was always the radio. Within a few days he no longer felt the urge to flick on the television as soon as he arrived home. He even found himself enjoying *Payback*, which had climbed to number one in only its second week of release.

He'd already listened to the song dozens of times when he first heard the whispering.

It was an indistinct sound, a susurration below the level of clear audibility. At first he thought it was just surface noise, a bad recording that the radio station hadn't replaced. But by the time the song had ended, its final notes rising to a crescendo and abruptly cut off, he had grown convinced that there were actually spoken words scattered within the white noise. Once he even thought he had heard his name.

The undertones were there the next time he heard *Payback* as well, and on every occasion thereafter. He was never quite certain what was being said, no matter how closely he listened, but with each repetition, he became more convinced than ever that it wasn't just random noise, that there was some hidden message lurking, waiting to be deciphered.

So he decided to buy a copy of the CD and play it where he could adjust the bass and treble and try to bring some clarity to the fuzzy sound.

The Dead Beat Society's second album, *MELODY DRAMA*, was already rising on the charts, bolstered by the popularity of the lead single. Jason had no difficulty finding a stack of them piled up in a display in the front window of Raspberry's Stereo Shop. The picture on the cover was a shot from the video, the musicians standing at the top with arms upstretched, a half dozen wandering souls emerging from the mist below.

One of the faces was unquestionably that of Mark Walton.

"Hey, fellah. You all right?"

Jason glanced toward the man at his side, disoriented. "What? What's the matter?"

His sudden companion looked to be in his mid-twenties, dressed in low key punk style. "You looked really bummed out. I thought maybe you were sick or something." A cigarette stuck out pugnaciously, its end glowing red, and Jason found his eyes drawn to focus on that slowly crawling flame.

"No, shit no." He shook himself back into something like composure. "Just got to thinking and lost myself." He turned away, cutting the conversation off. After a second, the other man shrugged and walked off.

He bought a copy of the CD, carefully avoided looking at the picture, relieved that the bags at Raspberry's weren't transparent like at Music City.

Even with his relatively high quality equipment, it took considerable experimentation before he was able to improve the clarity of the whisper significantly, and even then he was only able to make out a few fragments, fragments which seemed almost to be answers to the lyrics themselves.

"A song unsung, by anyone," sang the Dead Beat Society, ending the first verse, and a trailing whisper added, "a life undone." The final line of the next was "Facing life with resignation" to which was appended, "hello Jason." And finally, following the concluding line, "Paybacks sometimes can be sweet" came "soon we'll meet."

Troubled, he turned off the CD player and glanced down to the floor where he had discarded the cover.

The too familiar face stared up out of the fog, smiling but without humor.

The next several days passed, each indistinct in his memory. Jason tried to stay high as much as possible, but his dreams remained disturbed, filled with fiery images of accusation. Although he worked pretty much on his own at the Concert Hall and was not popular even with the rest of the custodial staff, several people asked if he was feeling well, including, eventually, his uncle, who insisted he take a couple of days off, with pay of course.

Jason found that he could not bear to listen to the radio any longer; the possibility always existed that the next song to be played would be *Payback* or some other piece by the Dead Beat Society, and he didn't want to hear that whispering again. He had not removed *MELODY DRAMA* from his CD player, but had no intention of listening to it again. Ever. He had already thrown the cover into the garbage.

After two days, he forced himself to shower, shave, brush his hair into something approaching order, dress as neatly as possible in his unpressed, infrequently washed clothing, so that he could return to work. Something about his expression seemed to disconcert his co-workers, but there was nothing overt that they could object to, and he was soon set to replacing the posters in the display cases out front.

That's how he learned that the Dead Beat Society was booked to play two concerts at the hall, and only three weeks off. Jason was suddenly possessed of the certain knowledge that his answers lay there, if he could only find the right questions to ask.

The intervening period passed with dreamlike slowness, and it was with a certain degree of surprise that Jason awoke to the realization one Saturday afternoon that the arrival of the Dead Beat Society was only a few hours off.

Normally the maintenance staff was expressly forbidden to enter the stage area while the performers were present, but Jason's family connections had allowed him to bend the rules from time to time, although it was tacitly assumed that he would be circumspect in the matter. Tonight, he didn't care what the consequences might be; he was going to be in the wings when the group went onstage.

He waited until he was certain that the musicians were already in their dressing rooms behind the stage before working his way forward, carrying an overflowing box of trash for camouflage until he had reached his chosen waiting place, a jumble of infrequently used props, sound equipment, and other unidentifiable flotsam that had accumulated slightly to the rear and away from the audience, out of their line of sight, concealed by the curtain and the supporting structure for the light bars and other paraphernalia elevated above. When he was sure that he was unobserved, he slipped behind a rack of extension cords and crouched, waiting for his moment, and without realizing it, nodded off, dreaming of human figures dancing through fire.

No one noticed his slumping form as final preparations were completed for the evening's performance. Nor did he notice any of them.

"YOU SAY YOU'VE WAITED FOR ME, WELL I'M WORTH WAITING FOR," the opening line of *Cold Love* shocked Jason back to consciousness. He flailed about with both arms, disoriented, before remembering where he was and why. By the time he had recovered enough to peer out of his hiding place, the Dead Beat Society was working its way through the refrain. "YOUR HOT BLOOD IS NO MATCH FOR MY...ICE COLD LOVE."

Already the stage was obscured by an ankle high layer of mist rising from the fog makers below the stage, curling up around the feet of the musicians, spilling over the side and dissipating just before it reached the front row seats.

Now that the moment was upon him, Jason realized he had absolutely no idea how to proceed. Something had told him that he needed to confront the Dead Beat Society concerning Mark Walton's lingering presence, but how? Rush out on stage and shout accusations of supernatural powers, or act with more diplomacy? "Excuse me, sir, but could you tell me how it happens that a dead person appears in your video?" Sure, he could do that. As the last notes of *Cold Love* faded, Jason found himself near panic. Why hadn't he planned for this moment?

Motionless Emotion followed, the Society's first single, a moderately successful hit that had been eclipsed within weeks by the group's first million seller, *Paying the Dues*, into which they segued without pause. The closing instrumental section continued then, material not on either of their albums, perhaps spontaneous jamming even as he listened. Like most of their music, it was dominated by the relentless, inventive percussion of the drummer, a hermaphroditic type fortuitously named John Tapper, the least reclusive of the atypically reticent rock group. The keyboards played a shrill counterpoint that wove around the beat, while the three guitarists chased one theme after another, sometimes independently, always working their way back toward a regular, unified rise in volume that brought a small rush of inappropriate applause from the audience each time it crested. The mist became more pervasive, even penetrated into the wings, and the stage manager was working the lights to emphasize the flowing currents, highlighting the heads and torsos of the Dead Beat Society as they swayed above the roiling, earthbound cloud.

The music crashed to an abrupt stop and the audience exploded into shouts, screams, and more traditional applause. The artificial fog rushed out in ever greater volume, and the stagehands retreated before it. Jason took advantage of the cover to move closer to the musicians, but none of the staff looked in his direction as he advanced.

Deeper into the fog.

The uproar from beyond the stage lights died away while the members of the Dead Beat Society stood motionless, not responding to the evident adulation. They were a strange group, lacking a dynamic stage personality but undeniably exerting a considerable degree of charismatic power over their audience. But as time passed and the silence grew, their fans grew restive, and there were impatient and puzzled whisperings from the darkness. Jason pressed forward, almost close enough to be seen from out front.

Without warning, the Dead Beat Society broke into the opening chord of *Payback*.

Jason froze, left hand raised to brace himself against the hanging curtain. His knuckles clenched the tough fabric, his nails scoring its surface. Fog billowed and drifted on every side. The Society had deliberately dropped the sound level, so that the audience was forced to remain quiet, unconsciously leaning forward to better hear the lyrics.

"A song unsung, by anyone," they whispered into the darkness.

Directly behind him, someone whispered, "A life undone."

Jason closed his hand even more tightly, felt the hard edge of fingernails against his palm despite the heavy curtain. As the second verse began, he continued to watch the performers, unwilling or unable to turn to see who, or what, might be behind him.

"Facing life with resignation," breathed the Dead Beat Society.

"Hello Jason." And this time something touched his shoulder.

Pivoting slowly on his left foot, still refusing to relinquish his hold on the curtain, that last anchor to the physical world, Jason turned toward the barely visible figure looming behind him. The strobing lights from the stage did little to dispel the darkness, and the mist was at shoulder height now, impossibly thick and clinging. Surely something must be wrong below the stage; this was far beyond the usual effect the crew had been able to manage in the past.

"Paybacks sometimes can be sweet," came the final line of the refrain, and the unknown other stepped forward, close enough that Jason could recognize his companion.

"Again we meet," said Mark Walton, smiling.

Jason released the curtain and staggered back, out onto the main stage. The Dead Beat Society was deep into an innovative jam session now, again straying from the recorded version by building one variation upon another, all playing with the original theme but none entirely true to it. They seemed to pay no attention to him, nor was there any indication that his presence had been spotted from the packed house beyond.

Smiling, Walton followed.

Jason's immobilizing terror broke and he spun away from the advancing figure, unconcerned now whether he caused a scene. Almost immediately, his feet became tangled in the electrical cords leading to the gigantic amplifiers emblazoned with the stylized "DBS" that had already become a popular trademark. He threw out his hands to break his fall as his head dropped within the bank of fog.

Effectively blinded by the all encompassing mist, Jason squirmed about on the floor, kicked free of the power cord, and scrambled back to his feet. The instrumental background continued.

He was even more disoriented now. The fog flowed on every side, periodic ripples making the surface heave and subside. He had lost sight of the Dead Beat Society, although he could still hear their music. Strangely, it seemed to come from every side, as though he had stumbled right in among them, although he couldn't see their chalk white costumes anywhere.

In fact, he couldn't see the audience either. Or the wings. Or any other identifiable point of reference. The stage lights seemed to be diffused, decentralized, and he couldn't quite decide where they were positioned. And somewhere, concealed by all this, was Mark Walton.

Jason forced himself to keep moving, arms groping about to avoid collisions. He set one foot in front of the other, counting as he moved in a more or less straight line, convinced that if he could only find one end of the stage or some other concrete reference point, he could determine his location and escape. But long after he knew he had walked at least twice the length of the raised stage, he remained enshrouded in the mist.

And the Dead Beat Society was still developing its impossibly prolonged jam session.

Just as he reached the point of despair, the fog began to recede. There was no clear line of demarcation, but with each forward step, the clinging wisps receded slightly, down from his shoulders, across his chest, to waist then hip level, then below his knees. It was still incredibly dark ahead and he could see nothing clearly, but somehow he knew instinctively that the audience was ahead, that he was finally moving toward something rather than away.

The fog was swirling around his ankles when he ran into the barrier.

It was as though he had run into a shield of plexiglass, smooth, cool to the touch, featureless, almost but not quite transparent. It spread from right to left and as high as he could reach. What's more, there was a strange, electric sensation when he touched it, something weird but familiar, something he knew he should recognize.

"Shit, no!" He jerked his hands away as though they'd been burnt. "No fucking way, man!" It was the same sensation he had felt when he had reached out and touched his television screen the first time he had spotted Mark Walton's face. Except this time he was on the same side as the mist.

"Oh, there you are, Jason. I wondered where you'd gotten to." Mark Walton emerged from concealment, one arm extended. "I have something for you, old buddy. It's payback time."

And as the Dead Beat Society broke away from the instrumental variations into the refrain of the last verse of *Payback*, a tiny flame sparked in Mark Walton's fist, reminding Jason of the fiery figure whose immolation climaxed the video of this very song.

"Paybacks CAN be sweet," Walton whispered softly.

LITTLE EVILS

The note Kristi received from her father's lawyer was in a plain envelope. "Our instructions were to deliver it to you on this date. We were never told what it contained or given any other instructions. I'm sorry." He hadn't sounded particularly sorry.

The relationship between Kristi and her father had never been simple. She had loved him dearly and had believed that he reciprocated. But he was a strange man with a great many secrets and it had been difficult to get close to him except for brief moments when his guard was down. She had suspected paranoia, and later even worse when it became obvious that his interest in the occult had advanced to the point of obsession. On one or two occasions toward the end of his life she had expressed false interest in his hobby in an effort to understand what was happening, but he had insisted that she wasn't ready yet.

"The time will come when you'll understand. There's something coming, Kristi I know when and where but not exactly what it is. It will be bad, though."

He had died of a stroke a few months later without ever explaining.

It was a very brief note, an address in nearby Taunton, Massachusetts written in bold, block letters, followed by a neatly typed paragraph:

"It is imperative that you visit this location tonight, June 5th, after the fall of darkness. Bring a weapon..The authorities are not equipped to deal with the situation. Keep this note with you. I can't tell you what to expect but remember that every large evil consists of many little ones."

It would be very foolish to walk into a probable trap, but the unstated risk of exposure was unnerving.

Arriving at the small, nondescript split level where she lived in rural Managansett, Kristi parked in the driveway and entered, moving directly to the closet that masked the entrance to her equipment room. Sliding the rear wall aside, she entered the narrow space lined with racked weapons, infrared goggles, a starlight scope, plastique and other incendiary devices, and other items she either owned – legally or otherwise - or had "borrowed" from the Agency.

She considered ignoring her father's message; it was probably just an illusion. But the specifics of it were intriguing and she was on leave and bored. Just past her twenty-seventh birthday, Kristi hadn't been nicknamed "The Shadow" by her fellow agents by accident; a resourceful and aggressive operator, she disagreed with some of the tactics of her employers, but had never let such qualms interfere with her performance. Thoughtfully, she selected a few items, carried them into the bedroom, sat down on the bed and addressed the picture of a middle aged man that was mounted on the near wall.

"Well, Dad, maybe I'll finally found out what had you so worked up. I don't believe you're up there some place watching me, but if you are, you might have been a little more informative." She lay back, stretching her arms above her head, willing the tension to abandon its grip on her muscles.

She often spoke to her absent father. Arthur Scott had been an unusual man, a successful entrepreneur who built a healthy business in a highly competitive market without ever finding it necessary to sacrifice the welfare of his employees to the imperatives of commerce. "It's the little things that count," he'd told her on more than one occasion. "Treat people fairly. Show some interest in them as people. Be honest about problems. Sooner or later, it's the people who work for you who decide whether you're a success or a failure. Whoever's on top might make the big, showy decisions, but it's the accumulation of countless smaller choices that makes a company. Or breaks it."

Her father had chosen his employees well. He had sold the company to them on his fiftieth birthday and retired to his hobbies.

Kristi had never decided whether or not he had approved of her career choice. "Sometimes you have to be ruthless to survive, Dad."

He didn't answer, of course, but a stray breeze stirred a nearby curtain, and the fluttering shadow gave the illusion that Arthur Scott was shaking his head.

It was still daylight when she passed the sprawling building complex the first time. The address was that of Crook Inc., a giftware manufacturer whose doors had closed by way of bankruptcy two years earlier. Most of the buildings were elderly, brick faced, part of an old mill complex more or less converted to house a successor industry which had also passed away, victim of the failing economy of the Northeast. The buildings were interconnected by smaller, more recent additions, some of them obviously prefab metal shells. The entire facility was enclosed by a six foot hurricane fence that stretched back to a heavily wooded strip along the banks of the Taunton River. On either side and in the lot opposite, similar empty buildings loomed like dying mammoths, some still displaying posted seizure notices. The parking lot was empty, with no indication of a guard. She slowed her car slightly as she passed but refrained from stopping.

Kristi ate a leisurely supper in town, drove past the complex three more times over a period of two hours. At dusk, a single floodlight illuminated a portion of the main parking lot; scattered lights went on within the nearest building as well, probably on a timed circuit. There had been no detectible human activity, only windblown leaves and trash whispering across the parking lot.

She parked on a side street over a mile away, walked down to the river, followed it cautiously back through the trees. The starlight scope made it somewhat easier to pick a path through the heavy growth. The swiftly flowing water masked any slight sound she might have made. At no time did she see or hear anything indicating she was expected, not even when she climbed a tree and dropped to the ground inside the fence.

Soundlessly, she scaled the side of a small outbuilding, then clambered from window to window until she reached the framework of a massive blower system. A minute later, four stories above the ground, Kristi walked cautiously across the roof of one of the larger buildings, using a flashlight to examine the windows of another, taller structure that abutted this roof. As she had expected, several of the windows were broken. On her second attempt, she found one where she could reach inside and release the lock.

This entire level appeared to be empty, perhaps originally warehouse space; there wasn't even a security light. She moved carefully in her soft soled shoes, playing the narrow circle of brilliance on the floor ahead so that she wouldn't alert anyone to her presence by treading unwarily.

The stairway door was closed but not locked.

"Well, if you're going to do it, now's the time," she whispered to herself, then quietly, but determinedly, opened the door.

An hour later, Kristi wondered if the entire affair hadn't been a practical joke of some kind after all.

She had wandered through room after room, offices, corridors, one very large and several smaller storage areas, a shipping and receiving room lined with truck bays, several manufacturing departments, silver and gold plating, small assembly, polishing, inspection stations, a sample room. Enough of the equipment had been abandoned to rust for her to make tentative identification. Her exploration was efficient and professional; she shielded her own light at all times, walked so that she would not display an unnecessary silhouette or shadow when near open windows. There were no light, probably no power. Several times she was startled by sudden noises, but each appeared to be random sounds from the corpse of a once thriving business. Despite her growing conviction that nothing was going to happen, she maintained her concentration as she moved from building to building.

That's why she noticed the smell so quickly.

She had just entered a series of interlocking open spaces, all occupied by oversized mechanical presses, double and single action, massive pieces of equipment that now stood silent and powerless. A kerosene fueled smelting furnace stood in one corner, flanked by two fifty gallon drums. The moment she entered the area, Kristi picked up a slightly sweet scent, and as she progressed deeper into the gloom, it grew stronger, almost nauseating, with a hint of a second, more acrid fragrance in the background.

Then she discovered the mound.

There was no other word to describe it. In a remote corner of the press area, the concrete floor seemed to have been forced up from below, a circle five meters in diameter, tapering to an opening approximately one meter across at its apex. As she cautiously approached, Kristi crouched, played the flashlight over the side of the conical structure. At its base, the concrete was splintered and cracked, as though rent by an intrusive force. But higher, the concrete floor seemed to have been shattered and reshaped, the surface rough but still fairly even. Its texture felt wrong.

It reminded her of an anthill.

Slowly she made her way around the periphery, puzzled, wary, but not particularly alarmed. The close attention she was paying to the mound itself was the reason she almost stumbled over the first of the bodies.

"Shit!" Her anger was at her own inattention, not the discovery of an obviously dead man lying at her feet. In her line of work, such a lapse could result in serious if not fatal consequences. Kristi had seen dead bodies before; on a few occasions, she had caused them to die. In some cases, she even felt that they deserved their fate. In the others, she had deferred to the wishes of her superiors.

The expression on the corpse's face was calm, eyes closed, arms and legs spread to the side in near symmetry. There was no sign of trauma to the head or limbs, but when she played her light down the torso, she almost lost her composure.

The body had been gutted from just above the crotch to the sternum, the ribs and all internal organs removed. The surface of the spinal column was clearly visible, nested in a swathe of muscle tissue. Crouching, she realized this was the source of the sweet smell. There was no indication of decay. What remained of the flesh was still flexible, although it felt unnaturally dry and warm to her probing fingertip; it was as if someone had sprayed the remains with a preservative.

There didn't seem to be any blood.

When she pointed her light into the shadows beyond, she saw a second body, then a third. Stepping carefully over the first corpse, she made her way completely around the mound, counting seven before stopping. There were four men and three women, ranging from one teenage girl to the oldest, the middle aged man over whom she had stumbled. All of the bodies were laid out in the same fashion, each had been eviscerated and emptied. Adrenaline poured through her body but despite its stimulation, she was unwilling to explore the shadows beyond.

"All right, Kristi, you have a serial killer here," she told herself silently. "A pretty strange one, admittedly, but nothing you shouldn't be able to handle. All you have to do is leave and make an anonymous call to the police." But that didn't explain the mysterious note and its assertion that the authorities were powerless here. Could the killer have written it, and for what purpose? She crouched, reached into the pocket of her slacks, pulled out the folded piece of paper, determined to read it again, perhaps find something she had overlooked the first time.

The text was exactly the same as before, except that new words had appeared at the bottom of the note.

"It's not as simple as you think. The police cannot help."

There was no technical problem treating paper so that a message appeared after the passage of time; the mechanism of the change didn't trouble her. But how could anyone have, once again, anticipated her thoughts?

Something moved inside the mound.

Kristi set aside her puzzlement and speculation swiftly in response, slipping the paper back into her pocket. It was a tentative sound, like the susurration of cloth rubbing stone; it persisted for several seconds then stopped. Kristi drew her weapon and began to edge around the circumference, head cocked to detect any recurrence however faint. The apex was slightly more than two meters high and the sides were too steep to climb without making enough noise to alert whoever was concealed within. She was still trying to decide whether to scale the cone when one of the bodies stood up.

At least, that's what appeared to have happened, although when the man stepped out into the light, she could not recognize him from his profile as one of those she had examined. His chest rose and fell as he moved with a perfectly natural gait, apparently unaware of her presence. She waited until he had made his way past the mound and out of the immediate area before following.

He left through a side entrance into the main parking lot, first placing a piece of wood to keep the door from closing and locking. Kristi followed, her weapon still drawn and ready. Her first inclination had been to call out, apprehend the man and turn him over to the local police, but there was still something wrong with this entire situation and she wanted more information before committing herself to such a definite course of action.

She shadowed him as he made his way through a gap in the fence where it met the river, across an adjacent lot, then down the sidewalk, past the darkened hulks of buildings, finally turning to cross over a small bridge into the outskirts of the commercial district. He never looked back.

Over the course of the next two hours, Kristi found herself witnessing a series of petty vandalisms and cruelties that seemed an absurd contrast to the horrifyingly mutilated bodies she had discovered earlier. Her quarry trampled gardens, snapped aerials off parked cars and used the broken ends to gouge the paint in long lines from bumper to bumper. He swore viciously at two young girls who walked past, smashed a discarded bottle against the side of a store, and overturned several trash cans onto the sidewalk.

Although there were few people walking the streets at this hour, there was rarely a time when he was not within sight of others, but whether because they failed to see what he was doing or just didn't wish to become involved, no one intervened or even made a comment. Not even when he opened his pants and urinated on the illuminated sign on the front lawn of the Methodist Church. Kristi felt mild outrage at the small cowardices that led to such universal apathy, but then it occurred to her that she was not entirely free of that taint herself and was momentarily startled by this surge of atypical self criticism.

She followed carefully, fascinated, convinced this was the same man who had killed and mutilated at least seven people, now directing his attention to annoying but comparatively trivial acts of vandalism. It would have been quite easy for her to abandon the pursuit, walk back to her car, pretend she'd never seen anything, and let the authorities deal with the situation. Certainly procedure required that she do nothing to draw attention to herself, even if the consequences of such inaction were, as in this case, unfortunate.

Then a short, bearded man in a tattered coat lurched out of a doorway on a deserted side street.

"Mister, you gotta dollar for some coffee?"

Without a sound or a moment's hesitation, the taller man attacked, both hands leaping directly to the beggar's throat. His cry was cut off so quickly, it took a second or two for Kristi to realize what was happening. Then her reflexes took over.

She closed the gap with a few quick, running steps, raising her weapon at the same time.

"All right, let him go! Raise your hands above your head and step away or I'll fire!"

The struggle continued exactly as before. The beggar was flailing ineffectively at his attacker's face, pressed back into the doorway.

"Let go, I said!" She lifted her arm, aimed at the back of the man's head.

When she was ignored a second time, Kristi stepped forward, deciding at the last moment not to use her weapon. Summary execution had always bothered her and besides, there were still a lot of questions to which she wanted answers.

The butt of her weapon smashed heavily against the back of the man's head, a blow that should have completely immobilized him. Indeed, he did freeze for a moment, half turning in her direction, before moving his arms convulsively. The beggar's head snapped to one side with a crack and he ceased struggling, crumpled limply as his assailant turned away.

In the wan moonlight, he seemed to have a perfectly normal face; his expression remained calm, almost abstracted, despite the fact that he had just killed a man.

"Raise your hands!" Kristi was startled to hear a tremor in her voice. She'd been in danger of her life many times in the past, but this was the first instance in which she felt the tentative touch of panic. There was something distinctly wrong here, something she couldn't quite define.

She had expected him to speak, to shout obscenities or make excuses or even break down into tears. Experience told her to watch for the tensing muscles that indicated an imminent attack, and she was almost taken completely by surprise when he moved with no apparent preparation.

The expression on his face when she shot the killer through the left shoulder was almost comical, a blend of surprise, confusion, and outrage. Kristi expected him to capitulate now, perhaps even faint with shock. Instead he recovered and lunged forward with preternatural swiftness, swinging with his uninjured arm. She took an instinctive step back and her foot turned on something lying unseen on the sidewalk. As she fell, Kristi threw herself desperately into a roll, sprang back to her feet with her weapon ready.

He was gone.

She spotted him within seconds, running back the way they had come moments earlier. The streets were, if anything, more deserted than they had been only moments ago; she hadn't even heard a vehicle pass during the entire encounter. With a disgusted sound of self contempt, Kristi set off in pursuit.

He led her through alleys and along railroad tracks, through vacant lots and well-tended backyards, sometimes losing ground but always staying far enough ahead that she would not risk another shot. It was soon obvious where he was headed; the commercial and residential neighborhood gave way once more to the long stretch of empty warehouses, closed factories, and failed businesses lining the near bank of the river.

Abruptly she remembered the propped open door; if he got there before her, he could lock her out long enough to do whatever he intended, crawl back inside the mound perhaps. Ignoring burning lungs and protesting muscles in her thighs, she stepped up the pace.

Although she closed the gap appreciably, she was unable to overtake him before he reached the factory entrance.

He pushed through the door and turned, one hand reaching to slam the door in her face. Only a few meters separated them and by instinct more than design, she fired twice, two sharp cracks in the night air. At least one of the rounds struck; his upper body jerked backward as his knees buckled, dropping him to the floor. The door was caught against one leg, unable to close.

Kristi hit the door with her shoulder, almost losing her own balance in the process. "Now...you bastard..." Before she could recover, he twisted away, jumped to his feet, and ran off into the darkness.

"Damn it!" Exhausted, she was slow to react, then fired twice before he rounded a corner and disappeared from sight. Kristi drew a deep breath, changed to a fresh clip, and followed.

He was scrambling up the side of the mound, one leg dragging limply, hampering his progress.

"This is the last time I'm going to warn you," she called out calmly. "Climb down right now and lie on the floor or you're a dead man."

He ignored her completely, reached the opening at the top, rose to his full height. Kristi suddenly realized he was going to jump down inside unless she stopped him. Smoothly and without hesitation, she raised her arm and shot him through the side of the head. He posed motionless for a second, then fell away from the opening, landing with a dull thud somewhere out of her line of sight.

Kristi cautiously approached the body.

He lay on his back, eyes still open, limbs outstretched in the same fashion as his apparent victims, one entire side of his head obliterated. There was no chance that he might have survived the wound.

Which is why Kristi was so surprised to see that his chest was still moving.

Except that it wasn't really his chest, it was lower, and irregular, not at all like breathing. The dim light concealed details and she retrieved her flashlight from its place on her belt.

As she watched, the dead man's shirt peeled back of its own volition, revealing his chest and abdomen. An exit wound just under the heart showed where one of her shots had passed completely through his body.

"What the hell?" Unease became alarm as the flesh of the torso suddenly split and opened, revealing what lay concealed within.

Something living moved inside the hollowed out cavity of the man's body, but nothing she had ever seen before. Shocked into immobility, Kristi watched uncomprehendingly as long, sinuous, bluish white tubes were retracted from within the arms and legs, curling up against a spindly, featureless body. A fifth tendril ran up behind the sternum, apparently into the throat, and now it was withdrawn as well, a broader variation, fringed with constantly moving cilia.

It looked like an oversized, attenuated starfish.

With a convulsive movement, the creature flexed all of its limbs and extended them, then scrambled out of its housing with a spiderlike motion, quite obviously heading for the cone. Kristi's free hand flashed out, caught one of the lesser appendages, gripped it tightly despite its intensely cold and unpleasantly moist nature. Twisting her body for leverage, she lifted it from the floor and threw it off into the darkness, unwilling to maintain contact, but determined that it should not reach whatever sanctuary it sought.

As she raised the flashlight to locate the creature, there was a rustle in the darkness and another of the bodies became animated and sat up, this time the teenage girl. The eyes were open and alert.

"You have to let me go." The girl's voice lacked inflection but was entirely human. The cavity was closing over the alien form even as it manipulated its puppet's vocal chords.

"The hell I do." She fired twice, once through the forehead, the second time striking the falling torso at the point where she believed the intruder's central mass resided. The girl, or her body anyway, collapsed soundlessly.

This time there was no indication that life still persisted within the motionless body. Kristi watched carefully before crouching to move the blouse aside. The two flaps of flesh had almost joined, but through an inch wide gap, she could see a line of pale blue. Suppressing her revulsion, she used the barrel of her weapon to widen the seam, gradually working each flap of flesh aside, revealing the gutted interior.

There was a charred hole where her round had penetrated the starfish creature at the thickest part of it body. There was no blood, but neither was there movement.

"Sorry friend, but I couldn't let you get away. I don't know if anyone's going to believe this no matter what the evidence, but at least this way there's a chance."

She was actually contemplating removing the intruder from the girl's body when its skin began to stretch, small points of movement as though something were probing from beneath.

Or more precisely, from within.

Kristi drew her hand back just as the first tiny claws emerged, retreating even further as a dozen or more diminutive creatures erupted from the ruined body of their host, then climbed out of the girl's abdomen slowly and with great effort. They were all identical, oversized centipedes with two sets of claws, except that their antennae -- if that's what they were -- were numerous, distributed evenly over the surface of their bodies.

Stunned, she remained motionless as each made its laborious way out of the corpse, across the floor, then up the side of the mound to the lip of the central hole. There were small clicking noises as they moved, sounds which continued in more muted fashion even after they had dropped out of sight. The only reason she was able to react in time to stop the very last one was that part of its body had been crushed by the bullet she had fired into its host (or into its host's host). It left a trail of slime as it struggled to drag its crippled body over the rough surface.

Rousing herself, Kristi stood, took three quick steps, then raised her right leg and smashed the last of the centipedes with the heel of her shoe.

From its mangled body, a score or more tiny serpentine forms emerged, each squirming frantically. They might almost have been earthworms except for the fact that their bodies were apparently covered with fur.

She retreated hastily this time, unwilling to experiment further, making no effort to interfere as the dozen or two new forms inched their way up the side of the cone. She didn't want to see what might emerge if one of them died.

It only took her a few minutes to make a decision. Her career had taught her to take the initiative whenever it seemed warranted by events. With considerable effort, she rolled one of the drums of kerosene over to the mound and used the hand pump to spray most of its contents into the subterranean darkness. She hesitated only briefly before spraying the remainder over the mutilated bodies; under the circumstances, it was probably best if friends and relatives never did learn what had happened to these people.

She ignited the dome first and only turned back to the bodies after several dozen of the wormlike creatures emerged, their bodies engulfed in flame, reduced to ashes within seconds. Nothing emerged like a phoenix from the inferno.

When she started the second fire, it spread even more quickly than she had expected. The beams and floorboards were so infused with oil and resins, they served as gigantic wicks. She left hastily through the main door, and was gratified to see that the entire complex would be in jeopardy within seconds.

When the sirens started in the distance, she walked to her car and drove home.

Nevertheless, as she sat on her bed, she felt more at ease with herself, and more resolute about the future, than she had for some time. The mysterious note lay near her hand, with a final sentence appended.

"There are more of them. I'll be in touch."

DOMINION

"The world was designed for mankind, not for animals!" Steve Kostka's braying voice was audible from one end of the tavern to the other. "It's ours to rule as we see fit."

"But we're animals too!" a young woman protested.

"Well, some of us are anyway." Shelly Arruda moved closer to her boyfriend, who stood with his arms folded, inviting further argument. But his opponents had finally been worn out by the endless cycle of clichés and insults, and those few who hadn't already faded away did so now, leaving the belligerent twosome unchallenged masters of the field of battle. Or at least of one corner of the Tabor Street Tavern.

Steve chose to interpret their departure as an admission of defeat, and was silently congratulating himself when he noticed that there was still one figure sitting at the table. It was an older man who hadn't participated in the debate, whose face held a faint hint of amusement that Steve found immensely irritating.

"Do you really believe that people are the rulers of the world?" The man's voice was low, controlled, and carried an undertone of sarcasm that grated.

"Of course. It's obvious. We don't even have any close rivals."

"Yeah, if we're not on top, who is?" Shelly leaned forward, her face reddened with enthusiasm and drink. "I don't see anyone challenging us."

"Would you like to?"

The question caught them both by surprise. The couple exchanged puzzled glances before Steve responded. "Are you making fun of us, dude?"

"Not at all." The man leaned forward, his voice neutral but his eyes still amused. "I just wondered if you'd be interested in seeing the real masters of the world. I could show them to you if you like."

Shelly looked mildly uncomfortable now, but Steve was laughing. "I suppose you got pictures in your wallet or something, right?"

"No, but see them if you're willing to take a little drive with me."

Steve hesitated, more cautious now. "What makes you think I'd go anywhere with you, friend? I got no idea who you are and I'm sure not getting in your car."

"Actually, I don't own a car, but I imagine you do. It's just down the road a short way."

"And that's where we'll see the real masters of the world?" Steve tried to inject sarcasm into his voice.

"What's the matter? Afraid to face the truth?"

Steve hesitated, began chewing his lip indecisively. "It's not far, you say?"

Shelly reached over and grabbed his arm. "Steve, I don't think that's such a great idea."

He shrugged her arm away. "This is bullshit, man. Why should I waste my time?"

The stranger sat back and smirked. "I didn't think you'd have the balls."

Steve's face darkened and he leaned forward, pressing his palms flat against the table. "You better watch what you say, asshole. I'm more of a man than you ever dreamed of being."

"Then let's go for a little ride, shall we?'

Shelly tried to talk him out of it, but Steve had been sufficiently provoked that he wouldn't be easily dissuaded. He told her she could wait in the tavern, but she glanced nervously at their former antagonists, now clustered around two adjacent tables, and shrugged.

"I'm not hanging around with these losers. Let's go." But she didn't sound happy about it.

Steve drove, somewhat unsteadily, two miles down an unlit, country road. The stranger sat in the back seat, silent until they reached a row of stunted poplars. "Park along here," he said quietly.

The night had been hot and dry, but now there was a damp, cool breeze that left an unpleasant film on their exposed skin. The stranger pointed to a narrow pathway that led through the poplars into an overgrown field. A full moon washed the area with soft light.

Steven balked. "What is this shit, man? This is the middle of nowhere."

"I'm forty pounds lighter than you, ten years older, and unarmed. And there are two of you. What's there to be afraid of?"

"I'm not afraid. I just don't see why I should waste any more time on this crap."

The man sighed. "It's a ten minute walk from here. What have you got to lose?"

"What's in this for you, anyway?" Shelly's voice cracked with tension. "Why'd you drag us out here?"

"I want to see the look on your faces when you see how wrong you are," he said quietly. "Failing that, I'll be satisfied seeing you squirm out of this and run home."

"No one's backing out." Steve took a tentative step forward. "Let's get this over with."

The stranger led them straight across the field. There was a low stone wall at the far end, but they passed easily through one of several gaps. Another untended field stretched before them, but the man stopped at the edge.

"Stay here. They'll be along in a minute. They pass through pretty steadily on nights like this."

"They who?" Steve's temper was rising again. He suspected he was being made the brunt of an elaborate, peculiar practical joke. The stranger was in for a surprise though. He planned to leave him here to walk back on his own.

"Just watch. It won't be long."

And it wasn't.

"Whatever you do, don't move!" The stranger's voice was suddenly tense. "You don't want them to notice you because if they do . . . well, let's just say you wouldn't like it much."

Steve was about to make a smart remark when he heard Shelly's sharply indrawn breath. "What the fuck is that?"

He turned his head to follow the line from her eyes to the distance and saw, at the opposite end of the clearing, movement. It was vague and shadowy, but large. Whatever lurked there was nearly as tall as the towering spruce beyond.

"It's one of the real masters of this world, young man. This field is a crossing spot of some sort. Every night at about this time they pass through it, but they're not always visible. Sometimes only a few of them, sometimes a great many."

"Bullshit," Steve replied, but he answered in a whisper. Shelly was holding his arm so tightly that it was painful, and she wasn't saying anything at all.

There were three of them now. The first had reached the center of the field, an amorphous shape like a bank of clouds that seemed to be constantly dissolving and reforming itself. It was a smoky dark color that blended with the background so well that it was a few seconds before they realized that they could see the shapes of the distant spruce trees through the body of the thing.

Its companions were very different. One towered above the trees, its body thick and wide at the base and tapering to a comparatively tiny apex. It was a shimmering white that glowed almost blue in the moonlight, and there were hairlike filaments covering its body that moved and shifted, not always in response to the night breeze. The third stood only a few meters tall, but its broad, crablike body straddled almost half the clearing. These two were also partially transparent, and all three moved with absolute silence, disappearing at last into the near tree line, vanishing there as though they'd stepped through a gateway to another world.

"What the fuck was that?" Steve's voice was thin and wavery.

"The owners of our world," the stranger replied. "Just as I promised you. They've ruled here since time immemorial, and we remain for the most part totally ignorant of their existence."

"Steve, I want to get out of here." Shelly spoke in clipped, brittle syllables that were clearly a thin crust over panic.

He ignored her. "What is it, some kind of movie projector?"

"There was a pack of wild dogs living near my house a few years back. They were led by a tough old mongrel who kept the younger dogs in line by knocking them down and grabbing them by the throat, then took his pleasure with the bitches when they were in season." The man rushed on when Steve tried to interrupt. "That dog thought he was king of the world until I got tired of having him challenge me every time I went for a walk. That last day, he probably thought my shotgun was some kind of a trick too, until the shells brought his reign to an end."

"So what's that supposed to mean?"

"It means, don't kick over the ant hill until you're sure the ants aren't better armed than you are. Watch now, there's more coming."

Another of the crab things was visible now, followed by an undulating form that writhed out of the darkness and approached without revealing its opposite end. The serpentine form diverged from its fellow, the massive head weaving about, coming closer to where the three humans stood than had any of its predecessors. Its body was studded with spikes, from which hung tangled masses of gristle, parts of which resembled some of the smaller creatures that had begun to enter the clearing, as though they'd ventured too close and become impaled by their larger fellow.

Shelly shrank back a step.

"Don't move, you fool!" hissed the stranger. "It won't see you if you remain motionless."

As translucent as the others, the serpent form continued to emerge from the distance, its body impossibly long. Smaller creatures were more abundant now, hopping, walking, and otherwise advancing across the uneven ground. Some were remotely humanoid; others so alien that the eye couldn't quite follow the curves of their bodies. One creature moved its millipedal legs with relentless precision, even though the two halves of its body were not joined, and in fact another form passed between them and moved on.

Steve was so terrified that he couldn't have moved even if he'd wanted to, but Shelly's eyes were fastened on the serpent head, now only a few meters away. Her face lifted and for a second the creature's eyes seemed to lock on hers. It was an illusion, for she had not been seen, but it was persuasive enough that she broke and fled back the way they had come. The oversized eyes blinked then and the head was motionless for a second.

"Don't move if you value your life," said the stranger.

The crowd of passersby thinned and finally disappeared, all but the serpent thing which remained motionless except for its eyes for a very long time. Then it continued its inefficient progress toward the distant trees and eventually vanished with its fellows.

"We can go now."

Shelly was lying on the back seat of the car, curled into a ball, her face wet with tears. "Get me out of here."

Steve just nodded, climbed into the front seat, his plan to maroon the stranger completely forgotten. But the latter made no move to enter the car. "I'll walk," he said quietly.

"Mister, I don't know how you managed that crap, but that was some kind of show you put on." Steve turned the key.

The man leaned close to the window. "It saw her." He nodded toward the back seat.

"Yeah? So what?"

The stranger looked away. "Nothing. Just. . . I'm sorry. I hadn't meant it to go this far."

"What's that supposed to mean?" But Steve was talking to thin air. The stranger was gone.

When Steve woke the following morning, he'd completely forgotten the events of the night before. As usual, Shelly was up before him, but when he reached the kitchen, the usual pot of coffee was missing from the table. He wandered through the apartment, wearing just his undershorts, and found her on the patio, sitting in the recliner and staring across the parking lot toward the adjacent strip mall.

"Hey! Where's my coffee?"

"There's something moving down there." Her voice was so taut with strain that he didn't recognize it. She raised one army and pointed down toward the parking lot.

"Just a garbage truck."

"Not there. On the roof."

He squinted and there did seem to be a dark shape crossing the flat expanse atop the nearest row of stores. "It's just a cloud shadow." But the sky was cloudless.

"It saw me, Steve."

He blinked, and fragments of the previous night returned to him. "That was all bullshit, Shelly. Some kind of trick he played on us. Forget about it."

"I don't think I can." But she said it softly, and Steve was already back inside the apartment.

"Where's my coffee?" he shouted.

Shelly moped around the apartment all day, jumping at shadows, refusing to eat or go outside or even watch television. By suppertime Steve was thoroughly pissed off, but even when he shouted at her, she refused to react, didn't even appear to hear most of what he was saying. Finally he stormed off to find himself something to eat, and drink.

"Bitch better straighten up quick or I'm moving on," he told himself, and later a couple of newfound drinking buddies. "I got 'em standing in line wanting me to move in."

It was almost midnight when he returned to the apartment. Shelly was still there, still sitting at one end of the couch where she'd been when he walked out, stilling wearing the ugly orange housedress that she reserved for days when she was sick, or depressed.

"You feeling better yet?" He tried to sound sympathetic. Despite his earlier bragging, he needed to stay at her place for a while yet. He'd just started a new job after a long layoff, and his bar tab the last couple of nights had used up most of his first paycheck.

Shelly didn't answer at first, and he thought she might be asleep. But then her head turned and she spoke, but her voice was leaden. "They've been here, in the apartment. I see them sometimes if I don't look too hard, going from one room to another. Through the walls, you know? I can feel them looking through my things, looking at my body."

Steve stood motionless, wondering if Shelly had completely cracked. "Yeah, well I'm going to bed. You coming?"

But she had turned away and after waiting a while longer for an answer, Steve did just that. The hell with her, he thought.

Steve woke in complete darkness, the shadowy memory of a thud lingering in his consciousness. He sat up in bed, noticing immediately that Shelly's side remained empty. The apartment was quiet, the night outside disturbed only by distant traffic noises and the faint sizzle of a neon sign from next door.

There was nothing to indicate that he wasn't alone in the apartment, but somehow he knew that he had company. Shelly, he told himself. Dumb bitch must be stumbling around in the dark, knocked something over, woke me up. No consideration at all.

The apartment remained silent.

Steve had just about convinced himself to go back to sleep when a faint movement caught the corner of his eye, just visible in the dim light that entered through the bedroom's three slit windows. Over on the far wall, between the dresser and the closet door. He squinted, trying to make it out, almost reached for the bedside lamp, then hesitated, warned by some unsuspected sixth sense. The skin on his arm tingled and he began to sweat.

The movement became more noticeable but it was several more seconds before he could make out the shape, a gigantic serpentine head issuing from the bedroom wall. It began to slide back and forth as it approached, and its crest disappeared into the ceiling. Steve shrank back under the covers, watched in stunned disbelief as the now familiar monster continued to pass by, or rather over him, its head disappearing into the outside wall. And more and more of it continued to emerge, including those spiked protrusions and their grisly adornments.

Steve was so paralyzed with fright that his muscles locked and his mouth opened in a scream that remained silent, silent until another spike appeared, this one bearing a struggling form wearing an ugly orange housedress. He glanced up at her contorted face, realized that he could see right through her body, and then she was moving past him and disappearing into the wall, and he slid down completely under the covers and remained there until morning, hoping it was all just a dream.

But he never saw Shelly Arruda again.

THE HANDYMAN

They were able to see the pool of blood through the screen door as soon as they mounted the porch. There was no chance that it might be something else. The smell was unmistakable.

"Shouldn't we wait for our backup?" The rookie was crouched to the right of the front door, his eyes frightened. He'd never had to deal with anything more dangerous than an aggressive drunk until now.

Grolan shook his head. "They're all tied up with that train derailment. Besides, if the bastard's gone, there's no reason to wait, and if he's still inside, we've gotta take him down before he gets away. You know he only works on Halloween." He smiled. "We might get a citation out of this one, Alan."

Alan Pelletier, nodded but it was a shaky gesture, not entirely convincing. Not for the first time, Tom Grolan wished his ex-partner, old Matt Staples, was still with him, but the gunshot wound Matt had suffered the previous spring, though minor, had been enough to convince him to start the paperwork for early retirement.

"Look, kid, there's probably another door around back or on the side. You go and cover it. If he's not on the ground floor, I'll call you in once I've checked it out."

Pelletier nodded. "I'm on it." He took a deep breath, then walked to the side of the porch, vaulted over the railing, and disappeared into the darkness.

"Just don't shoot me when you come in," Grolan whispered into the night. He was honest enough to admit to himself that he really didn't want to open that door and venture inside, but it was part of the job and part of his image. Grolan could never have lived with himself if he'd backed down from a challenge like this. If they'd been greeted with a hail of gunfire, he'd have waited for support without hesitation, even though that meant someone else would get the credit for the arrest. But the house was quiet; it felt empty. The neighbors had reported a scream but it was Halloween after all, and no one would have taken the call seriously if they hadn't been expecting it. This would be the fourth consecutive Halloween since the killer had made his first shocking appearance. The streets were empty, kids kept at home or shunted off to well chaperoned parties, even though the killer had never targeted them specifically before. He preferred to get inside and take his time.

Grolan had figured the scream was a cat or a television show or some kid who'd slipped out despite the ban to taunt a neighbor. He'd expected this to be just another false alarm, until he'd smelled the blood.

With his free hand, Grolan pulled the screen door open and slipped through, then eased it shut soundlessly behind. The hand holding his service revolver was steady.

The ground floor was well lit, but silent. From the vestibule, he could see part of a dining room to his right, a more comfortable sitting room to the left. The furniture was of good quality, but obviously well used. At the far end of the dining room was what appeared to be a swinging door leading into the kitchen. The rest of the ground floor consisted of a broad staircase built over a tiny room, probably a half bath.

A second pool of blood spread across the floor. It was almost a meter across and had already started to congeal. Just inside the dining room lay the body of a middle-aged woman, face down, blood no longer flowing from the deep gash that ran along one side of her throat. Grolan saw a more familiar mutilation as well, and knew the Handyman had struck again.

"Oh shit!" It was what he had expected, and what he had feared, and what he had hoped never to see the likes of again. Two severed hands were arranged on the table, their fingers twined around a knife and fork. The woman's arms ended at her wrists.

Grolan struggled to remain dispassionate as he edged his way along the short hall, weapon ready, stepping over the sticky tentacles of darkening scarlet. When he reached the door jamb, he whirled and stepped into the living room, both hands clasped around his weapon now, watching for a target.

The second victim, a slightly built man in his forties, was slumped across the couch. He had evidently been struck from behind, perhaps while watching television, although it was now turned off. There was no mystery about the murder weapon, a poker from the nearby fireplace. It remained lodged firmly in what remained of the man's skull. The expression on his face was one of surprise.

As with the other victim, both hands had been severed at the wrist, leaving ragged stumps behind. Grolan spotted them almost immediately. One was in the fish bowl, the other had been impaled on a pair of scissors and propped upright. It almost looked like it was waving to him. The stumps had stopped bleeding, but only just, and the cushion beneath the man's buttocks was dark and shiny.

There wasn't much else to see in the room, and no place to hide. Grolan quickly decided that no one was lurking bloody handed in a corner waiting to pounce.

The dining room was also clear as was the kitchen. Grolan opened the back door and called quietly to Pelletier, who emerged from the shadows with his weapon drawn, eyes jumping anxiously from side to side.

"C'mon in," Grolan said softly. "But keep your voice down."

They checked the first floor bathroom together, Pelletier covering while Grogan opened the door. It was empty. The basement door to one side was secured by a sliding bolt. Grolan ignored it for the moment. Unless the Handyman was a magician, he couldn't have retreated downstairs and locked the door from this side.

"Let's check upstairs."

Pelletier glanced at his watch. "Shouldn't we wait?" Grolan and his partner had been first on the scene at the first Handyman killing and the odds were against that happening again. He and Pelletier had expected to find themselves in the middle of nothing more serious than a frenzied family quarrel. The younger officer cocked his head as though he could hear a siren at the very limit of audibility, but it might have been wishful thinking. He would be much happier if there was someone else here to take the lead. Although he had a lot of respect for his partner, he knew that Grolan was prone to unnecessary risks.

"They'll be a few more minutes yet," Grolan assured him, having correctly interpreted Pelletier's expression. "What's the matter? Want to live forever?"

"Yes, as a matter of fact." Pelletier's voice shook, but at least he hadn't lost his sense of humor.

Grolan's face twisted into a clumsy approximation of a grin, quickly gone. "Cover me until I reach the landing. Watch yourself."

A minute later, Pelletier joined his partner in the upstairs hall. There were five doors, two open, three shut. The open ones were closest.

A full bath was located directly over the staircase, spotlessly clean and orderly. A nude teenager floated in the tub, the hilt of a kitchen knife protruding from between her breasts. Both her hands had been amputated. They were mounted not far away, right hand for hot, left hand for cold.

Pelletier gave a little moan and lurched back into the hall. His face had gone pale and he was convulsing, trying to suppress the urge to vomit. Grolan felt pretty sick as well but he forced himself to give the room a quick once over before rejoining his partner. The younger man was bracing himself with one hand against the wall, struggling for composure, but Grolan was pleased to see that his weapon was still raised and ready. The kid was doing all right. There might be a policeman lurking inside him after all.

"Let's check out the rest of the rooms."

The open door opposite led into a small sewing room that seemed to double as a walk-in closet. A rack of winter coats stood in one corner, and there must have been several dozen bagged sweaters piled on a set of wire shelves. The windows were heavily curtained and shadows were everywhere, but none were large enough to conceal a lurking killer.

"Nothing here," said Grolan.

Pelletier had regained most of his color by the time they opened the first of the closed doors and found themselves in the neat but dimly lit master bedroom. They checked the closet and under the king-sized bed, but there were no indications of an intruder, and no mutilated victims. Grolan felt a slight easing of the tension in his gut, but it returned quickly when the next room revealed a fourth body, a boy in his early to mid-teens.

He'd been hit across the bridge of the nose with his own baseball bat, just once apparently, but hard enough to be fatal, splinters of bone driven back into the brain. His entire face seemed to have collapsed in on itself. In contrast to the rest of the house, this room was extremely disorderly, and it actually took a minute or two before they found the boy's hands. One had been stuck inside a catcher's mitt lying on the bed; the other was sitting on a closet shelf, the fingers curled around a softball.

Both men hesitated before approaching the final door. Grolan knew the odds were low that the Handyman was still in the house, but he was nervous. This was the fourth family to fall victim to the

Handyman, whose Halloween attacks had made the national news, and despite optimistic statements made to the press over the course of the previous three years, the officers investigating the killings had yet to find a single useful clue. Grolan had never admitted how deeply he'd been affected by the events three years earlier, but he considered the failure of the authorities to apprehend the killer a personal shortcoming.

Impatient with his own equivocation, Grolan signed for Pelletier to stay back, then pushed the door open and stepped through, his weapon ready.

It was another bedroom, obviously the girl's. A pair of bunk beds stood to the right, twin dressing tables to the left. The walls were decorated with pictures of rock stars and the mirrors were almost completely covered with snapshots of high school kids, at the beach, at a dance, at a picnic.

Someone was sitting at one of the desks.

Moving cautiously, Grolan stepped to one side so that he could see better and as he did so he experienced a brief moment of unreality. It was the teenager from the bathroom, he realized, recognizable despite her slashed throat. Except that that was impossible.

"Jesus! Twins!" It was Pelletier who spoke, having silently followed, and Grolan felt a surge of relief, realizing belatedly the significance of the bunk beds.

One of the girl's severed hands had been placed inside her blouse, pressed against her left breast. The other appeared to be inside her jeans, between her thighs; Grolan didn't investigate further.

Once they were satisfied that there was no one alive upstairs, they returned to the ground floor. In the distance, they finally heard sirens, and Grolan glanced at his watch, startled to realize they'd been in the house only about five minutes.

"All right, let's go back outside and wait for them. There's nothing more we can do here."

They had just started toward the front door when they heard the sound.

There had been movement somewhere inside the house, furtive and brief, but distinct enough that both men reacted by drawing the weapons they had holstered. Grolan was pretty certain it had come from one of the rooms in back, perhaps from the basement stairway. He put one finger to his lips unnecessarily; Pelletier was disciplined enough to remain silent.

Seconds later, they stood on either side of the basement door. Since it was locked from this side, Grolan doubted very much that the killer could be lying in wait beyond, but he was too good a cop to take foolish chances and what he'd seen in the last view minutes had spooked him. Pelletier was raising a cautious hand to slide the bolt back when something moved in the shadows beneath the staircase, less than a meter from Grolan, who leaped away, turning and crouching in a single movement.

"Come out of there, slowly, and with your hands where I can see them!"

There was a storage closet tucked under the stairs, almost invisible unless you were looking for it, It was too small to have sheltered an adult, but when the door swung open, a young girl emerged, perhaps eight years old. She held a large, disreputably frayed teddy bear in her left arm; her right hand, clutched tightly against her side, was caked with blood.

Grolan relaxed and lowered his weapon, relieved and suddenly hopeful; this was the first time there had been a survivor of one of the Handyman's attacks, someone who might be able to provide a clue about the killer's identity.

"Are you all right, honey?" He put his weapon away and approached cautiously, not wanting to startle the girl. She watched him warily and clutched her teddy more tightly as he gently touched her bloody arm and side.

"Is she hurt?" Pelletier had moved away from the basement door, but his voice remained tense and he still held his weapon ready.

Grolan shook his head. "I don't think the blood's hers." He glanced at the girl's fixed stare and wondered if she was slipping into shock. "Probably tried to rouse one of her parents before she realized they were dead. Poor kid. What's your name, little girl?"

At first, he didn't think she'd answer. But her lips twitched and she whispered, "Mandy", without changing expression.

"Everything's going to be okay, Mandy." He stood up. "Take her outside, Alan. She doesn't need to see any more than she has already."

Pelletier nodded, reached for the hand holding the teddy, but Mandy immediately shrank away. He nodded, more to himself than to her, then gestured toward the back door. "Let's go outside, Mandy. Would you like to sit in a real police car for a while?"

After a momentary hesitation, she moved forward with slow, measured steps. Pelletier started to follow, then noticed his partner's hesitation.

"What's the matter, Tom?"

Grolan shook his head. "I don't know. Something's bothering me about this; something's not right. I got a kind of sixth sense about things some times, and it's telling me that I'm not seeing what's right in front of me. Go on outside; I'll be with you in a minute."

Pelletier shrugged and followed the little girl through the swinging door into the darkness. Grolan turned and stared back into the body of the house, convinced that he was overlooking something important. He mentally retraced his steps, the discovery of each body, the examination of every closet, alcove, and lurking space that might have concealed an intruder. Everything seemed to check out, but he couldn't shake the feeling that something was incongruous, something obvious.

The sirens were very loud now, coming up the long deserted stretch of Reservoir Road from Managansett center; they'd arrive within a minute or two. Grolan suppressed his misgivings and crossed to the door at the rear of the house, then stepped out into the back yard.

He stood, blinking, trying to focus his eyes in the dim light cast by the half moon overhead and what little diffused illumination escaped the house. Mandy was standing a few feet away and to one side, her teddy still clutched tightly. Just beyond, a larger, darker figure was half crouched in the darkness, little more than a silhouette in the night.

It wasn't his partner. Alan Pelletier lay prone on the ground, unmoving. The second figure had pulled one arm away from the fallen officer's side and was hacking at the wrist with what appeared to be a meat cleaver.

Grolan gave an inarticulate cry of rage and drew his revolver, realized just in time that he might well hit Pelletier instead of the Handyman if he fired in the poor light, instead rushed forward, swinging his weapon like a club. There was a gratifyingly solid impact as the barrel connected with the side of the killer's head and he lurched backward, dropping the cleaver and falling to his hands and knees.

"You son of a bitch! You stay right there and don't move or so help me God I'll blow you away!" Grolan's voice trembled with rage and fear and he had to summon all his strength to keep from pulling the trigger anyway, pulling it again and again until there were no rounds left to fire.

Whether cowed by the threat or stunned by the injury, the fallen man remained motionless and silent. Not even a groan. Pelletier wasn't making any noise either.

Holding his revolver as steadily as possible, Grolan gestured for the girl to come to him. "Come over here, Mandy. He can't hurt you now."

Obediently, she crossed the small distance that separated them. Grolan raised his free hand to steady his grip, shaking with emotion, so intent upon keeping the Handyman covered that he didn't realize that Mandy had spoken to him until the words had percolated a bit in his mind.

"You hurt my daddy," she said softly.

Grolan blinked. "What...?" He dropped his eyes just in time to see Mandy withdraw a long bladed knife from inside the torn body of her teddy bear and plunge it forward into his abdomen. As the tearing pain stole his strength and the revolver dropped from suddenly numbed fingers, he realized what had bothered him back inside the house.

There'd been nothing to indicate that a child of her age lived in the house, not even a bed.

A TIGHT SITUATION

Cherie never would have crawled into the hole in the first place if she hadn't been desperate.

For the past two nights, she'd slept in an abandoned lean-to in the woods not far from where she first heard the men talking. Her father's anger had grown deeper and more violent recently, and being conveniently at hand, Cherie was its most common target. She learned by hard experience that it was safest to stay out of sight, and reach, until the moods passed and this wasn't the first time she'd packed a few things and slipped off into the undeveloped part of Managansett to wait out the storm.

"But the Narragansett Indians weren't mound builders!" She'd been picking berries when the voices grew loud enough to hear, had slipped quietly through the heavy underbrush to a point where she could listen without being seen.

"These weren't Narragansetts; the carvings are completely atypical." The taller of the two men was gesturing at the steep rock face that lined the cleft where they stood atop an oblong mound of earth about ten meters long. Someone had cleared away part of the blanket of vines and lichen revealing bare rock decorated with fading shapes and symbols.

"But there's nothing in the local archaeological record to suggest such a thing!" The shorter man was more animated, kept walking back and forth while he talked. "This has to be some kind of hoax!"

"Look around, Hal. This isn't a recent formation; the flora are too well established. And the weathering on the carvings looks authentic. I don't know what we'll find under that capstone, but I wouldn't be surprised if this is one of the most valuable discoveries ever in this part of the country. There's probably a chamber down there, a hidden room where they could hide from their enemies. It's a treasure chest waiting to be opened."

She'd been losing interest in the conversation but that last sentence caught her attention. When Cherie dropped out of school on her sixteenth birthday, no one tried to talk her out of it. She wasn't unintelligent, just uninvolved; algebra and the history of Egypt and the difference between xylem and phloem didn't seem relevant in a world that included alcoholic fathers with heavy fists and a mother who hadn't spoken or left her hospital room in four years. Teachers had long since given up expecting class participation, let alone homework, and were secretly glad to see her go.

Cherie may have flunked economics, but she knew that money meant independence, escape from the trap she found herself in.

"What do you suppose is down there?" Hal knelt and examined something on the ground, something invisible to Cherie even though she craned her head above the brush, risking discovery.

"We won't know until we look, and we can't do that without equipment and help. Let's put it back the way it was for the time being and get to the car before it gets dark." Storm clouds had already brought a premature dusk to the world, emphasized here under a heavy mantle of foliage.

There was a brief silence as the two men struggled to accomplish some mysterious task. "That'll do for now."

"Right. The weather's supposed to be clear by morning. Let's plan on getting here by eight."

She waited until she could no longer hear the sound of their passage before descending.

At first, Cherie couldn't figure out what they'd been talking about. The mound seemed perfectly natural to her, a rounded swelling of soil covered with denuded blueberry bushes and some bracken. There was a litter of stones, mostly fallen from the cliff face, a few larger ones half buried in the earth. Funny figures and symbols were carved on the exposed rock above her head, but she saw nothing there that held either interest or meaning.

Then she noticed that a largish rock near her foot was also decorated with carvings, three stick figures. Two of them were primitive reproductions of the human form, each with a horizontal line drawn beneath the feet; the third was similar except that the body was drawn in a series of sharp angles, as though to suggest that it was similar to but different from that of a human being. In this case, the horizontal line was above its head. The stone was almost perfectly circular and when Cherie knelt down and felt around the edges, she realized it lay within a concave depression with an almost exactly complementary shape.

It took fifteen minutes to remove, and even then she only managed by finding a long pole and levering it inch by inch out of its resting place.

Light didn't penetrate very far inside and because the opening descended at a forty five degree angle, she couldn't gauge its depth by dropping a stone. Cherie sat on the edge, dangled her legs inside, thinking. It looked like it might be a tight fit, but she figured she could manage it. If she dared.

She'd have to act today since the two men planned to return in the morning, but she couldn't just climb down inside without some kind of plan, some preparation. Cherie forced herself to think things through, and a few minutes later scrambled to her feet. When she returned from the lean-to, equipped with a flashlight and a full canteen of water, she was wearing jeans and an old sweater over her blouse.

First decision. Head or feet first? She didn't know what was down there, maybe some animal had made its lair inside, and the idea of sticking her face into a nest of snakes or rats or whatever was unnerving. Bugs didn't bother her, not much anyway, but there were limits to her tolerance there as well. On the other hand, if she descended with feet ahead, she wouldn't be able to see what she was getting into until it was too late.

The walls looked tight, even for her slim body, and there was as much rock as soil, some of it rough and sharp enough to be dangerous. Impatient with her own indecisiveness, Cherie stuck her head inside, used the flashlight to examine the space ahead, and squirmed forward.

The descent was gradual at first, and she used the flashlight regularly to avoid surprises. There were a couple of places where the walls pressed tightly against her body as she passed, particularly at hips and shoulders, but in each case a twist of her body allowed free passage. The canteen created an additional problem, but she was unwilling to give it up and kept shifting the strap so that it pressed against different parts of her body, depending on the configuration of the walls. The closeness was oppressive but she refused to think about the possibility of getting stuck. The whole idea was freighted with unpleasant images from an old horror film she'd seen as a child, where someone was buried alive and panicked inside the coffin.

About five meters down the tunnel leveled, although it was still too narrow for her to rise to hands and knees. The ceiling was mostly chunks of rock, some with sharp edges that occasionally scraped against her back. The earth was dry and crumbling and rivulets of sand rained down, getting inside her blouse and jeans. Cherie was already damp with sweat; the evening air was cool but squirming through the earth was more work than she'd expected. She paused long enough to painstakingly remove the sweater, with barely enough room to manage the maneuver. When it was finally off, she used one hand to push it back down the length of her body toward her feet before continuing.

Seconds later she found the dagger. Only the hilt was visible, rising from the earth in which it had been buried, and she might have dismissed it as just another stone if she hadn't noticed the carving. The wavy limbed stick figure again, this time completely enclosed in what might almost have been a vase. Cherie pulled it from the ground, noted the crude metal blade, almost discarded it before she realized it might be helpful if she needed to widen the tunnel later on.

She slid it point first inside the canteen cover where it couldn't come loose.

The passage stayed level for a few more meters, then turned steeply downward. Cherie's discomfort grew more intense, and she wondered if she might have been better off leading with her feet. Too late to change now, she realized. To retreat would mean to crawl backward, awkward and uncomfortable at best. One of the men had mentioned a hidden room; she'd just have to continue until she found it and turn around there.

There was nothing to indicate animals used this passage, no droppings, bones, animal hairs, nothing at all. In fact, she hadn't seen any insects either, no earthworms, ants, spiders. It was quiet down here, she realized, a funny sort of leaden silence that pressed against her ears. And the soil smelled vaguely sour, acidic, reminding her of chemistry class. Test tubes with corks in them.

The angle became so steep that she paused, wondering if perhaps this wasn't such a good idea after all. Claustrophobia wasn't a problem; before she was old enough to fend for herself in the woods, she'd hidden from her father's rages in various places in the house, closets, inside a wardrobe, under the kitchen sink. If anything, the closeness of her surroundings provided a sense of security. There was such a thing as too close, though. But Cherie had a stubborn streak that had led to increasingly dangerous confrontations with her father in recent years, so she wasn't about to quit without a much better reason than simple uncertainty.

Ten minutes later she reached a junction.

There was a cross tunnel, an intersection large enough that she could almost sit up by rolling over and pulling her knees close. Her muscles had been cramping badly and this new position felt wonderful after the first few seconds of blinding pain.

"This had better be worth it," she said aloud, just to break the silence, but the walls seemed to soak up the sound and left her feeling vaguely disquieted. There'd be no problem reversing position here, and she could crawl back to the surface with no difficulty. And she almost did it, almost abandoned her explorations, might have done so if a sudden memory of the towering, raging form of her father hadn't flickered across her consciousness.

There were worse things than crawling through earthen tunnels.

The flashlight didn't reveal anything informative in either direction, so she chose the right fork more or less at random, started forward once again.

It was easy going at first, the tunnel level and larger than before, although the surface was rough enough to tear at her clothing and abrade flesh, particularly knees and elbows. She'd learned to ignore pain. Cherie settled into a regular rhythm, moving a few meters, then pausing to catch her breath and use the flashlight to illuminate the way ahead.

Then the angle started downward again, just a little at first, then sharply. Earlier the tightness of the walls had retarded her movement, now the comparatively wider passage made the going dangerous. Twice she lost her balance and slid forward jarringly before recovering. After that, she braced her legs against the walls of the tunnel, advancing more slowly but more securely.

When the tunnel changed direction sharply, almost straight down, she hesitated.

Even with the flashlight, the darkness seemed to press in from all sides. Occasional sounds reached her from elsewhere in the tunnel system, probably falling sand, the earth stretching its own muscles. Cherie thought of all the reasonable explanations, but couldn't shake the feeling that she wasn't alone down here, that someone else was present, aware of her, even watching somehow despite the inky blackness where her own light didn't touch.

She was also aware of the real danger that she might injure herself and never be found. This latest downturn was particularly frightening, and Cherie even made some tentative efforts to back away, discovering that it was indeed as awkward as she had expected. But then it occurred to her that the very difficulty of the passage might be a clue to its resolution, that if there was indeed any treasure to be found within the mound, its former owners might well have made access as difficult as possible.

She reversed course and started down.

Ten minutes later, disaster nearly struck. The walls had zigzagged twice, a sharp edged "S" curve which she'd negotiated with great difficulty, extensive cursing, and at the cost of scraped palms and a bump on the side of her head. Then the tunnel straightened suddenly, widened, and she almost slipped, recovered only by desperately pressing her arms against the walls, losing the flashlight in the process.

It fell into the darkness.

Fortunately, it didn't have far to go, and even more fortunately, it didn't break when it landed. Once she'd recovered her composure, Cherie descended the rest of the way, finding herself in a dead end. No treasure, just a thick carpet of what looked like twigs but which she eventually realized were animal bones. White, pencil thin, dessicated and brittle. They looked very old and there was no smell of death or decay. Judging by the skulls, they were field mice, or perhaps squirrels. There was no sign of flesh or fur to confirm either alternative.

There was also insufficient room to turn around.

Cherie had a headache, possibly because of the unusual exertion and tension, more likely because she'd essentially been standing on her head for the past twenty minutes. Now she had no choice but to crawl back, upside down, despite the tremors that were rippling through her arms and legs.

But there was no alternative, and waiting in her present position would only make things more difficult. Cherie twisted slightly, pressed her body as far to one side as possible so she could play the cone of her light back the way she would have to go, trying to decide how best to proceed.

Something moved up above, something which might just have been a trick of the shadows. Or might not. The lower end of the "S" curve obstructed her view.

Shadow or animal, trick of the light or poisonous reptile, Cherie had no choice but to climb back out, essentially blind until she reached the level tunnel above, and after that she'd still have to crawl backwards at least till the junction, which now seemed almost impossibly distant.

It was even more difficult than she had expected. A sharp point of rock caught the seam of her jeans at one point and slit open half the pants leg on that side, scratching the flesh of her calf painfully in the process. She didn't think she was bleeding but had no way to check. The first angle of the curve was so difficult she had to rest for several minutes with her body contorted into an uncomfortable shape, and when she finally tried to continue, cramps immobilized her. Cherie blinked away tears of pain and exhaustion as she used her fingers to relax the rigid muscles.

She hadn't owned a wristwatch since her father smashed her brand new Swatch under his heel a year earlier, so she had no way of measuring time. It felt as though she'd been underground for days, weeks even, and surely it must have been at least a couple of hours. The ache in her head had settled to a dull throbbing and she'd turned off the light to conserve the battery; at this point she could learn more from the sense of touch than sight.

Her mood improved when she finally cleared the top half of the curve. The realization that she was through the worst provided the strength to keep her moving in a steady progression of knees and forearms. It wasn't until her feet discovered an anomaly that she began to panic.

At first it was just puzzling, a spur of rock where she didn't remember having encountered one before, at least not anything of this size. It seemed to jut down directly from above rather than from one of the side walls, which made no sense, and when her probing feet could provide no further information, she pressed herself to one side and resorted to the flashlight.

There were two passages leading up, divided neatly by a wedge of stone, each indistinguishable from the other. Obviously she hadn't noticed this divergent passage on the way down. Both routes were at roughly the same angle but separated from each other, with nothing to distinguish either one. She had turned so many times during her descent and subsequent return, she had no way of guessing which led back to the surface.

Suppressing her growing fear by refusing to think about anything but the immediate decision at hand, Cherie chose the rightmost path and continued her backward crawl.

It was soon obvious she'd chosen incorrectly because when she at last found herself on level ground, and under level ground as well, it lasted for only a short distance, then started to drop away. For the first time since she'd started, Cherie was descending in a relatively upright position. Once again she hesitated.

"Get your ass out of here, girl." Her voice was even stranger this time, echoing in the distance, truncated so that it came back sounding as though someone had answered, "Gonna get your ass, girl", which was clearly impossible. Common sense told her to go back to the fork, work her way around it, and return to the surface, get out of here for once and all. But now that she wasn't quite so uncomfortable, even her headache having faded to an almost negligible pain, it occurred to her that retreating now would mean the entire episode had been for nothing. And for all she knew, an incredible horde of buried gold or jewels or something equally valuable might lie ahead.

"Shit!" She used the flashlight to explore below her feet, half hoping to discover another dead end, but the passage curved away from the cone of light and continued deeper. "Maybe I'll just go a little further."

The echo replied, "Go a little further". And she did.

Twenty meters and two gentle curves later, she groped with one foot, felt the rock she was grasping turn under the palm of one hand, tried to shift her weight and lost hold completely. Her rear end skidded down a sandy slope for a split second before she suddenly became airborne, briefly, ending with a stunning impact.

She'd dropped the flashlight again but it was still working and Cherie discovered she' fallen into an underground room of some kind. The chamber was tall enough that she could stand up after a fashion, although even at five foot three, she was forced to crouch. The floor was roughly circular, measuring about four meters in diameter. Walls and ceiling were lined with stones, most of which were decorated with stick figures similar to the ones she'd seen above. A second passageway, indistinguishable from the one by which she'd just entered, led upward from the opposite side. The floor was hard packed earth, the smooth surface decorated only by a handful of broken stones. And a small ceramic pot or urn.

At first she thought this was it, her fortune was made, imagining Ali Baba finding a bucket of jewels in a cave, already wondering how she'd go about converting whatever she found to cash. But the urn was empty and her disappoint was so intense, she burst into quiet tears, wiping them away with the back of one filthy hand. Even the pottery itself was a washout; a large chunk of stone had fallen from the ceiling, shattering the lid and sending cracks spiderwebbing down through the sides.

Cherie slumped next to the entranceway, sitting with her back against the wall. She was angry with the men who'd lied to her about there being a treasure here, illogical as that anger might be, angry with herself for pressing forward when she had known it was time to cut her losses and retreat. But most of all she was exhausted, her body crying out for rest, and eventually, despite a growing anxiety about the situation into which she'd thrown herself, Cherie turned off the light and set it down beside her hip, leaned forward with her arms crossed and supported by her knees, and fell asleep.

It couldn't have lasted long in such an awkward position, and when she raised her head after some uncertain period of time, she had a sense that she had never really lost consciousness at all. What disturbed her was the undeniable feeling that she was no longer alone, that someone had touched her hair a moment before, just brushing it slightly.

"Hello? Is anyone there?" Of course there wasn't, but she was just sleepy enough not to be entirely sensible. Her voice was raw and thin, and even a few sips from the canteen did little to help. She fumbled for the flashlight, but it seemed to have rolled out of reach.

Cherie spread her arms wide, moving them back and forth in ever widening circles.

"Now where in the hell did that get to?"

There were no holes in the floor, no real features that might have concealed it. On all fours, she increased the range of her search, carefully at first, then with increased desperation. Then panic. She crawled from one side of the chamber to the other, back and forth, then diagonally, turning and twisting each time she thought she sensed an unexamined patch of ground. Nothing. Her frantic, disorganized search only ended when she banged her head against a stone embedded in one of the walls with enough force to jar her back to rationality.

But when she methodically repeated the search, a systematic back and forth pattern that covered every inch of the chamber at least twice, she still hadn't found the light. Which meant it wasn't here at all. Which meant someone or something had taken it.

She wasn't alone.

A light came on suddenly, very faint, from out of the throat of one of the exit passages. As though someone had just turned on a flashlight. As indeed was the case.

Cherie moved to the opening, hesitated. Was this the way she had come in, or the unexplored tunnel? During her momentary panic, she'd lost her orientation. Not that it mattered. Whatever risk might be involved, she was going toward the light. It was bad enough being alone in the dark in this place; discovering she was no longer alone in the dark was even worse.

She crawled in.

The light kept moving, beckoning her onward through a series of level sections and slight inclines and drops, finally emerging into a second chamber, this one much larger than the first, oval in shape, perhaps twenty meters long. At the far end, her flashlight was wedged into the ground, the cone of light extending straight up toward the ceiling.

The walls and ceiling, even the floor, were riddled with scores, hundreds of small tunnels, none bigger than her thigh. It was like being inside a gigantic, barren honeycomb. There didn't appear to be any other exits, and no sign of whoever, or whatever, had led her here.

"I'm warning you, stop messing around!"

The echoed whispered, "Messing around."

She took a tentative step toward the flashlight, scanning her surroundings. In addition to the small tunnels, there were dozens of shallow niches carved into the soil, each of which was filled with something she couldn't identify at first. But as she advanced toward the flashlight, she could see more clearly that they were insects, earthworms, centipedes, ants, crickets, slugs, all dead and all sorted quite thoroughly into the separate cavities.

She had crossed half the distance to the light when something struck her in the shoulder.

It was a small stone, propelled with enough force to bring a cry of pain. Cherie staggered to one side, rubbed her shoulder and tried to spot the source of the attack. As far as she could tell, she was alone in the chamber.

Something moved behind, or rather within, the wall, something not seen, almost not heard, but definitely sensed. Cherie backed away cautiously, moving toward the flashlight.

Another small stone struck her on the left kneecap and she stumbled, skinning both palms as she broke her fall. A third whistled past the side of her head and ricocheted off the far wall. Cherie rolled away, banging her already wounded knee painfully in the process. But her roll was toward the flashlight and a second later she was holding it in one hand.

From the opposite wall, something was coming out of the warren of small tunnels, a tenuous form that unfolded as it emerged into the semblance of a small child. It had a head and arms and legs, but the limbs weren't quite right, there were curves rather than joints and the head had just the suggestion of a face.

It stood watching her, motionless at first, then raised one serpentine arm to point to a feature of the chamber Cherie hadn't noticed before. Along one side wall, portions of the floor had been scooped out to create a concavity similar to those that had been filled with the corpses of insects. But this was much larger, large enough to accommodate a human body.

And the face that wasn't really a face smiled. Inhuman as it might be, the smile was a familiar one, the humorless grimace her father affected when he was using a belt or his hands or a length of knotted rope to instill what he called "discipline" in his daughter.

That's when she remembered the knife.

It wasn't much of a weapon, but it was the best thing she had. She stood slowly, favoring the injured knee even though the pain was already beginning to fade. As she did so, the tenuous apparition advanced toward her, incredibly menacing even though it seemed insubstantial, little more than a trick of the light. The knife seemed to slip into her hand of its own volition and she cocked her arm and tossed it overhand, watched it tumble end over end, right into...and through...the figure's chest.

Something screamed soundlessly inside her head and the creature, whatever it was, seemed to shatter, each of its limbs seeking refuge in a separate crawl hole. It was still there though, on both sides now; she could hear it moving behind the walls.

She limped across the chamber and retrieved the knife before climbing into the exit tunnel while behind her something chattered in silent rage.

Cherie's fatigue was washed away by a flood of adrenaline and she moved steadily, not even pausing for breath when she reached the chamber with the shattered pot, then headfirst back into the tunnels. She had to reverse herself at the fork and wriggle back feet first, but she did so without hesitation, rarely even using the flashlight. The terror behind her was worse than anything the dark might conceal.

Or so she thought.

Then the larger junction where she was able to sit up, flex her aching muscles. It should be easy from here, along the horizontal passage, then up to the top. Once she thought she heard something moving back the way she had come, faint, furtive. There was no question of it being an animal; she knew now that there were only two living things in these tunnels.

Assuming the creature was a living thing.

Her fear diminished as she crawled forward, but the tunnel seemed much longer than when she had entered. At the bottom of a shallow trough, something soft moved under her hand and she almost cried out before realizing what it was. Her discarded sweater. She knew where she was now; in a few minutes, she should be on the surface.

And she would have been if the ground above hadn't suddenly given way.

She wasn't buried exactly; in fact, very little dirt fell, just enough to make it difficult to move her arms and legs. But a very large chunk of stone had shifted, dropped lower, just low enough that no matter what she did, she could move neither forward nor back.

It took Cherie a while to figure that out though, and only her physical weakness prevented her from flailing about in frustrated rage. But calm returned as she realized that at the worst, she simply had to wait until morning. When the archaeologists returned, she could call to them, and they'd get her out, one way or another. They wouldn't be happy to find her there, but that's life, right?

Cherie arranged the bundled sweater under her head and decided to try to get some sleep. She might have succeeded if it hadn't been for a sudden loud noise in the distance, unrecognizable at first, then quite clear. Thunder. The rain came a few minutes later.

It was a pretty heavy downpour. The dry walls of the tunnel absorbed the water at first, but it came too fast, began to reach the floor of the first level in a trickle at first, then a steady stream. Cherie wasn't alarmed initially, not until she realized her hair was soaked and her left cheek was lying in a pool of water.

The dampness spread down her body, the water backing up from the fallen earth. Cherie used the flashlight to examine the problem, then carefully used her hands and feet to dig a narrow channel. By the time she was successful, her neck was stiff from holding her head above the rising water.

But when she finally broke through, the level dropped with astonishing speed, and she let her head fall back into the mud with a sigh of relief, listening to the tiny sounds of running water, surprised at how wonderfully they sounded.

Cherie began to laugh then, realized it was the beginning of hysteria, but couldn't do anything about it. The tension had to be released somehow. In the morning she'd be rescued, pulled loose like an impediment in a drainpipe, made to look a fool, and probably sent back to her father besides. And it had all been for nothing.

"Damn it all!" She shouted at last, finally returning to something like calm.

The sound of running water had changed somehow, but she didn't realize what was going on until the pooled water climbed up past her chest to her chin. With the flashlight, she could just make out the low earthen barrier that had been pushed into place just below her feet, just out of reach.

And then came the belated, almost echo once more.

"Dam it all," it said.

TRAPPED

When Liz woke up, she was alone in the bed. That didn't immediately alarm her because she figured Jason was in the bathroom. He was still recovering from a urinary infection and was up at least a couple of times a night to empty his bladder. She was mildly surprised that the bathroom light wasn't on, but maybe he hadn't bothered. It was easy enough to find your way in the dark. All hotel rooms were basically the same. It wasn't as if he could get lost.

She glanced at the clock. Exactly midnight. Jason would be up at the crack of dawn, of course, anxious for breakfast and an early start on the tourist circuit. He had never learned how important it was for her to waken properly in the morning, and in her own good time, never realized how much it irritated her to be jostled awake to "come see the robins playing in the birdbath" or some such nonsense. Jason was the one who had planned this vacation, sorting through brochures and visiting websites for months in advance. It was the first time in years that they'd been able to schedule their time off from work simultaneously and he had allocated what she considered a somewhat too generous fraction of their savings to pay for the trip. "It's a chance for us to get to know each other again. You know, like a second honeymoon." Liz would have been just as happy to spend the time sitting in the back yard at home, with a book in her lap and her feet up. She hadn't particularly enjoyed their first honeymoon when she was excited by Jason's obvious devotion, and the prospect of another at this late stage, when she felt trapped by youthful impulse and practical necessity did nothing to brighten her life.

The room was very quiet. Liz opened her eyes again. "Jason? Are you all right?"

There was no answer. She glanced again at the clock, which still said 12:00. She was sure that more than a minute had passed. If the clock was broken and the alarm didn't go off on time, Jason would be very unhappy. She sat up and snapped on the lamp, blinking as light spilled out into the room. "Jason, I think there's something wrong with the alarm clock." She picked it up and looked at it helplessly, then set it down again. "Are you all right in there?"

Still no answer. Feeling just slightly anxious, Liz slipped out of bed. The room was chilly and she picked up her bathrobe from the chair where she'd dropped it before climbing into bed, slipping it on as she walked toward the bathroom. The light switch was mounted outside the door and she flicked all three levers up at once. Two overhead lights in the main room and one in the bathroom came on with a faint, electric shushing noise.

There was no one in the bathroom. She even looked in the shower. Puzzled, but still not alarmed, she decided he must have left the room for some reason. Maybe a drink? The bar was open until midnight, she remembered, but Jason wasn't usually a late night drinker. She stepped out of the bathroom and turned to the door. It was bolted on the inside, including the safety chain. Jason could not have relocked it from the outside, which meant that he was still in the room.

Except that he wasn't.

Liz made a thorough search, even though she could think of no reason why Jason would hide in the closet or crawl under the bed. It only took a few seconds. The room wasn't that big, and there was no connecting door. The window? She opened the drapes and looked down onto the lighted parking lot, but they were several floors up and in any case, she couldn't find any way to open the windows.

"This is ridiculous," she said aloud, but her voice sounded funny and there was a tremor in it that made her feel even worse. Her watch was on the dresser and she picked it up, but the battery must have gone dead because the two digits that indicated seconds were not changing. The hotel alarm clock was blinking "12:00" over and over, so that didn't help.

She thought about going back to bed. If this was all just a dream, she'd waken to normality. But it didn't feel like a dream. In fact, she knew it wasn't. Somehow Jason had left the room. Maybe she'd gotten up and, half asleep, locked the door after he'd gone. Liz wasn't a sleep walker normally, but she wasn't used to traveling, sleeping in strange beds in strange rooms. She had used this as one of several arguments against taking this trip, but Jason had brushed it aside, just as did anything she said that didn't coincide with his plans. It was possible and it fitted the facts. If Jason had come back and found the door chained, what would he have done? Knocked, of course, but it might have been impossible to wake her without making so much noise that it would have disturbed the other guests. Jason detested making a scene. He wouldn't even complain when a waitress messed up an order. It was always Liz who had to speak up.

So what would he have done then? Liz decided that if she'd been in that position, she'd have gone to the lobby and phoned the room. If that hadn't worked, she'd have curled up on one of their couches or, if they objected to that, she'd have rented another room for the night. Probably that was what Jason had done.

She decided to go down to the lobby and take a look around. Shedding the bathrobe, she pulled on slacks and a sweater over her nightgown. A quick glance at the mirror told her she didn't look completely disreputable and she went quickly to the door. The chain slid smoothly out of its slot and fell free. The door bolt, however, would not turn, no matter how much pressure she applied. Furious, she yanked on the door handle, which refused to rotate, and pounded her fist on the door. "God damn it!"

Liz was startled to realize how fast her heart was racing. It almost required a conscious effort to breathe and she backed away, telling herself to calm down, that she would accomplish nothing by panicking. It wasn't as if she was in any danger, after all. This would all work out in due course and later she and Jason would turn it into an amusing anecdote to tell their friends back home.

So what next? The telephone, of course. She would call the front desk and explain that her door was jammed shut and they would send someone up to take care of it. A glance at the instructions told her to dial 1-2-3 to reach the front desk.

"Yes? This is the night desk. How may I help you?" It was a woman's voice, low and throaty, with just a hint of an accent.

"Hi. This is Mrs. Parker. I seem to have a problem with the lock on my door. I can't get it open."

"Perhaps you are trying to turn it the wrong way. You should turn it to the left, not the right."

Liz clenched her teeth, telling herself not to lose her temper. "I realize that. I tried both directions. It won't move either way. The mechanism must be jammed."

"I don't know anything about that, Mrs. Parker."

Liz waited, but the woman remained silent. "Can you send someone up to let me out?"

"There is no one here except me at this time of night, Mrs. Parker, and I can't leave the desk. I wouldn't be able to help you anyway. I don't know anything about locks."

"There must be someone you can call. This is an emergency."

"Are you injured in any way, Mrs. Parker?"

"What has that got to do with anything? No, I'm perfectly all right, except that I'm locked in my room and my husband is missing."

"He is not there with you?"

Anger seeped into her voice. "Well, if he's missing, he's certainly not here with me. That's what the word 'missing' means."

"It is not necessary for you to be rude, Mrs. Parker. I am only trying to help."

"Well then help me get the goddamned door open!" Liz was immediately shocked by her own vehemence, took a deep breath. "I'm sorry. I didn't mean to shout at you, but I'm worried about my husband and I'm a little bit claustrophobic." She wasn't, but it made a reasonable excuse.

"Perhaps your husband went for a walk and to the bar." The clerk's voice remained calm, reasonable, and that was even more irritating than it would have been if she'd shouted back.

"The bar closed at midnight."

"They stop serving, yes, but sometimes gentlemen will sit there afterwards for a while and talk or play cards."

Liz remembered the clock. "What time is it anyway?"

A short pause. "It is just a few minutes after midnight, Mrs. Parker."

A sudden inspiration came to her. "Listen, if there was a fire, I wouldn't be able to evacuate. That's a serious violation of the law. I could sue the hotel if you don't let me out of here."

This time there was an audible sigh. "What is it that you want me to do, Mrs. Parker?"

Liz spaced the words evenly, speaking each distinctly. "I want you to find someone to get this door open and I want it done right now."

Another sigh. "I will call my superior. Can you please tell me your room number?"

Liz thought about it, but couldn't remember. Jason had registered, led the way to the room, and had kept the key. She didn't even know exactly what floor they were on. "I don't remember. My husband took care of everything. Can't you just look at your switchboard and tell what room I'm calling from?"

"No, ma'am, I can't do that. This is an old phone system. Your room number should be on your key card."

"Hold on." Liz made a quick, efficient search. "It's not here. My husband must have taken it with him when he left."

"I cannot help you if I do not know where you are."

"Well, look in the register. Jason and Elizabeth Parker."

"Our computer system is down at the moment. We had a power failure."

"What kind of a goddamned hotel is this anyway?" Liz felt tears running down her cheeks. Tears of rage and frustration, and something more, something she couldn't define. "I'm warning you, get me out of this room or I'll sue your ass and the hotel and everyone else I can think of!" Terrified that she would break down even further, she slammed the receiver into its cradle, breaking the connection.

It took several minutes before she calmed down, minutes in which she paced back and forth through the small room, periodically rattling the still immovable door handle, slowly regaining her composure. Only after she regained relative calm did she make her next observation.

All of Jason's things were gone. She remembered his old, battered suitcase sitting in one corner of the room, his shaving gear and toiletries on the left side of the sink in the bathroom, his topcoat hanging in the closet. A quick search revealed that everything was gone, everything except for his straight razor, which she found on the bathroom floor, behind the waste basket, as though it had fallen there unnoticed when the other items were taken away.

Taken away by whom? And why?

She thought about secret passages and remembered you were supposed to rap on the walls to find them, but she wouldn't know the sound of a solid wall from a fake one, so she didn't even try, although she did make a cursory search for concealed levers or buttons. It was only after she tripped over a chair leg and banged her elbow that she stopped to think how irrationally she was behaving.

There are no secret passages in hotel rooms, she told herself. But another voice asked, if that was so, then where had Jason gone, and how? Not to mention why?

She called the desk again, got the same voice.

"When will they get here?" she asked perfunctorily.

"When will who get here, ma'am?"

"The people you called to let me out of this room."

There was a hint of surliness this time. "Oh, it's you, Mrs. Parker. Have you remembered what room you're in yet?"

"I'm in the room with the door that won't open! When are they going to get here?"

"I haven't called anyone. There's nothing to be done until I know your room number. If you're in the hotel at all."

Liz was momentarily stunned. "What are you talking about? Of course, I'm in the hotel."

"I only have your word for that, Mrs. Parker. If that's really your name. I have no way of knowing if this is an internal call or whether you're calling from somewhere else entirely. We've had several prank calls recently – bomb threats, mostly – and you have to admit that your story sounds pretty unlikely. You've conveniently forgotten your room number, your husband isn't there to help, and you are trapped and want someone to come help you but you don't know where you are."

"I'm on the eighth floor, or maybe the ninth. And we turned left when we came out of the elevator. I remember that much."

"There are 36 rooms on each floor, Mrs. Parker, half of them to the left. I can't ask a locksmith to break into 36 rooms."

"He can rap on the doors until I answer."

"And wake many of our guests on the chance that your unlikely story is true? I don't think my superior would be very happy with me. I think, Mrs. Parker, that this is all a very bad joke. I don't think that is really your name, or that you really have a husband, or that you're here in this hotel. I think you are a very lonely woman whom I should feel sorry for and would feel sorry for if you were not making things so very difficult for me. So I will say goodnight, Mrs. Parker." And she hung up.

Her first reaction was to call back, but she was shaking with a fury so intense that she kept missing the right buttons on the phone and she finally threw it across the room. She immediately regretted the act and retrieved it, when she held the receiver to her ear and pressed some of the buttons experimentally, her suspicion was confirmed. There was no dial tone. It was out of service. Like the door, she told herself silently.

Liz suddenly felt very cold and very uncertain of herself. She tried to turn up the heat but the unit remained silent even when she set it to the maximum. Shivering, she went back to the bed, climbed under the covers, and pulled them up across her chest. Somewhere along the way she had picked up Jason's razor, the only physical proof she had that he was real, that he had been there with her. It was comforting somehow, and she held it tightly as she closed her eyes, telling herself just to go to sleep, that in the morning she'd wake up and find that all of this had just been some very strange, very realistic dream.

Lieutenant Mohr stared down at the bed where the dead woman had been found. The sheets were soaked with blood, which had also spilled down into the carpet. The razor with which she'd cut her own throat had been lying on the floor in front of the night table, but the technicians had already photographed, tagged, and removed it. The medical examiner's preliminary estimate put the time of death at around midnight. There really wasn't any reason for him to stay any longer. It seemed a straightforward suicide. The door had been locked and bolted, she'd registered by herself and that name matched the driver's license and credit cards in her purse. Elizabeth Parker. There were pictures in the wallet of the dead woman with a tall, prematurely balding man, presumably her husband. They were trying to contact the man to notify him of his wife's death.

The room smelled very badly. The Parker woman must have turned the heat up to high before killing herself. Even with the windows open, it was still unnaturally warm. He'd talked to the night clerk, a young Pakistani woman who spoke impeccable English, but without learning anything useful. The phone had been ripped out of the wall at some point and lay in one corner.

Mohr was just turning to leave when one of the uniforms – Jennings - entered the room hurriedly, excitement obvious in his expression. "Lieutenant, I have something for you. The vic's husband is dead too."

Mohr's eyes widened but his expression didn't change otherwise. He'd worked homicide too long to be surprised any more. "How'd that happen?"

"They found him last night. A neighbor went over because the dog was barking and saw his body through a window." His face changed and he straightened his back imperceptibly to emphasize the significance of what he said next. "His throat was slashed. No murder weapon at the scene but they think it was a thin knife or a razor." He emphasized the last word for Mohr's benefit. "They've been looking for the wife. Seems like they hadn't been getting along too well lately."

"Well, they won't be arguing anymore."

He started to walk toward the door, but Jennings made an involuntary move to cut him off. "One more thing, sir. Something strange."

"Something stranger, you mean. Well, what is it?"

"They found something at the crime scene that they can't quite explain. The husband, the dead man, was holding it in one hand."

"Holding what, Jennings?" Mohr asked impatiently.

Jennings looked uncomfortable. "It was one of those electronic passcards that hotels use instead of keys."

Mohr could see it coming and had a sudden urge to leave before he heard the rest, but his feet refused to move. "It was for this room, sir. They can't figure out how it got there."

TWISTED IMAGES

It was on a Friday evening when I first heard sounds from my mirror. I know the day, if not the date, quite specifically because I invariably pay my bills promptly after supper on Fridays and I was searching through a dresser drawer for a pen when it occurred. It was a brief but quite distinct sound, as though some heavy piece of furniture had been moved across a hardwood floor, and since my bedroom is entirely uncarpeted, my first reaction was a mixture of outrage and fear at the thought of some interloper in my apartment. My parents' home had been burglarized twice while I was still living with them, but somehow that seemed a lesser violation, an invasion of their privacy but not of my own. Despite the fact that I had been living independently of them for only a few months, I had already developed a deep rooted sense of place and property; at this point, I had never even allowed a guest into my rooms, let alone some stranger.

The absurdity of that initial thought was self evident. The tiny apartment would have provided little concealment for a field mouse, let alone a human being, and my bedroom would have passed for a walk-in closet elsewhere. The bed consisted of a mattress and box spring, the latter flush against the floor, no headboard, and my dresser was a cracked child's bureau I had carried laboriously home after spotting it waiting on the curb for the morning's trash pickup in the relatively more affluent neighborhood four blocks away. The bottom drawer was falling apart and sustained the weight of a few handkerchiefs, nothing more. Its cheery lime green exterior clashed with the dingy off-white plaster walls, but it was still an improvement over the collection of tomato crates which had formerly housed my presentable but rather unimaginative wardrobe. Together, these two items were the sole furnishings for the room in which I was currently spending at least one third of the hours of my life.

Plus the mirror, of course. And whatever inhabited it.

I had discovered this particular apartment more by luck than design, although I had not yet decided which brand of luck that might be. Certainly it was less expensive than anything else I had seen, relatively convenient to the center of town, only two blocks from the bus stop that would take me into Providence, but still far enough from Main Street that I rested at night undisturbed by traffic noises. Not that Managansett saw much traffic after eleven o'clock, which was the hour when I normally surrendered my grip on the day. For that matter, there wasn't much traffic before eleven either. Managansett was a sandbar around which the tides of development and change nibbled to little effect.

"It's nothing special, but it's clean, convenient, and inexpensive, Mr. Sheridan." Jeri Kaplan, the landlady, a young woman who might have been attractive had she not been so intense, barely concealed her skepticism about renting the room. "In a college town, I'd have no trouble moving it, but out here..." She made an all inclusive gesture with both arms and sighed theatrically before continuing. "Even by local standards, it's too small, too old fashioned, located in the wrong part of town. But it is affordable. Affordable is how we slumlords avoid saying 'cheap'." The flash of humor, accompanied by just the faintest ghost of a smile, was incongruous but paradoxically helped put me at ease.

I had attempted an appreciative smile but feared my face was contorted into its usual nervous idiot grin, tried to cover up by assuming an emotionless, businesslike pose. It's very unlikely I fooled her. After all, finding one's first apartment away from home at eighteen, even in a backwater town like Managansett, is something of a milestone in a young man's life.

"I had really hoped for something furnished," I replied at last. "This is my first apartment, you know, so I really don't have any furniture, not even a bed."

My prospective landlady met my eyes steadily, with such intensity in fact that I remembered my mother telling me to make a point of staring down each new dog she brought into the kennel, to establish myself as a superior beast in the pecking order of life. That memory lent me the strength to return her stare without blinking, until she finally relented and turned away. I have no doubt she knew exactly what we were doing, and abandoned the field of battle out of kindness rather than weakness.

"There's a mattress and box spring in the loft you can use, I suppose, but you'll have to bring them down yourself. If you can salvage any of the other stuff that's up there, go right ahead; the door isn't locked. In fact, there isn't even a door any more. Just follow the stairs up until you can't go any further and don't make a mess. But I'm afraid there's no other furniture in the apartment itself, just an old stove."

Which wasn't quite true. The mirror was there as well.

In Canton, China, there is a legend about mirrors. In ancient times, the Cantonese believe, there was free passage between the specular world of the mirror and our own. Free passage at least until a great battle broke out, with the mirror people attempting to gain suzerainty over both realms, repelled by the magical powers of an ancient Emperor of China who not only closed the doorway between the worlds but enslaved the mirror creatures, forcing them to mimic the appearance and actions of anyone who chanced within view of their now circumscribed universe. A third race of creatures inhabited the water, closely allied with the mirror world, and when they saw the power of the Emperor, they pretended to have fallen under the same spell, imitating through subterfuge rather than compulsion, waiting for the day when their allies beyond the mirrors' surface could break the slowly weakening spell and resume their conquest. The water creatures were far more vulnerable, of course; a single ripple could disrupt their image.

I didn't know this story at the time, of course, because I had not yet met my neighbor, Chen Li, and she had not yet told it to me. But even in my ignorance, when I first set eyes on -- or perhaps into -- the mirror in my bedroom, I sensed that it was a special object, incongruous within its shabby surroundings.

The frame was quite impressive in an aggressively ugly fashion, the intertwined bodies of naked women forming a rope of make-believe flesh that completely circumscribed the glass itself. Except that wasn't quite accurate; close examination revealed a much more diverse pattern. The topmost carving was an exquisitely rendered miniature of an attractive oriental woman, slender tapering limbs, breasts stylishly small, almost boyish, coils of long hair draped over one shoulder. But as the ornamentation progressed clockwise around the circumference of the mirror, the details of each subsequent figure were less human, more feline, toes gradually turning to claws, the long hair into a tawny mane, the nose and jaws coarsening, widening, eyes growing deeper, brighter, fiercer. At the very bottom, the woman had turned into a tigress, fully rendered, remarkably lifelike. Once past that point, the transformation reversed itself, each stage shedding some of the bestiality of the previous, returning symmetrically to its origin when the circuit was completed. The frame had been painted a bright, almost phosphorescent orange, probably fairly recently since it was uniform, unblemished, unscratched.

The mirror thus ornamented was itself a smooth, unbroken expanse of glass fully two meters high and half as wide. It dominated one wall of the room and was so firmly fastened, by some means I was too lazy to investigate, that I quickly abandoned any idea of moving it to the loft. I am not, by my nature, fond of mirrors. On the verge of my twentieth year, acne still reigns triumphant on my face, and my comically weak chin, too narrow nose, close set eyes, and worst of all, a raspberry colored birthmark across the left cheek so frequently disconcert those who meet me for the first time, I have almost ceased to notice their reaction. Almost. Faced with its intractability, I contented myself finally by positioning my bed so that it was behind me as I slept; I would never have to waken to the sight of my own peculiarly unpleasant appearance.

Besides, the painting on the opposite wall was far more interesting, so striking in fact that it was a major element in my decision to take this decaying (but affordable) third floor apartment.

Jeri Kaplan had apologized briefly for its garishness when she brought me through, explaining that the previous tenant had painted it directly onto the wall without her knowledge, that she had only learned of its existence once the police had taken away the body and finished their investigation. "Yang kept to himself, like most of these Chinese. But he always paid his rent on time, so I had no reason to come up here. I could probably get the owners to pay for a couple of cans of paint to cover it, but you'd have to do the work yourself."

"No, no," I protested, perhaps a bit too vehemently. "I like it. It's different. Where else could I find an apartment with a giant blue dragon on the wall?"

It was at one time a simply rendered likeness, but also on some unconscious level, enormously complex, each brushstroke implying far more than it illustrated. The dragon was unmistakably oriental, a full frontal view with the enormous head positioned alertly over recumbent haunches, spiked tail raised suggestively above as if it were some retriever who had just caught sight of live prey. It was also unmistakably male, which probably explained Jeri's clear embarrassment, the fully erect penis clearly visible beneath its glistening body. The eyes were large and, unlike the remainder of the painting, completed in very elaborate detail, almost human in shape and expression with distinct eyelashes drawn individually, the pupil dark black but with a hint of highlights, the rest of the eye chalk white, but faceted like an insect's. They stared directly across the room into the depths of the mirror and, oddly enough, even when I stood squarely in front of the painting, I had the impression it was looking right through me, or around me, unconcerned with anything except contemplation of its own image. Or rather its reflection. Or rather its lack of one.

In the mirror, the opposite wall was completely blank.

I'm uncertain whether or not you will believe me, but I really didn't notice that anomaly until the mysterious sound first drew me into a detailed examination of the mirror, and by then I'd been in the apartment for almost three months. For most people, the mirror is an opportunity for self examination; it's almost the only circumstance in which we see ourselves in the context of our world. In the depths of our mirrors we chase youth, beauty, success, and happiness, while telling ourselves we're examining a blemish, strayed hair, crooked tie, or unwelcome zit. I've never had any illusions on that account; my parents alerted me to my ugliness at an early age, and drove the lesson home at every opportunity thereafter. One night, when I was ten years old, I wakened to hear my parents arguing, and I understood just enough to realize my father's accusation that the dogs were a substitute for an ugly son she could not bring herself to love. I sometimes think my mother's chief concern about my moving out on my own was that I might forget that lesson and blunder into the fantasy that I could fit in with normal people. In a sense, her fears in that regard were ultimately realized, although that wasn't until I had met Chen Li, and we haven't come to that part yet.

Or maybe we have.

I knew there were other tenants in the building of course. Jeri Kaplan had warned me that most of them spoke little or no English, that they were a heterogeneous mix of Orientals and newly arrived Europeans, lured for the most part by the domestically undesirable production line jobs being offered by Eblis Manufacturing, my current employer and virtually the only non-retail business in town. Shang Yang, the man who had died in what was now to be my apartment, had reportedly come from China ten years earlier and was the building's oldest resident, but he had rarely stirred from his room and no one knew how he supported himself. His tenancy dated from two sets of owners back, and Jeri had only worked for the realtor involved for the past two years; she did know that he had accepted a small rent increase without comment the previous year, and had turned down the offer of a better room when they had last had a vacancy.

"There's another Chinese family in the building," she told me. "Much more scrutable than Shang Yang. Apparently they're from a far different part of China, and they knew very little about him, had never spoken to him other than an occasional quick greeting in the hallway. Yang was pretty much a hermit. Chen Li, she's the niece, told me her uncle had sent her to invite Yang to supper shortly after they moved in, and he wouldn't even open the door to talk to her, just told her politely but firmly to go away. She's a nice girl, quiet, caught halfway between the culture of her ancestors and an understandable desire to fit in here. Anyway, after the accident, I went to see about boxing up his personal belongings, but they were all in such a deteriorated condition, I finally just threw most of it out." She gave me a quick, apologetic look. "There wasn't any furniture to speak of. Just a few odds and ends, woven mats, some pottery, things like that. He had a little, pedal powered lathe and used it to make all sorts of little knickknacks. I don't know why; maybe he sold them somewhere and that's how he made his money. They looked pretty ugly to me; all out of round, no symmetry at all. I put most of them up in the loft in case we ever run across any family or anything, but I can't imagine them having any value. Can't imagine how he worked the clay with those long nails and all."

"What happened to him exactly? You said that he had some kind of accident."

She looked uncomfortable. "Drowned in the bathtub." For a moment, I thought that was all she would say, but her eyes became distant for a second and I waited, sensing she was seeking to match words with thought. "The police said he must have passed out during some kind of epileptic fit while drawing the water. He was on his knees, outside the tub you know, and sort of fell forward, over the edge, so that his head was below the water level. I'm the one who found him; I went up to collect the rent and found his door unlocked, and there was this peculiar smell, you know?" She shook her head. "Sorry, I don't mean to bum you out."

"No, that's all right," I protested. "I'm not superstitious or anything. It's kind of romantic, living in an apartment where someone died mysteriously. Maybe I'll get to see a ghost; that'd be a treat."

She grimaced. "Not this one, you wouldn't. Even when he was alive, he was pretty bizarre, had these tattoos on his face and his nails were real long, not like a woman's, more like Nosferatu in that old movie." I looked puzzled and she measured a distance several inches past the tips of her fingers. "That was the other funny thing about his death, you know, the reason the police wouldn't let us show the room for so long. All of Yang's nails were broken off and floating in the bath water when I found him, as though something had pulled them off or he'd been hammering at something with his hands. There was dried blood on the ends of his fingers." She gave a little shiver which was not, I suspected, entirely feigned. "He always kept his nails painted blood red; definitely not playing with a complete deck of cards. But he kept to himself, paid his rent like I said, and none of the other tenants had any complaints about him. The police don't like loose ends, but they couldn't even find any indication of robbery. They asked the other tenants a lot of questions, but they finally had to give up."

We had been walking through the small rooms as she spoke. The bathroom was clean but old fashioned, claw foot tub of white porcelain, an incongruous site for mysterious death, cracked tile walls, paint peeling ever so slightly on the ceiling, pedestal style sink with a medicine cabinet. No mirror, just a plain, painted surface.

"That's funny," Jeri remarked. "There must have been a mirror there at some point." She frowned. "I don't know if there's anything upstairs you can jury rig."

"I can manage."

She crossed to the sink, twisted a faucet. Within seconds, tendrils of steam rose. "Plenty of hot water even up here. The one thing new in this entire building is the heating system, piping's only about ten years old, new boiler and burner put in last year. Pressure's good too; you won't have to worry about running out of the hot stuff for your bath or when you shave."

She pointed to a small linen closet just beyond the toilet. "You'll have to provide your own sheets and towels and stuff, but there's a stock of light bulbs and some toilet paper there to get you started." She gestured toward the fluorescent above the sink. "If that goes out, give me a call, but it should be okay. I replaced it when I moved Yang's stuff out. The bulb that was in there was all smashed, and judging by the amount of dust in there, it hadn't been working in years. As a matter of fact, all of the lights in here were burnt out or broken. It was almost as if Yang kept this room perpetually dark. There's no outside window and there couldn't have been much illumination from the rest of the place."

"I guess he just didn't mind washing in the darkness."

The day I moved in, I caught my first glance of Chen Li, although I didn't know her name at the time. I was carrying the second tomato crate of shirts up to my room when I saw her briefly at the far end of the second story landing. I might almost have believed her a ghost, she was so slight of stature, and the white kimono and long black hair gave her an aura of unreality, like an image from an old black and white movie. She disappeared quickly through a door before my eyes had focused, so quietly that I wasn't certain I really had seen her.

It was Odrodek who told me her name finally. Odrodek was a Czechoslovakian national who had fled to America in the 1980s to escape the Communists, claimed to be a Serbian prince who had been living in exile, a descendant of Vlad the Impaler, as well as a Macedonian separatist if he was in a romantic mood. Reality and truth were fluid commodities in Odrodek's universe, but his guileless transparency included you in his conspiracy of fictions. Despite his strangely articulated English, which I suspected was at least half an affectation, he was clearly well educated, though whether formally or through his own reading I never did learn. Certainly he almost always carried a library book or a bedraggled paperback whenever I encountered him, invariably dressed in a shapeless beret and worn trench coat. He lived somewhere on the ground floor, or at least so he led me to believe; he seemed to wander the building at random and I never did learn exactly which apartment was his. Perhaps he didn't really live there at all, or any particular place for that matter. Odrodek was more an environmental variable than a human being in some ways. He seemed distant, unreal, bigger and smaller than life.

I had already spoken to Odrodek briefly on a few occasions the day I actually met Chen Li. Invariably gregarious, he introduced himself (as a descendant of Tsar Nicholas fallen on bad times) while I was carrying in paper bags of those personal possessions I had chosen to take with me on the move from Cumberland to Managansett. Magically, he followed me up and down the stairs four times without offering to carry a thing, and managed to bring this off without seeming in the slightest offensive or ill mannered. Odrodek did not carry things; it just didn't seem a part of his nature. Royalty employed others for such mundane tasks. In the days that followed, he always seemed to be somewhere about, sitting on the front steps staring off into memories of his heritage...or heritages. He was a cashiered Bulgarian Secret Service operative the day I found him dozing in one of the chairs in the lobby, a gypsy brigand too well known to remain anywhere in Europe one morning when I heard him pacing in the corridor outside my room. Odrodek was one of those rarities, an adult whose eyes never strayed to my birthmark, who treated me as an equal from the outset, without condescension, without pretense. I don't think he ever told me a true word about himself, but he was almost immediately my closest friend.

There wasn't much competition for the job.

He and I were both descending the stairway to the ground floor one Saturday morning when the outside door opened and she came in, a small bag of groceries held close to her body. She was wearing western dress that day, after a fashion, a white silk blouse and black silk trousers. When she saw us standing above her, she dropped her head immediately and almost ran up the steps to my left. Once again I missed seeing her face in any detail, but the angle was such that I was granted a brief but stimulating glance inside her blouse. I turned away immediately, convinced she would feel the impact of my eyes on her flesh.

"Nice girl, Chen Li. You like her?" Odrodek ostentatiously let his eyes trail partway down my body. "Looks like to me." He laughed with a thin shrillness that reminded me of a dentist's drill.

I spoke quickly to cover my embarrassment. "I haven't met her, as a matter of fact. I think I've seen her once or twice before."

"Room six, your floor, Alan. Meet her uncle, old Tao Tieh. He's introduce you, you see. Pretty girl, no?"

Actually no, not particularly. Chen Li's face was thin and pale, her nose a trifle too large, but the individual features were softened into a not unpleasing whole. And who was I to criticize the appearance of others? "Yeah, I guess so."

"She like you too. Odrodek can tell. Gypsies can see these things with the inner eye."

"Odrodek, we haven't even met each other. I don't know whether I'd like her or not. And I thought you were a Russian nobleman?"

Ignoring my last remark, he tapped one finger against the side of his head. "Maybe you don't know it here, but here is different matter." And he touched his chest, just above the heart. Then, with a short laugh and an exaggerated leer, he added, "And one other place as well, my friend."

I didn't need a mirror to know color had rushed into my face.

Most people spend their lives relatively friendless, or so I have read, even though they conceal that fact with numerous levels of acquaintances. I've never had even that much consolation. My mother never allowed me to play with the other children in the area, because I was "too frail for their games" and "they'd just make fun of your looks and you'll come home all upset again". I had no siblings, my father periodically took off with one or another of his transient girlfriends, sometimes staying away for months on end, and even when he was home, his eyes were always somehow distant, his attention elsewhere. He and my mother had some sort of arrangement; I never really understood it, but she seemed not to take any offense at his derelictions. I think he sincerely felt affection for me but his estrangement from my mother placed constraints on all our inter-relationships.

Perhaps guilt was a wall between us. But whose?

Deprived of family and peers alike, I grew up taciturn, studious, introspective, and filled brimful with unexpressed thoughts, questions, concepts, ideas, speculations, observations, arguments, and opinions.

Which might help to explain why I began talking to the dragon.

When I was a child, just about the time I started school, I had a collection of stuffed animals. Each one had a name and a distinct personality, and I spent endless hours explaining things to them, telling them my dreams, eliciting from them their own, and at the time I was often able to convince myself that they were in fact real personalities.

When I came home from my first day at school, all of my friends had vanished, never to be seen again. "You're old enough to be going to school now, Alan, so you're old enough to keep your own company." My mother frequently spoke like that; I think she made notes when she was reading, saving phrases to use when the opportunity arose. But for whatever reason, she had disposed of my friends and I was forbidden to replace them. The ambivalent pleasure I had felt while being exposed to an entire room filled with disparate personalities that day was now fractured, inextricably wedded to my bereavement, not without a touch of outrage. Bradbury's "The Small Assassin" might have been inspired by a similar memory, so intense that it was still capable of raising my pulse fourteen years later. It was not so much an infringement on my property as an attack on myself; I was defined by my friends, real or unreal, at least in my own still pliant mind.

It was the first time I actually hated my mother.

But now that I was on my own, I was in command. I made the rules. I had even browsed in a toy store near the apartment from time to time, contemplating spending part of the barely adequate wages I received working as a floor boy (excuse me, as a material handler) at Eblis to purchase a stuffed bear, or an image of a familiar cartoon character. Most of my spare money went for pens and notebooks, in which I painstakingly scribbled the stories I felt compelled to write, and there never seemed to be quite enough left over to indulge myself.

But the dragon was even better, I discovered. I couldn't afford a television, of course, and without friends or any other social life, I ended up spending most evenings in my room, lying in bed, frequently writing, enjoying the possibilities of my freedom while simultaneously chafing at my inability to take advantage of this new state of existence.

So I talked things over with my new friend, the dragon. Funny, but I never did give him a name; he was always just "the dragon". It was if he were somehow above such things as having an individual identity, more as if he were a primal force, a symbol for an entire range of concepts which I could not put into words. He was the embodiment of everything for which I yearned, power, beauty, wisdom, and by addressing him, I felt I was confronting my own problems.

Gradually, despite the fact that those preternatural eyes embraced the mirror to the exclusion of everything else in the world, I came to believe that he reciprocated the feeling in some fashion, that he was conscious of my existence and found me tolerable, if not admirable. I could be content with that; my expectations were never great.

One evening, shortly after I had arrived home from work, someone knocked on my door. I experienced a moment of pure panic; this was the first time in my entire life that someone had come to call upon me, a visitor to my room. The place wasn't really a mess; I didn't yet own enough stuff to create more than a minor disorder; the only furniture in the front room consisted of two decaying chairs I had recently salvaged from the loft and a small makeshift table that consisted of two egg crates covered with an extra blanket I had sneaked out of the house when my mother wasn't looking. (Needless to say, she looked upon the entire move as a "foolish adventure into unhappiness and a needless expense", although she approved my having found employment, however humble.)

I opened the door to one of the most incongruous sights in my experience, and I am appalled to admit that I probably gaped with every bit as much consternation and even revulsion as I imagine many people feel the first time they are introduced to me. To this day, I feel shame for that moment.

Tao Tieh, uncle to Chen Li, was one of the most grossly fat men I had ever seen. He reminded me of a sumo wrestler, with multiple chins, a midsection so bulky he could not possibly have seen his feet in years, an overall soft pudginess that looked distinctly unhealthy, particularly when coupled with his pale complexion and short stature. Even after I grew to know him better, I had difficulty convincing myself that he bore many of the same genes as Chen Li, whose fragile frame and slender limbs seemed an absolute antithesis. This behemoth of a man wore a western style suit and tie, obviously specifically tailored to his proportions, white shirt with cufflinks and a tie tack, the tie twisted into a meticulously symmetrical Windsor knot.

He bowed just slightly as I opened the door, then offered his hand. "I am Tao Tieh, your neighbor from room six."

I took his hand mechanically, still seeking orientation. His English was almost without accent.

"As we are neighbors, I thought it prudent that I present myself and my family. If it is convenient, we would be pleased to have you join us for dinner tomorrow evening at six o'clock, so that I may introduce you properly to my niece."

Under ordinary circumstances, I would probably have risked offending Tao Tieh by rushing into some elaborate excuse to avoid appearing in public. Even after finally making the break with my mother, I knew the fetters with which she had bound me would not be cast off so easily. But even as a flurry of excuses clamored for expression, my mind skipped back through time to that brief flash of flesh I had seen on the staircase, and I was stuttering my acceptance before I quite realized what I was about.

That must have been on a Wednesday, because it was the night after I formally met Chen Li that I heard the sound from the mirror.

I have wondered since then whether it was an accident, or a deliberate act to attract my attention. I may never know the answer, although I suspect the latter. I had almost ceased to recognize the mirror's existence by now, my eyes automatically avoiding even the most fleeting glimpse of my own image as I passed back and forth in front of it. But somehow my mind had linked the clandestine sound with the mirror, and within seconds I was standing directly in front of it, staring into its depths.

I noticed two disparities that evening, one subtle, one not. The subtle difference between the reflected image and the reality outside it almost escaped my attention. When I had laboriously carried the box spring down from the attic to this room, I had been uncertain whether it would in fact fit along the wall that ended with the doorway to the front room. It had been a great relief to discover that it did, with exactly one board width of the hardwood floor to spare.

In the mirror, there were exactly two board widths between the foot of my bed and the doorjamb.

I realize that's a pretty outlandish statement, and that most of you who have followed my account thus far are probably pausing now, wondering if there is any point in reading further this account of someone either insane or a charlatan. The situation only becomes less credible however. Not only did I observe and accept this violation of the physical laws of our universe, I didn't tell anyone else about it.

Is that so hard to believe, after all? For almost two decades, the most intimate secrets of my life were subject to review by my mother. Did I mention that she routinely searched my room, seeking such contraband she had forbidden me as science fiction magazines, "trashy books", records or tapes by rock groups of whom she disapproved – which was pretty much all of them. My secret library was concealed in a remote part of Sheffield Park, carefully wrapped in layers of plastic wrap, buried in a hole I had painstakingly lined with clandestinely collected boards, shingles, and other materials in a mostly futile attempt to keep the moisture out. I kept two diaries as well, one brief and bland, "concealed" under my mattress so that mother could fancy she had plumbed my inmost secrets. The real one, filled with character sketches, juvenile musings and observations, painstakingly copied quotations I felt spoke specifically to my situation, I risked keeping closer to hand, usually in the back of the hall closet where she "knew" I never kept any of my things.

Is it any surprise then that, having discovered a miracle of sorts, I was reluctant to share its existence?

And then there was the second anomaly, one which I found simultaneously exciting and disturbing, exhilarating and frightening. It was a mystery and a revelation at the same time, affirmation of the endless variations of reality and proof that not all explanations were to be found in logic and reason.

In the mirror, the far wall of my bedroom was blank. The dragon did not exist in the mirror world, not one scale, not one eyelash, not one stroke of the painter's brush. His absence was so palpable, I looked back over my shoulder, convinced Jeri Kaplan or the mysterious owners who employed her had sent someone into the apartment in my absence to vanquish the offendingly sexual creature from the wall. But in the real world, or in my real world anyway, he was as intent and alert and as present as ever.

At first, I was afraid to experiment. The distortions apparent in the mirror were clearly more than a trick of the lighting, or the cut of the glass, or the placement of the pane of the mirror in relationship to other objects in the room. During the first few minutes, my uncritical mind entertained these possibilities, of course, but they were quickly dismissed. No matter how carefully you arrange things, you cannot superimpose a blank wall where a painted one exists. I experimented by interposing my hand, noting where the shadow fell, saw an exact mimicry in the mirror world.

But the dragon just wasn't there.

My next thought was to move the bed, so that I could more closely examine the disparity in the number of exposed floorboards. Initially I resisted this temptation as well, terrified lest by applying logic and organized investigation to what might well be some metaphysical phenomenon, I might disperse whatever occidental or oriental magic held sway in this tiny corner of the cosmos. But the desire to know more overcame my reluctance at last.

I moved the bed, lifted it by the foot and leaned the mattress and box spring up against the outside wall of the room, exposing the floorboards completely. Down on my hands and knees, I counted the floorboards from far wall to door frame, across the frame, then to the wall where the mirror rested. I did this twice, to make absolutely certain I was correct. Then I rose and peered into the mirror, craning my head this way and that, trying to do the same. Unfortunately, short of removing the mirror from its mounting, I could not physically count the nearer boards. Frustrated, I tried to remove the mirror, but it was so rigidly fastened to the wall, I could barely make the frame tremor despite my exertions, and I finally desisted, afraid that I might cause some damage by tearing it loose unexpectedly.

I wanted to talk to someone about it. I also wanted to keep it as my very own secret. Who was there to tell, after all? Odrodek? He would nod sagely and tell me about a similar mirror in his royal father's moldering castle in Budapest. My mother? She would dismiss it as an early symptom of mental disorder caused by disregarding her advice and setting out to make a life of my own.

So I talked to the dragon as I replaced my bed in its former position. The discrepancy in the flooring was still there. Was it real magic, I inquired, or some new law of optics previously unheard of? And what, if anything, was I to do about it? I spent over an hour examining the far reaches of my quarters, both in their natural state and by reflection, placing a row of coins on the floor and counting them, examining whorls and pits and scrapes on the painted walls, comparing them to their reflected relatives. In all other respects, the mirror appeared to be performing normally. "I've got such a lousy apartment even the mirror doesn't work," I joked.

I had forgotten the sound, didn't remember it until later when, finally having lost interest, I wandered out into the front room to read. It was louder this time, a soft scraping sound, as though something heavy were being moved. I recognized it immediately as an amplification of that earlier interruption, but I realized something else as well. It was meant to be clandestine, but obviously clandestine; this entire phenomenon was dressed in contradictions.

I stepped back into my bedroom, my eyes moving first to the dragon. He had not moved, of course, but my imagination told me his expressi
on had changed, that those all too human appearing eyes might be fixed immutably on the mirror, but that he saw what was happening elsewhere as well. The expression and the posture spoke of strength, confidence, and safety, but there was warning there as well. I had never before noticed how tautly coiled the tail had been drawn, how the short but powerful legs were flexed as though in preparation for a spring.

There was neither movement in nor sound from the mirror (and I was still convinced beyond all possibility of doubt that the mirror was in fact the source), but I approached cautiously, uncertain whether or not I was in danger, mystified as to what possible danger could exist. Shang Yang had died in this apartment, I reminded myself. But not in this room, another voice whispered.

I looked into the mirror and saw my room. Except for the usual mirror imaging, it was an exact duplicate. Or almost exact. There was still no hint of the dragon's existence.

On the other hand, the disparity in the placement of my bed no longer existed. The reflected bed had been moved.

I was very nervous when I knocked tentatively at the door of room six for the first time. It was opened so quickly that I wondered if Tao Tieh had been standing on the other side, just waiting for me to arrive. He nodded and silently gestured for me to enter, his expression neutral. I stepped through the door, then had to move around an elaborately decorated screen which had been set just inside. I was later to learn that this was a K'uei screen, designed to prevent the entry of the spirits of the dead. Chinese tradition says that the souls of those who die accidentally must linger on earth until they can induce another to find the same fate and replace them. Tao Tieh may have embraced western modes of dress and speech, but he had retained his Chinese heritage and, as I learned later, meticulously adhered to certain traditions. Their rooms, for example, were explicitly Chinese, lacking western furniture other than a small end table with a portable television set. Everything else consisted of pillowed seats, thick mats, wicker tables, and intricately woven and illustrated screens.

"Welcome to our home, Mr. Sheridan." I never did find out how he learned my name; perhaps he asked Jeri Kaplan, or perhaps he saw an address on the junk mail that was already appearing regularly in my mailbox in the lobby. "This is my niece, Chen Li, whom you may have seen about the building. It is the custom in our homeland that unmarried females never speak to strangers until they have been properly introduced by a male relative. Since we are to be neighbors, it seemed appropriate to satisfy custom before you thought us rude."

The words reached my ears in an abstract, distant fashion. I nodded and possibly even made some inane reply, but all of my attention was on Chen Li, once more dressed demurely in a pale kimono, egg blue on this occasion, her hair swept back and tied into a double ponytail. She had emerged from behind a bamboo screen, eyes downcast, sketched a small bow as she approached, then raised her head almost defiantly.

Chen Li was ugly. Chen Li was beautiful.

I realize that my story has been full of anomalies and contradictions and that each one, building upon the edifice of those that preceded it, can only lessen my credibility. So be it. I am committed to the truth, not to plausibility.

Each individual element in Chen Li's face was unassuming, possibly even unattractive. Her features were delicate, eyes small and dark, nose narrow, aquiline, lips thin, mouth a shade too narrow but not terribly so. But the planes of her cheeks were slightly wrong, and the separate parts of her face had all rushed toward the center, skewed away from their normal positions. The gestalt was, by contemporary American standards, unfortunate, perhaps even tragic.

As an added insult, Chen Li had a beautiful, unspoiled complexion, a bit pale perhaps, but not unwholesomely so, and her figure was slender, but with good lines, definitely sexy. Her posture implied respect and vulnerability at the same time that it was self-confident and alluring. I had never before felt so sexually attracted, not even in the privacy of my room at night, thumbing through my meager collection of men's magazines. I turned back to her uncle in embarrassment.

"I'm pleased to meet you both. I didn't know what was appropriate so I brought this. I hope it's all right." I offered him the inexpensive (we never say "cheap") bottle of saki I had picked up earlier that day, the first time I had dared use my altered driver's license in a package store. He accepted it with a grave nod.

"Intentions in these matters are more important than accomplishments. A gift to the host is never required but always honored. Please, be seated."

Much to my surprise, Tao Tieh soon put me at my ease, inquiring about my family and my job, my plans for the future. Naturally reticent, I discovered a flood of words had been set loose, perhaps a reaction to the loneliness I continued to feel even now, having escaped my mother's clutches. Even after several weeks at Eblis, I had made no real friends. Those with whom I worked were separated from me either by age or position or disposition; the few in my age group seemed interminably interested in sports, automobiles, and sex, none of them topics with which I had had much experience. Most lunchtimes and coffee breaks I spent sitting alone, usually reading a paperback, while the rest went out for a smoke, or played cards at the back of the cafeteria. But Tao Tieh listened intently and with evident interest to every word I said, even when I caught myself babbling on about my literary ambitions. When I realized how breathlessly I had been running on, I stopped in some confusion, stumbling over my own words. Tao Tieh nodded and put me immediately at ease.

"The desire to create is a wellspring that frequently overflows our lips." He chuckled. "Confucius didn't say that; I just made it up. Don't be embarrassed about your enthusiasms; they are an expression of your inner qualities."

I tried several times to include Chen Li in the conversation, but she always deferred to her uncle, or replied in monosyllables.

When he excused himself at one point, climbing laboriously to his feet, I tried to draw her out, but she kept me politely but firmly at bay. "In China, a woman does not intrude upon the conversation of the men of the house."

"But we're not in China; those rules don't apply here, Chen Li."

For a second, I thought I saw humor flash in her eyes, but it was gone in an instant. "You would have to ask my uncle about that, Mr. Sheridan. He has been known to suspend the rules in his house," she smiled briefly, "but only with those who have shown themselves worthy of such an accommodation."

The meal was wonderful, the best I had eaten since leaving home; for all her faults, mother was a skillful and inventive cook. Chen Li did most of the preparation, some in the kitchen, some right at the table, although I noticed that her uncle watched her intently and occasionally said something in Chinese. It was stir fried chicken and vegetables, only some of which I recognized, cooked in a mildly spicy oil that had no aftertaste at all, sprinkled lavishly with slivered almonds. We drank the saki and then, when it was gone, another similar rice wine that came in an unmarked bottle. I wasn't used to that much alcohol, and by the time I excused myself to return to my room, my head was spinning and I was uncertain exactly what I was saying or hearing.

But of one thing I was absolutely certain.

Tao Tieh had eaten more than Chen Li and myself combined, and the food was so good I had gorged myself with considerable enthusiasm. He had consumed a proportionate amount of wine as well, and by the time I was making my departure, he was at least as far gone as was I. Or at least, so he led me to believe; in retrospect, I think his sleepy withdrawal from the conversation was feigned. Under the circumstances, it was understandable that he might choose to ignore the byplay between Chen Li and myself. If he really did miss it. I'd like to think that he recognized in me a person who would treat his niece with respect and honor. I remember reading that Chinese traditionally have a less than admirable view of the value of female children, but if that's a fair characterization, then Tao Tieh was atypical, or perhaps he had spent enough time among westerners to modify his outlook. Whatever the reason, he excused himself shortly after the meal had ended, but quite clearly indicated that I should stay as long as I desired.

Chen Li had done most of the cooking, all of the serving, all of the cleaning up despite my admittedly diffident offer to help. Once her uncle had retired, her manner eased slightly. I found it difficult to keep the conversation moving, but whenever I was clearly at a loss, she would volunteer an opinion or a comment that would provide just enough of a handle that I could respond. We talked about modern music, about which she knew far more than I, a few books we had both read, movies, television -- though briefly; I hadn't watched anything in more than a month now, and had been an infrequent viewer even while living at home. Chen Li had graduated from the local high school the year before and was currently working as a part time sales girl at a local clothing store.

Throughout our conversation, I became steadily more interested in her, and on various levels. Although she did nothing overtly, Chen Li was far less shy than I had imagined. While clearing the table, she had provided me a fleeting glimpse of a softer landscape within the silk of her blouse. More than once, I rearranged myself on the pillows to obscure my growing sexual interest. Once, I think I caught her laughing silently at my uneasiness, but there was nothing malicious in her humor.

I had great difficulty sleeping that night, instead lying awake imagining various scenarios in which I protected her from villains, rescued her from the ravages of hurricanes and earthquakes, and finally, as my thoughts grew used to the idea, as I undressed and bedded her. But when sleep finally claimed me, my dreams were filled with unseen creatures lurking - impossibly - under my bed. I remember one image with great clarity; I was falling into the surface of a gigantic mirror and turned my face back to the real world, hopeful of rescue. Tao Tieh and Chen Li hovered above, oversized images shutting off the sky. She was naked, at least as much body as I could see, her breasts appearing unnaturally large. My eyes were riveted to them even as I fell down, down into the unknowable depths of the mirror.

"Don't be embarrassed by your enthusiasms," leered Tao Tieh, and that's all I remember.

Any romantic aspirations which I might have developed that evening were tempered in the days that immediately followed. Not that Chen Li was unfriendly; indeed, in contrast to her former reticence, she greeted me frequently when we encountered each other in the hall, or occasionally outside the building. In each of these meetings, I tried to remain alert to every nuance, convinced that she was sending me sexual messages which I only had to interpret correctly to achieve my ultimate goal, intimacy on some level that to this point I could only imagine. Chen Li remained polite, friendly, even mildly flirtatious at times, but there was always a clear line of demarcation beyond which I was not permitted to go.

I grew increasingly frustrated, angry at myself for not knowing how to proceed, angry at Chen Li for failing to show me the way. My elation over the discovery of the anomalies in my mirror suddenly lost value, particularly now that one had already ceased. I even entertained the possibility that I had imagined the entire incident, although if that were true, my continued inability to see any reflection of the dragon in the mirror could only be construed as evidence of my own mental instability. It occurred to me to find another pair of eyes to confirm, or deny, the reality of my experience, but the old reluctance to share what was uniquely mine with anyone else reasserted itself. Besides, with the opening pangs of what I fancied was my first true love, all other considerations became secondary. Not that Chen Li was providing any encouragement. Alternately I avoided leaving my room for long periods to show her how hurt I was, or spent long hours sitting on the stairs, waiting for a chance to see her, or speak to her. If she took any notice of my wild mood swings, she gave no indication, greeting me with cool, polite, friendly detachment whenever we met. This continued for several weeks before I finally grew frustrated enough to act.

I knew that Chen Li went to the Chinese grocery store down the street every Wednesday evening. We hadn't spoken for three full days and I had finally mustered the resolve to dispense with polite posturings and approach her directly. It was a hot August night, and humidity had turned the wooden banisters lining the stairways clammy, the air indoors stale and rank. I couldn't afford an air conditioner, of course, and the rooms were so poorly ventilated that I spent much of my free time reading in the lobby (secretly hoping she would pass my way).

I waited outside for her that evening.

She was wearing her invariable silk, this time a patterned yellow blouse and dark green slacks. Descending to the street, she appeared unaffected by the intense heat, although when I moved to intercept her, I detected the glimmer of perspiration on her upper lip. The silk seemed to cling to her body with an intimacy of which I was instantly jealous.

"Chen Li, may I talk to you?"

She met my eyes squarely to prove she could, then dropped them demurely. "I am on an errand for my uncle, Alan Sheridan, but I'm sure he would not take offense if I allowed you a moment or two."

Irritation and sexual frustration overcame my normal reticence. "Look, Chen Li, I'm not very good at this, but I thought you and I could be, well, friends."

She nodded. "I have much admiration and respect for you, Alan Sheridan, and would be honored to be considered your friend."

I was beginning to feel foolish, but was unwilling to be put off again. "That's not what I mean..." I started, realizing I didn't know exactly how to say what I did mean. "It's just that, you know, the night we met, I thought there might be something special between us..." I trailed off, realizing I was drifting into an embarrassing cliché.

Chen Li's head was up now, her expression unreadable (inscrutable, I suppose). "What are you trying to say, Alan Sheridan?" I opened my mouth once, twice, then threw up my hands theatrically, completely at a loss for words. I had the distinct impression that she was laughing at me, but her expression was so guilelessly serious, I could not take offense.

"I don't know, exactly. Forget it. Forget I said anything at all." But before I could turn away, rushing towards the sanctuary of my stiflingly hot room, she reached up and grabbed my arm with one hand. She was surprisingly strong, and her grip was not gentle.

"Did you think I might sleep with you, Alan Sheridan? Are those the words that will not come? Are you frustrated because the poor little Chinese whore wants coaxing before she jumps into your bed?"

The words were meant to sting and they did; they were meant to shock, and they did that too. I was stung by their unfairness, and humbled by their accuracy. There was truth in her accusation and no truth at all, and if this is a contradiction, then Whitman was right and we all encompass contradictions we cannot reconcile. I wanted her to be innocent and untouched and pliable at the same time I wanted her to be sensuous and available and without inhibition.

I hesitated, caught among emotions that included panic, the desire to escape, rage, the need to hit back, fear, affection, pain, hope and hopelessness, an entire gamut of conflicting feelings and fearings. Caught in an irresolvable situation, I retreated into the ultimate refuge of my childhood.

I broke down into tears.

To this day, I don't recall exactly how Chen Li got me away from there. I have this fragmented memory of sobbing on her shoulder, trying to explain to her how I had never had a friend of any sort, let alone a girlfriend, that I had no idea how to act in her presence, what might please her, what might offend. I think I raged about my mother for a while, but that might be a phantom memory from one of the many dreams I have had in which I finally revolt against her patronizing, domineering insistence that I will be forever unable to deal with the world on its own terms, that I will always need her to intervene for me, to protect me from the sharp edges of life.

But I do remember what happened as we sat in the darkness in the small, litter strewn park at the end of the street, on a metal bench set back under a gigantic copper beech. I remember her arm around my shoulders and then mine around hers, and her hand on mine, guiding it beneath the satiny smoothness of her blouse to close around the equally satiny smoothness of one small, almost boyish breast. And the kiss that seemed to go on and on because I was afraid that if contact was once broken it might never be renewed.

We didn't sleep together that night. I don't think either of us was ready for it. But I think I already knew it was inevitable when we finally separated, she to complete her errand, me to the conundrum in which I lived.

I haven't mentioned my experience in the bathroom yet, have I? The room where Shang Yang met his end, bent over the rim of the claw footed tub, his head completely immersed, his painted fingernails adrift in the scum of bath water. As you might expect, it was tiny, little more than a cubicle, containing tub, sink, toilet, closet, and room for one person to stand. The mirror over the sink was still missing; I used a small hand mirror I had picked up at the local hardware store, propping it up behind the faucets. The bathing facilities were primitive but serviceable; nevertheless, I missed the convenience of a shower and had already considered reworking my budget to include one of those hand held shower heads that you can clamp onto a faucet. The toilet refused to flush from time to time, but I had already managed to figure out how to jiggle the float in back and correct the situation. I was learning to cope.

The second night after I moved in, I attempted to take a bath. I mentioned earlier that I am not superstitious, and that's the truth. My mother did instill in me a profound respect for the rational. She called herself an agnostic, insisted that everything believable was provable, and raised me to be skeptical but open minded. It was one of the few valuable gifts she provided. I had no fear of ghosts, felt no need of a K'uei screen to keep the spirit of Shang Yang from urging me to follow his example, and I was really looking forward to a warm, relaxing bath.

But I just couldn't get into the tub.

I later decided it was an optical illusion, created by the sharply delineated lines of the room, the distortions of the stained fluorescent fixture over the sink, and the suggestive patterns of discoloration in the enamel of the tub itself. Whatever combination was responsible, I discovered that the shadows and reflections in the drawn water were disturbing, almost frightening, and I stood there naked looking down into the motionless water, seeing motion, catching glimpses of my own homely features twisted into even more gruesome form, and I could not summon the strength to set foot into that chaos.

The sensation eventually passed, or I managed to suppress it, although I never spent any unnecessary time in the bath, or in that room at all for that matter. It was as if in what should have been the most private room at all, I was most exposed. If Shang Yang's ghost, complete with clanking chains and grisly wounds, had appeared in person, I would not have been surprised.

But nothing happened at all. In the bathroom, anyway.

I would like to possess the kind of imagination that allows belief in ghosts; it would have been a real hoot to be able to tell myself that I lived in a haunted room. But it wasn't the spirit of Shang Yang I feared at all; I never for one second believed his spirit lingered after his body had passed away. But there was some other presence in those rooms. It was unobtrusive, but I found myself constantly waking in the early hours of morning, or looking up from the book I was reading, or hesitating while I cooked the simple meals I felt confident preparing, convinced that I was not alone, that I was not the only consciousness present.

Two weeks after our tearful, fledgling intimacy, Chen Li and I had sex together for the first time. We did so in the darkness of Sheffield Park, far back under the untended bushes, lying stretched full length on a blanket she had foresightedly brought along. She undressed me first, then herself, insisting that it was her place to do so, then stretched out beside me, wrapped her long legs around my own, and the feel of her flesh against mine was orders of magnitude beyond anything I had imagined while staring at touched up photographs of overly endowed women in my private moments.

We met again two nights later, and irregularly after that, sometimes every second night, sometimes after longer intervals. I never knew what excuses she made to Tao Tieh for her frequent absences, never really cared, to be completely honest. I suspect to this day that he knew, or at least suspected, what was going on. Honor, as I understood it, required him to act only if he could not avoid indicating knowledge of the situation; as long as he could pretend ignorance, face was saved. I believe that Tao Tieh realized the happiness that Chen Li and I had found together, and would not willingly move against it. Perhaps, recognizing his own advancing years and their lack of any other family or means, he felt it more important that she forge some new bond of emotional support than that the old forms be preserved to their very letter.

When we weren't making love, Chen Li was telling me much of her culture and tradition. It was on one of these nights that I heard the story of the Yellow Emperor and his war against the specular world, and I thought immediately of the ornate mirror in my bedroom. I heard also of the four dragons who were set to guard the Earth, one in each hemisphere, north and south, east and west, and that also reminded me of the mirror. She told me stories of creatures good and evil, warriors heroic and dastardly, and introduced me to an entire tradition of which I had virtually no experience. She tried to explain yin and yang to me, and grew frustrated when I tried to compare the concepts to the Christian view of good and evil, or the duality of Ahriman and Ahura Mazda, insisting that I was missing the point entirely, that good and evil were qualities of measurement, not absolutes.

I kept trying to convince her to come to my room. Once the first flush of sexual fulfillment had faded, I grew increasingly afraid of being discovered, by the police, by vagrants, by prowlers, by my mother. I had no plan at that time to tell her of my discorporate roommate, of the difference between reality and reflection. To be entirely truthful, I had managed to all but forget much of the experience. My only thoughts in those days involved the proximity of flesh to flesh, the physical wonders Chen Li had already revealed to me and those we had yet to explore. As August slid into September, the nights grew cooler, and I tried to supplement my irrational fears with more cogent, practical arguments.

"A proper Chinese woman does not go unaccompanied to the room of an unmarried man," she insisted.

It did no good to point out that nothing could happen in my room that hadn't already happened a dozen or more times already. I had visions of being forced to make love in snowdrifts come the winter, but faced with her steadfast refusal to budge on this issue, I finally stopped urging her.

At which point, of course, she did an abrupt about face.

When she first suggested that we go to my room that terrible night in October, I was initially confused about her intentions. A really spectacular rainstorm was thundering on the roof and against the windows of the building, and when we met by prearrangement in the lobby, I had expected her to call off the evening's tryst. Instead, she seemed unusually bold, not even checking to be certain we were alone before embracing me. Standing there, staring down into her upturned face, feeling the press of firm female hips against my own, her fingers pressing into my buttocks, I was immediately convinced that tonight would be something special.

"Where can we go?" I asked hoarsely. "The rain..."

"Your room," she answered without hesitation.

"But proper Chinese women don't go to the rooms of unmarried men."

"Tonight, I will be an improper Chinese woman." And the smile she gave me then transformed her homely features into something beautiful beyond measure. Chen Li was homely. Chen Li was beautiful.

We separated and were starting up the stairs when Tao Tieh emerged onto the landing.

I was frozen with guilt, even though we were chastely untouching long before he could have seen us. Chen Li, on the other hand, seemed totally unbothered, turning to whisper "ten minutes" to me before greeting her uncle warmly and moving to his side. Tao gave me a friendly wave before turning to talk to his niece in Cantonese and I passed them on the way to my room with an assumed nonchalance that I felt certain was completely transparent. It was the first and only time I felt guilty about what Chen Li and I had been doing, and even then the guilt was for the deceit, not the act.

Inside my apartment, I rushed around cleaning up the debris of my lifestyle, fast food wrappers, old newspapers, a magazine I preferred Chen Li not see, and some dirty socks dropped thoughtlessly several days previously. Then into the bedroom where I made an effort to straighten my bed, thanking the heavens I'd washed the linen only the night before. Finally I confronted my friend.

I still talked to the nameless dragon on my wall, though not as frequently. He'd been my confidant while I was courting Chen Li's affections, and I had continued to recount the details of each assignation when I returned, soliciting his opinion on my technique, my interpretations of her moods, my hopes for the future. I wouldn't have wanted Chen Li to think I was the kind of guy who kissed and told, but surely she couldn't object to the dragon. He was certainly in no position to repeat the stories.

But I was faced now with a peculiar uneasiness. The thought of lying naked with Chen Li in front of my confidant was unsettling, somehow obscene. I grabbed an extra sheet and climbed atop the bureau, anchoring it to four runners on the picture rail so that it fell down across the wall, completely obscuring the painting. As I did so, for the very first time I thought the eyes were actually taking notice of my existence, and their look was reproachful. Dismissing this as fantasy, I told myself I was avoiding offense to Chen Li's sensibilities, since the dragon's sexual organs were so prominently displayed. But in truth, I think I was more ashamed at the possibility of participating in some tawdry public sexual liaison. Not that I thought that way about Chen Li, of course, but I was still sexually and emotionally immature enough to be confused about right and wrong, guilt and pleasure, and there wasn't enough time right now to work out the details in my mind.

I had just pushed the bureau into place, anchoring the bottom of the sheet, when Chen Li knocked.

"Come in, Chen Li." I held the door for her.

She glanced around the room, interested, but thankfully avoiding showing the distaste I had feared. "You don't have much furniture, do you, Alan Sheridan?"

In my own room, I felt more confidence than normal, even though I was more excited than at any time since our first evening together. "Why do you always call me that, Chen Li?"

"Call you what, Alan Sheridan?"

"What you just did. You used both names."

"Are they not both your names?"

"Yes," I admitted with some exasperation. "But Sheridan is my family name. You know that. Why can't you just call me Alan?"

She smiled, but her eyes were serious. "And why do you call me by my family name, Chen? Why am I not just Li to you?"

It had never occurred to me before, that was why. "All right, Li. I'm sorry; I just never thought of it that way."

Her smile erased the last of my nervousness. "We must learn to think in new ways together, Alan."

I wanted to sweep her away to my bed right then, tear off our clothing, and strive to get so close together that the space between our individual bodies would cease to exist. But, as if sensing my mood, Chen Li (as I continued to think of her) turned to one side and began to open a drawstring bag she had brought with her. "We must brew some tea."

I'm quite fond of tea actually. Mother always insisted caffeine would make me hyperactive, but I was allowed tea from an early age and so never acquired a taste for coffee. This hardly seemed the time, but I was not about to do anything to upset Chen Li now. I was actually quite patient while she brewed a pot of tea from the leaves she had brought with her, then poured some carefully into a cup. When she moved to fill a second, I raised a hand.

"None for me, thanks."

She flashed me a smile. "It's not for you. These are for the gods. Wait. You'll see."

When the two cups were filled to her satisfaction, she picked them up and turned toward me. She lowered her head submissively, but not enough to conceal her flashing eyes and good humored expression. "Where is your bed, Alan?" Puzzled, I led her to the bedroom. She moved immediately to the makeshift headboard I had created out of two cement blocks and a piece of polished wood, placing one cup of tea on each end. "It is necessary to leave a cup of tea to appease Chuang Kung, the god who governs beds and everything that happens in them," she explained.

I nodded at the second cup. "He must be unusually thirsty tonight."

Chen Li laughed, full, rich, a sound which made my heart beat faster even as my body was anticipating the moments to come. "Why, that's for his wife, Chuang Mu. How could you think that the god who watches over bedrooms would not have a mate?"

The love we made together that night was better than anything that had gone before, and if Chuang Kung and Chuang Mu were responsible, then I would gladly set them a cup of tea any time they desire one. My room was rather chilly, since the building was poorly heated, inadequately insulated, and there was a cracked pane in one window, but we were soon so full of one another that heat seemed to pour from our bodies.

Despite my precautions, however, we did not go unobserved.

We were lying in the darkness sometime later, the sun having gone down, our limbs intertwined, mutually exhausted, completely satiated, when I heard a sound in the room, the creaking of a board. I sat up immediately, Chen Li's arms spilling off to one side as she rolled sleepily away from me. Almost immediately I dismissed the sound as just another result of the old apartment building settling on its foundation, but since I was already half up, I decided to make a quick visit to the bathroom before trying to stir Chen Li into another round of lovemaking.

I was halfway toward the door when Chen Li cried out, first in surprise, then in evident pain. I started forward, calling her name, suddenly afraid, and painfully aware of my own nakedness. The darkness was impermeable, obscuring even the most familiar lines of the room, and I stumbled across my own shoes, thrown there carelessly hours earlier. There was a sudden rush of pale light, as though someone had thrown open a door, but even as I raised my arms to shield my eyes, I realized the source of the light, impossibly, was the mirror behind the bed. Blinking, I peered between spread fingers, saw Chen Li struggling in the grip of a figure which seemed to be leaning forward and out of the mirror, a vaguely human form but distorted somehow; the surface of its body seemed to consist of a series of horny plates joined at odd angles, without curves or other softening.

Shouting out something inarticulate that was supposed to be virile and challenging, I leaped forward toward the bed. I never got there. A powerful, incredibly cold arm wrapped around my body from behind, lifting me from my feet, swinging me up into the air.

Pure luck saved me. As I swung helplessly in the grip of my attacker, one foot brushed the side of my bureau. Reacting without thinking, I planted both soles against its surface and pushed off, swinging my arms wildly at the same time. It was enough to unbalance my captor momentarily and he, or it, or whatever, turned quickly to re-establish its grip. One of my flailing arms caught hold of the sheet I had hung on the wall and, struggling for something to provide leverage, I ripped it free.

I don't know what happened after that, exactly. A rank, hot odor rushed into the room, and there was an awesome noise, except that I think it only sounded inside my head. Certainly none of the neighbors heard it, or at least never mentioned having heard it. There was a sense of struggle and I was suddenly free, flying through the air to crash headfirst into the wall beside the bed.

I rolled over and stared back toward the source of the almost physical roaring sound, but the brilliant white light from the mirror flooded the room, throwing shapes into silhouette, bleaching the color out of the world. The shapes I saw shifting there were so unexpected, so unlike anything in my experience, I believed myself dreaming for long seconds. Two figures moved to my left, superficially human silhouettes, although the planes of their limbs were too straight, the joints two angular, the proportions subtly wrong. I can't really describe what it was that was wrong about them because my eyes were drawn to the third figure, the one that towered above, somehow larger even than the room itself, a rearing figure with too many limbs, rampant wings, beaked head raised on a tightly arched neck, ready to strike, claw footed forelimbs in constant motion.

Everything happened very quickly then, but also in such distinct detail that I was able to replay events in my mind later. The clawed shadow struck the nearer of its two opponents, and when it made contact, the smaller figure fell rapidly away, back along a line of motion that didn't, or at least shouldn't, exist. The limbs spasmed as it fell/faded/imploded away, disappearing from sight, driven back to wherever it had originated.

The roaring was so intense, my head threatened to split open and I raised both hands, covering my ears, without any discernible effect. As I did, the second figure lunged forward, struck at its gigantic foe, which retreated in turn, the earsplitting sound it emitted increasing in both volume and pitch. I suddenly realized I could see no trace of Chen Li, and the need to know what I was facing, what creatures had invaded my quarters, became so immediate, so undeniably, that I overcame by fear bred lethargy, staggered to my feet, and turned on the lights.

There was a rush of movement in two directions, each preternaturally rapid, and as I blinked to accustom my eyes to the rush of light, I received impressions rather than images, a large, multicolored shape flowing, sinking into the wall to my right, taking with it the sound and fury which had filled the room. The second figure remained frozen in place, and in the split second before it recovered enough to move, I saw...something. It was all planes and angles and light seemed to reflect from it strangely. The tableau remained for less than a second, then my unwelcome visitor rushed past me, out the bedroom door into the front room. Stunned, still unable to comprehend what was happening, I turned and stepped over the threshold, focusing on the intruder once more as it paused indecisively in front of my closed door.

Then, with a shuddering motion, it stepped forward through the door. There was no sound, just a kind of blurring, everything in the vicinity becoming indistinct, then slowly coming back into focus. The door remained closed; the apparition was gone.

I came back to myself in an instant and turned, overwhelmed with relief to see first the arm, then the raised head of Chen Li as she rose from the floor on the far side of the bed. She was clearly stunned, and didn't recognize me initially when I rushed to her side, helping her to sit on the bed. A wide, angry red line crossed her back diagonally from shoulder to hip, perhaps the result of a blow. She sat docilely, holding her head in her hands while I wrapped a blanket around her shoulders and then rushed out to get her something to drink.

"I hurt," she said at last, reaching behind with one hand toward the livid bruise.

"It's all right, Chen Li. You'll be fine. They've gone now."

The confusion began to disappear from her eyes, replaced by a mixture of fear and curiosity. "What happened to us, Alan? Who were those people?"

I opened my mouth to reply, then shook my head. How was I to answer her question? The little I had seen only led to more questions, no answers. "I don't know. Something hit me," my own bruises were beginning to protest now, a wrenched shoulder, sharp pains along one hip, "but when I turned on the lights, whatever they were disappeared."

"Disappeared?" She drank some more of the tepid water I had brought, visibly fighting for self possession. "How did they get in? Didn't you lock the door?"

"Of course I did." I had. "I don't know. I don't understand."

She stared at me with disconcerting intensity. "You said 'whatever', not 'whoever', Alan. What did you see?"

I considered lying, unwilling to look the fool, but then I remembered, this was Chen Li. Even if I was willing to lie, she'd have seen through me in a minute. So I told her. I told her about the day I had found the difference between the placement of my bed in the real world and its placement in the mirror. I told her about the lightless, mirrorless bathroom, and the strange feelings I had there sometimes, the images that seemed to drift through the bath water just beyond the limits of visibility. I told her about the odd noises that seemed to originate inside the mirror. And at last, I told her about the dragon and its inexplicable absence from the mirror world.

At this last, she glanced up at the wall. My makeshift cover lay discarded in one corner now and he was revealed in all his glory, still obviously male. But after many hours spent speaking to this two dimensional creature, I knew every nuance of its appearance, its coloration, posture, expression, the curve of its tail, the way it curled under the anterior portion of the body. It was still the same dragon, the artwork indistinguishable from the original, the pose superficially the same as before. But I could see differences, subtle ones, but glaringly obvious to the educated eye. One ear was slightly folded now, the degree of furl of the left wing had increased, one less tooth protruded over the lower jaw on the left hand side. But most obvious of all was the small, straight wound that crossed a row of scales on the left forepaw, a diminutive smear of green blood oozing from the lips of the slash.

My shock must have made me deaf as well as immobile because the next thing I knew Chen Li was standing at my side, shaking my arm vigorously.

"It moved," I breathed at her, still not believing it. "It's not the same as it was before."

One more discovery was to add to our growing confusion before that evening ended. Chen Li had dressed herself somewhat jerkily, her bruised back was starting to stiffen up, and I had thrown on a pair of jeans and a clean t-shirt. It was later than we had ever remained together previously, but Chen Li assured me that her uncle invariably fell asleep by nine and could not be wakened by any normal means. She came and went without his knowledge pretty much at will and if he suspected that anything was happening while he slept, Tao Tieh apparently never let on. It was when I started to see her out that we had a fresh surprise.

I reached out to work the lock on the door so that she could leave, but stopped suddenly, my hand hovering inches from the door hinge. Except that there shouldn't have been a hinge here. The hinge was over on the right side of the door, near the wall to the bathroom. At least, that's where it should have been. Somehow the door had been changed, flipped side to side, the hardware all reattached in an exactly opposite configuration.

Like a mirror image.

Despite my bruises, the events I have just described seemed nothing more than a bad dream the following morning, at least they did until I noticed the still inflamed wound on the dragon's foreleg. The green blood I had noticed the previous evening had dried into a muddy brown stain. I was momentarily lightheaded at the sight, the implications and fantastic unreality of my experience were completely unnerving and I sat on the edge of the bed for several minutes, head bowed forward, struggling not to faint or throw up or in any other fashion betray my weakness. Slowly I regained my composure, but even when I felt well enough to rise, wash, dress, and make some coffee, I carefully avoided turning my head toward the mirror, afraid that I meet find something totally alien staring back at me. It occurred to me that I needed to speak with Chen Li, compare notes, confirm the reality of our shared encounter. But then another, more cowardly, part of my mind silently set that idea aside. So long as my only evidence was personal, it could still be illusion and self-deceit; confirmation by another would unsettle the cornerstone of reality as I perceived it. Until my equilibrium was a bit more stable, I preferred to nurture the ever more remote possibility that this was all just a product of my imagination.

It was Saturday, and although Eblis had been working half days on Saturdays ever since I had started there, only the senior material handlers were given overtime, so I had the day off. Under ordinary circumstances, I would have stayed in my room reading or writing. Chen Li worked just about every Saturday, from mid-morning to closing time in the evening, so I was free of that distraction. But today, the very thought of remaining indoors, particularly in proximity to the mirror and its silent, wounded guardian, made my gut churn acidly and locked the muscles at the back of my neck into a rigid band. I recovered the small amount of cash I had set aside for entertainment from its jar in my closet and left my room as quickly as possible.

The door to the hall was still backward but I refused to deal with that fact just then.

I took the bus into Providence and spent the day window shopping in the downtown, climbed College Hill to the Brown University and Rhode Island School of Design campuses, then wandered through a prosperous residential area before reaching Swan Point Cemetery and visiting the grave of H.P. Lovecraft. When I finally gave up and caught the early evening bus back to Managansett, ominous thunderclouds had already brought premature dusk to the area.

The bus depot in Managansett is on Main Street, not far from the commercial district, but thirty blocks from my building, a badly renovated Victorian monstrosity which could not possibly have ever been appropriate to this neighborhood. The streets were narrow and winding for the most part, and although streetlamps had been sprinkled through the area, fully a third of them remained dark. Town services had been reduced recently in an attempt to avoid deficit spending, and maintenance staff and supplies had been among the easiest things to cut. The thunderclouds had receded, but still cast a premature pall of darkness.

I moved slowly down Dunford Street and then across to Woodview. My feet and ankles were beginning to ache warningly and I have to confess to a certain degree of reluctance to return home. Although I thought I had put the matter out of my mind entirely, anxiety crouched in the corners of my consciousness, ready to spring to the fore at the least excuse.

I began to feel that someone was following me.

Just after turning onto Woodview, there was a screech of automobile brakes from somewhere to my rear. The sound obviously originated back on Main Street and there was no ensuing thud of impact implying that there had actually been an accident. Nevertheless, nervous tension had made me hypersensitive, and I spun about warily, momentarily disoriented.

Except for a brief flash of reflected light from a private yard at the opposite end of the block, there was no movement; the evening air was absolutely still despite the looming clouds, and the bushes and tree limbs could have been still life paintings rather than reality. I told myself I was letting my imagination run wild and turned back toward the north, but from that moment, I felt eyes upon my back. The urge to turn and look became irresistible, and just before reaching Walnut Avenue, I detoured slightly around a thick stand of white birch trees, casually turning as I did so to sweep my eyes across the route I had just followed.

The streets and sidewalks remained empty, and I was ready to admit my own foolishness when something glittered momentarily at the side of a house, a brief stab of intense light, gone so quickly that I would have dismissed it as imagination except that my eyes still stung from the impact. The full terror of the previous night returned now and I fancied I could hear my own heart beating in the still night air. It had cooled off when the clouds had rolled in, but my clothes were damp with perspiration and whatever therapeutic effect the day might have had was vanquished in an instant.

I turned and moved off at a fast pace, just short of breaking into a panicky run.

Up Walnut and across Drover to Peach then Ash, then along Ash to the split that wound around the high school and the adjoining athletic field, both surrounded by untended woodlots. At first I resisted the temptation to look behind me, but eventually I became more frightened not to know what might pursue. Without slowing, I cast frequent looks to the rear, but still was unable to spot even the most furtive movement. The flashes of light were not repeated, at least not while I was in a position to bear witness. There was activity in some of the houses, although I saw no one else out of doors. The urge to rush up to one of the front doors I passed and ring for entry, admission to a world of sensible, rational people was no match for my reluctance to make a fool of myself. This might well be a case of overactive imagination, after all. How would I ever explain that I had been terrified by a couple of harmless flashes of light?

To a certain extent, this realization brought a return of calm, and I slowed to a more sensible pace as I passed the high school, though I was still moving at a much faster pace than was acceptable to my sore feet. I had calmed enough by the time I reached the athletic field that I made the decision to cut across past the baseball diamond and take one of the diagonal paths through the woodlot on the far side. This would bring me out on Ashburnam, avoiding Dudleigh Court and reducing my route home by almost two full blocks.

I crossed the athletic field without incident, but hesitated at the break in the surrounding hedge of forsythia that marked the path to Ashburnam. It was growing rapidly darker, shadows longer and deeper, and the path was so thoroughly overgrown by trees whose limbs were intertwined with wisteria gone wild, it already looked like night had fallen within the woods. My only alternative was to retrace my steps and take the route I had originally planned; if I followed the line of woods, I would be stopped by the hurricane fence at the far end of the school property and would have to follow it back around the perimeter of the field to my point of original entry. Unwilling to add further time to the trip, anxious to have this entire unpleasant episode over with, I rushed forward impatiently.

Within just a few seconds, I knew I wasn't alone.

A branch off to my left shook violently for a second, then remained still, as though it had been pulled back, then released. I paused, then climbed up onto a rotting stump, peering closely through the intervening foliage. It was too dark to see much, and there was certainly no repetition of the flashing I had seen earlier, but the pooled shadows seemed to move in strange patterns, shifting purposely even though the feeble waning sun was the only light source and the night air was still motionless. There was no sound, not even insect noises, and years of watching old movies told me that this was almost certainly a sign of a foreign presence in the woods. I licked dry lips and jumped down, turning back to my original path.

This time I did break into a run, although I would like to think at least that it was controlled, without panic, a run toward safety rather than flight from fear.

I was perhaps halfway along the winding track when a dark shape loomed up suddenly in front of me.

"Hey, watch where you're going!"

My frantic effort to slow my headlong rush was almost successful. The newcomer was a year or two my junior, slightly shorter than I but heavier of body, sufficiently bulky that he absorbed my impact with minimal difficulty.

"Sorry. I didn't see you." The words were out of my mouth quickly, I was already glancing back the way I had come, fearing what might be pursuing me.

"This isn't a jogging track asshole." He didn't sound as though he was willing to accept my apology that easily. I smelled alcohol on his breath and wondered what he'd been doing back here in this lonely stretch of woodland.

"Look man, I'm sorry, okay?" I started to slip past him, but he raised a hand and grabbed by arm warningly. He opened his mouth to say something else, but then his eyes moved and he looked distinctly surprised. "What the hell?" I turned my own head and saw that we were no longer alone.

Whenever we use words to describe something to one another that we perceive with our senses, we are dealing in comparisons. When I say "big" you think of it in terms of something in your experience; when I say "humanlike", you envision a person you know or the generalized sense of what a human body is; when I say "brightly faceted" it may bring to mind jewels or a prism or perhaps even the eye of an insect. So when I say that the entity which joined us there was big, humanlike, and had a body covered by brightly faceted plates, you may think you know approximately what I'm talking about, but that's only because human words cannot describe an experience outside anything known to our world.

Its body was large in the sense that it was tall for a human being, and wide, but it seemed to have no depth; that is, there was the impression that if it turned to one side, it would almost disappear, even though it seemed massive and powerful. The overall structure was humanlike in that it had four limbs in the usual places, what appeared to be a head mounted centrally. But the joints weren't quite where the eye expected them to be, and the angle of thigh to torso, of arm and shoulder, were subtly but disturbingly wrong, more so than the grossest Hollywood makeup. And then there were the facets. The entire body was covered with shiny reflective plates, except that they didn't exactly reflect the light so much as distort it; the shadows around us danced unnervingly and unpredictably. They seemed to overlap but never quite to touch, and they were in a constant state of movement in relation to one another. As if sometimes they were there, and sometimes they were not.

It stepped through a bush as it approached us, and the leaves of that plant never wavered. But its appearance was somehow different afterward.

"What the hell?" My companion repeated his last comment, and they were the last words he ever made. One flashing, glittering, not-there-exactly limb swept forward and up and passed through his face. Fingers uncurled from around my arm and I fell back in shock, watching as his flesh at first seemed untouched, then developed thin lines horizontally across cheeks, nose, chin, eyes, forehead. The edges of the wounds separated with a motion that reminded me of claymation, sculpted models animated by stop motion photography. The flesh curled back, writhed in place, and slowly began to unravel from his face, revealing the musculature beneath.

The body was just beginning to fall as I whirled and ran off into the darkness.

I suppose it was somewhere behind me as I ran, although perhaps it remained to watch the death throes of its victim. Or perhaps to do something else the nature of which I could not even begin to speculate. I do know that in the days that followed, there were reports of a missing local boy, Bob Davis, but there was never any mention of a body found in the woodlot. I emergedonto Ashburnam at a dead run, turned blindly toward home without another backward glance. Several times I stumbled, once I fell and tore the knee of my best pair of pants, and on at least two occasions I passed pedestrians who turned to watch as I raced by.

Chen Li was waiting in the lobby.

She shouldn't have been there; she should have been at work. And she should have remarked about my disheveled appearance, but she didn't.

"We must speak with my uncle immediately, Alan."

I started to laugh, struck by the absurdity of the timing. Presumably Tao Tieh was about to call me to task for sleeping with his daughter, only minutes after I had been witness to a savage killing. The laugh came out ugly, choked, more desperate than mirthful, and I cut it off quickly. If Chen Li saw any sign of my disquiet, she refused to acknowledge it.

Fighting to control my hysteria, I nodded. "All right, let's go." She led the way upstairs without another word.

I had misjudged the situation. Whatever Chen Li had told her uncle about the night's events, and she demonstrably had told him something, if it had included our sexual relationship, he chose to ignore the situation.

"Ah, good evening, Mr. Sheridan," he greeted me as we entered the apartment, sidestepping the screen. When he rose to take my hand, I noticed that he was wearing oriental dress tonight, a silken robe of sorts, open in front in a thin sliver to his ponderous waist. The predominant color was a deep, rich purple and it was covered with Chinese pictograms.

I opened my mouth to speak, but he raised a forestalling hand. "Please, we must go to your room immediately. I must see this dragon of yours."

His words were so much at variance from what I had expected that I stood befuddled, replaying them in my mind, trying to force some sense into the situation.

"There is no time to waste." He was already moving toward the door, and I had no choice but to step aside. Eyes downcast, Chen Li followed, leaving me to bring up the rear.

They waited with deathly patience while I removed the key from my pocket and unlocked the door with shaking hands. If Tao Tieh noticed that the arrangement of hardware on my door differed from all the others, he gave no outward sign. Nor was I certain just what Chen Li had told him.

I opened the door and stepped to one side, but Tao Tieh and Chen Li waited until I invited them in before entering.

Chen Li led the way to my bedroom where her uncle examined the painted dragon in minute detail for several moments, then turned and subjected the mirror to the same scrutiny. I wanted to say something about my encounter in the woodlot, but could not muster the nerve to interrupt Tao Tieh's concentration. When he finally seemed satisfied and indicated that we should return to the front room, I could contain myself no longer.

"Do you know what this all means? The dragon and the mirror?"

"No, not in the slightest." Chen Li came and stood beside me and I felt a bit stronger for her presence.

"But you have to know something!" I burst out. "You're Chinese and that's a Chinese dragon."

"China is a very large nation with a very long history, Mr. Sheridan. Do you know everything of this country's own much shorter, much less diverse history?" He shook his head, answering his own question. "This is surely a Chinese style dragon, not surprising since it was painted by, or at least at the instigation of, my countryman."

"But the mirror, uncle..."

"Yes," he nodded in her direction, then slowly lowered himself onto the cushions I had arranged in one corner of the room as a makeshift couch. "It could be one of the Four." He seemed to age visibly as he made the admission.

That's when Chen Li told me the story of the mirror people and the water people and the ancient Chinese emperor who vanquished them.

"Then Shang Yang was one of the guardians of the gates?" This still had the feel of an oriental fairy tale, but my personal reality had been so fractured during the preceding twenty-four hours, there was plenty of room for new concepts to slip in.

"The guardians are eternal; they cannot die." Tao Tieh had remained immobile throughout Chen Li's narration. "The dragon must be the guardian, Shang merely the servant."

I shook my head. "That doesn't make sense. Shang Yang painted the dragon; he created it. If the guardian is immortal, where was it before then, throughout all the centuries since the original battle?"

"You mistake shadow for substance. The guardians are not living beings as we understand the term, they are talismans of some sort. If their origin is recorded, I did not hear or do not remember it." He sighed. "It was many decades ago when my father's father repeated to me the stories he had heard from an older generation, and much of the truth may have been lost or changed with the passage of time. The guardians could have many forms, their bodies constantly being destroyed and reformed. Perhaps Shang Yang used the substance of the guardian to paint his dragon." He shrugged. "And then he had a brief careless moment and the guardian was left without its servant."

I remembered the darkened bathroom and spoke without being told. "The water people."

He nodded. "In an unwary moment, Shang Yang must have allowed one to form fully. They're supposed to be very fragile creatures ordinarily; one touch while it was forming would have disrupted the process. Thus the guardian was deprived of his servant."

"So what do we do now?"

"First, young man, we thank our respective gods that you two escaped alive and that the guardian triumphed. Much evil could have entered our world had the way remained open."

That's when I told them about my journey home.

I opened the door to the loft and led the way. The entrance was almost too narrow for Tao Tieh's girth but he managed and laboriously followed, Chen Li trailing behind. I turned on the light switch and the overheads went on, two dim bulbs whose glow was filtered through cobwebs before it alighted on the corpses of discarded furniture. I had explored here earlier at Jeri Kaplan's invitation, and although there were a few real pieces of furniture - couches, chairs, beds - they had decayed so badly over time that I hadn't been willing to expend the effort to move them downstairs. A thick coat of dust covered most; we stirred some of this up as we walked about.

"I'm sure she said some of his things were in storage up here." I looked around helplessly. "Some pottery and books and things. But I don't see anything here."

It was Chen Li who noticed the passage at the rear of the room. I had missed it completely on my previous visits, a narrow opening through the sheetrock behind a partition that I had mistaken for part of the rear wall. Had it been any narrower, Tao Tieh would have been unable to follow us. The room beyond was smaller, a mattress laid on the floor to the left, piles and piles of books covering the floor to every side. A small pile of clothes was piled neatly in one corner.

"Odrodek," said Tao Tieh. "He must sleep here sometimes."

Confused, I looked back and forth between him and Chen Li. "I don't understand. Why doesn't he sleep in his own room?"

"Didn't you know?" Chen Li's look of surprise was almost comical. "Odrodek has no room here."

"Are you saying that this is his home?" I looked around in dismay.

"No," Tao Tieh said quietly. "Odrodek has many homes, and none. This is just one of the places he stays from time to time."

"This way, through here." Chen Li had found yet another exit, this time into an even smaller room, no more than a closet. The only light was what filtered through the entranceway, and with the three of us standing there, we blocked out most of that. But Chen Li made a small sound of triumph. "Help me with this."

The box we pulled out into the light was only the first of three containing what remained of Shang Yang's possessions. I felt vaguely guilty about sorting through the remnants of a man's entire life. There were little stoppered glass bottles of paint or pigment, some brushes, many misshapen bits of pottery with arcane symbols painted on their sides, very amateurish in execution but possessed of a simple, coarse beauty. There was also a scroll, ancient in style but of comparatively recent creation, decorated with a dragon very similar to the one on the wall of my room, and several lines of pictographs.

"Can you read it?"

Tao Tieh shook his head. "I don't understand this at all. I wouldn't necessarily be able to read an ancient Chinese dialect if it were reproduced here, but these..." he indicated the symbols that covered the bottom half of the scroll, "...these do not resemble anything I have ever seen."

"That's because they are written in the Generals' Code." The voice came from behind, and our three heads turned in unison. Odrodek had quietly entered while we weren't looking.

"We regret the intrusion, my friend," Tao Tieh replied respectfully. "But our need was great."

"A friend's presence is never an intrusion." Odrodek gestured toward the boxes. "I helped Miss Kaplan in her bringing of these things to this place."

"Do you know what this means?" I held up the scroll.

Odrodek smiled. "In my youth, my father the Prince of Bukovina sent me to study the art of war in the university in Tsientsin. There I learned the Generals' Code. When China was divided among many warlords, these leaders to protect themselves did devise a special code which not even their underlings could use to foster misunderstandings among them."

"And what does this say?"

Odrodek peered more closely. "That which bars the door shall call to its side those who must serve." He frowned. "And the servant shall take the body of the master unto its own body and shall strike as the fist of the master." It was incongruous that the most grammatical sentence I'd ever heard from Odrodek was his translation of an ancient Chinese coded message.

"Thank you, my friend." Tao Tieh caught my eye. "We should take these downstairs. There may be something here which can assist us."

And so it was that the three of us were shortly to be found carrying our burdens back down the stairs from the loft and down toward the apartment where Chen Li and her uncle lived.

The entire series of events was beginning to take on a surreal atmosphere, and I had to repress the feeling that this was all an elaborate hoax arranged for my benefit. Tao Tieh's personality was still impervious to my scrutiny; I had no idea at all how to interpret his actions or feelings. But I had gotten to know Chen Li deeply enough to care for her and to feel that the sentiment was a shared one, and I could tell from a dozen subliminal clues, the way she spoke slightly faster than normal, her rapid eye movements, the way she kept rubbing one hand over her hip, that she was under a great deal of strain. Knowing that someone for whom I felt great respect was genuinely concerned helped to dispel by growing feeling of unreality.

We were outside their door when Tao Tieh allowed his emotion to show in my presence for the first time. With a deeply indrawn breath, he raised both arms to hold us back, saying some short and low in Chinese which I strongly suspected wasn't fit for polite company. And then I realized what had elicited such a powerful reaction.

The lock, knob, and hinges on the door to their apartment had swapped sides, just as had happened previously to my own, when the mirror creature had passed through.

Which probably meant that it was inside their apartment this very moment.

"Quickly, to your room, Mr. Sheridan. I don't think it will risk coming too near the guardian."

Seconds later we were setting our burdens down in the front room of my apartment. Tao Tieh paced the room with furrowed brow, the most agitated I had ever seen him. I nervously checked the bathroom and kitchen for any evidence of intrusion, then moved to the bedroom. Everything seemed to be as I had left it, but I thought I saw something new in the dragon's expression, a glowered warning, possibly just my imagination.

Chen Li was sitting quietly watching her uncle pace when I returned to the front room.

"Do you have any idea what we should do next, sir?"

"Not in the slightest, young man. This entire situation is as far outside my experience as it is your own. In recent years, our family has been based in Hong Kong, the most westernized city in Asia in many respects. I came to this country as a young man and Chen Li has never been outside its borders at all. How much do you know about druids?" I shrugged. "The situations are parallel."

"We are safe here though, aren't we?" Chen Li was nervously looking back and forth between her uncle and the hall door.

He shrugged. "Perhaps. It appears that there was intervention on your behalf last evening. But I don't think we can presume upon Mr. Sheridan's hospitality indefinitely, nor is it likely he'd be willing to spend the rest of his life here."

But we did spend the next several hours there, talking at infrequent intervals. Chen Li and I took turns brewing tea until the last of my meager store was exhausted. I alternated between prowling the small suite of rooms restlessly, or sitting sullenly staring at the front door. Chen Li dozed off shortly after ten o'clock, stretched out across a pair of cushions. I was on the verge of doing the same when Tao Tieh laboriously climbed to his feet.

"Enough of this. I will not be barred from my own home any longer."

Chen Li stirred herself, blinking away the sleep, slowly sitting up. "Yes, Uncle?"

"It is time for us to go home, Chen Li." He turned in my direction. "I have no advice for you, Alan." It was the first time he had ever addressed me by my first name. "I will telephone the police and tell them of a prowler. Perhaps they will be able to do something." He didn't sound very hopeful.

"Sir, if it's waiting there in your rooms, you'll both be killed."

"What will come does come." He started for the door and I rose quickly to my feet.

"I'm coming with you." Chen Li had also risen, her expression calm, and I stepped to her side. "I feel responsible for all of this. If I hadn't covered the dragon..."

"It was meant to happen," he interrupted. "So formidable a being as the guardian could not be rendered ineffective so easily. There are purposes here which we do not understand. No good cause would be served if you accompany us. Either we will live or we will not."

"At least call from one of the other rooms, or the pay phone in the lobby. You know it's waiting there for you."

"That we do not know. I do not think the police will be of any assistance in any case. Don't you feel how narrowly circumscribed this situation is? The police are extraneous; the principals will decide the issue."

And the odd thing was, I knew what he meant. It felt wrong somehow to involve others.

I stood in the hall outside my door and watched them until they disappeared around a turn and headed toward their own room.

Back inside, I sat on the bed with my legs crossed beneath me, staring at the dragon, searching for inspiration. "What am I supposed to do, friend?" The dragon remained mute, but expectant, posture encouraging me to continue. "Would Shang Yang have been prepared, in case he had somehow let his guard down? Would he have kept a weapon of some sort?" I rose and dragged the three boxes into the bedroom, poked at the contents. Paint jars, pottery, no weapons, no obvious magical artifacts. If such an item had existed, perhaps it had been among those which had been set out for the trash collectors.

And then I noticed tiny flakes of color scattered about the "ground" beneath the dragon's feet and massive, coiled tail. I moved forward, stopping with my eyes an inch or less from the wall, trying to distinguish the diminutive shapes.

And suddenly I knew what they were. I found what I was looking for in the second box, slipped it into my pocket, and bolted from my room, not even closing the door behind me. Breathlessly, I raced down both legs of the corridor until I reached Chen Li's door.

The hardware was back to normal.

I knocked tentatively, almost afraid to know the truth, then with more force. There were long moments of absolute silence when

I knew they were both dead, realized it was my fault, the result of my initial ignorance and subsequent stupidity.

I was about to try the lock when the door suddenly opened.

Chen Li was barefoot, her body covered by a terrycloth robe. She raised one hand before I could speak. "Quietly, please. Uncle has fallen asleep in his chair and I don't wish to disturb him."

I tried to peer about the room, but the screen made this difficult. "It's not here then?"

"No, the door was changed again when we returned. Uncle believes that happened when it left."

Relief at finding her alive sucked some of the strength from my muscles and I felt momentarily giddy. There was also an immediate awareness of sexual tension between us; she had never looked more beautiful to me than at that moment.

"I think I've figured part of this out," I whispered. "Can I come in for a minute?"

She glanced back over her shoulder, bit her lip. "It's better if we talk outside." She carefully turned the latch so the door would not lock and eased it shut behind her as she stepped out into the hall. "If we keep our voices down, we won't disturb anyone."

But I never had the opportunity to explain. We were both struck speechless by an inhuman cry of pain from somewhere else in the building.

"It came from downstairs," she said softly.

"I'm going." Adrenaline rushed back through my system. "Go back inside and wait for me." I started for the stairwell, unaware at that point that rather than obey my instructions, Chen Li was following a few steps behind.

The cry had not been repeated, and when I looked down over the stairwell, I could see nothing below. There were protesting shouts from a couple of rooms, muffled, but they subsided almost immediately.

Tension was an electric charge running up my spine to the hairline.

Moving as quietly as possible, I descended to the second floor landing, where I paused only briefly before continuing down to the lobby.

Something writhed on the floor in front of the row of mail slots. At first I didn't recognize it as a human being, or what had once been a human being. All of the skin was gone, and the muscles and soft inner tissues were convulsing into organic fingers of flesh which struggled to tear themselves loose from one another. As the individual fragments tore themselves free and caterpillar crawled out from what remained of the figure's clothing, their movements became more spasmodic but less frequent, finally running down to complete quiet. Already the first few were beginning to deflate, shed their substance, as though they were evaporating or seeping into the cracks in the flooring.

I recognized the clothing. Odrodek had been wearing it when he discovered us in his loft hideaway.

There was a startled cry from my rear, and I turned to learn for the first time that Chen Li had followed me down.

"What is it?" Her voice had lost its customary even tone.

"It was Odrodek," I replied. "I told you to wait upstairs for me."

"We are not in China." Anger gave her voice some of its original timbre. "American women don't take orders so easily."

Whatever rejoinder I might have attempted at that point was pre-empted by sudden movement near the door.

There was a moment of haziness, as though the light from the streetlight outside had become unfocused. When it cleared, a massive figure stood just inside the still closed door. Points of light moved erratically across its surface, a roiling ceaseless motion. I retreated to the staircase.

From my pocket, I removed a small stoppered bottle of red pigment which I had retrieved from the box upstairs, almost dropping it as I did so. Grasping the top firmly, I twisted. Sweat slick fingers slipped on the smooth surface; I could find no purchase. "I have to get this open," I explained desperately to Chen Li, trying a second time. Once again, my fingers slid ineffectively around its circumference.

"Here, let me." Chen Li plucked the bottle from my hands before I could guess her intent. With three quick twists, she pulled the stopper free.

I held out my hands. "All right, pour some of it on the ends of my fingers. Quick, before it realizes what I'm doing." And silently I prayed that the pigment had not dried out, and that there was enough left to accomplish my purpose, and that I had guessed correctly in the first place.

The fluid was thick, treacly, and cool as it flowed out of the bottle. Chen Li held it at a deliberately shallow angle, so that the entire contents would not come out in a rush. I turned nervously back toward the door, realized that the intruder was moving in our direction.

"No time!" I grabbed the bottle and dropped it to the floor, smashing it under one heel. Crouching quickly, I pressed the fingertips of my untreated hand into the mess, wincing when a piece of jagged glass cut through the pad of my index finger, dragging my nails across the floor so that they would be completely covered.

When I stood up, the intruder loomed ominously close, one arm already rising to strike at me.

I raised both of my own arms and plunged my arms into the creature's body.

It was like stepping into the most powerful wind you've ever experienced. I was stopped short, my skin afire with millions of tiny pricklings, and a soundless roar rushed through my ears while invisible brightness assaulted my eyes. The taste of yellow filled my mouth and the odor of hatred my nostrils. After a moment of hesitation, I pressed forward, fighting the resistance, no longer aware of anything except the need to pass through this obstacle. Years seemed to go by in split seconds; I had been engaged in this task for millennia already and there was no end in sight.

And then I was through.

I fell forward, landing on my knees and forearms, momentarily dazed. The next thing I knew, Chen Li was helping me to my feet.

"It's gone, I think." Her eyes were wide, voice anxious. "You disappeared inside it for a moment and then..." She shook her head. "I don't know what happened exactly. It just shrank into nothing and you were there falling."

"It's the pigment," I explained. "The dragon was created with paint made from the body of the original guardian. This paint." I held up my sticky ended fingers. "That's where the strength is."

"No," she corrected me. "That's where the magic lies." She placed one hand on my chest. "The strength is here."

I still don't know how I feel about this situation. It was nowhere in my life plan to become servant to an ancient Oriental magic. I do know that I will never again be able to stare into a mirror with quite the casual interest as before. But I will never be able to doubt the reality of my encounter with the intruder; each time I examine my own reflection, the proof will be evident.

When I passed through the body of the invader, it passed through me as well. My raspberry birthmark is now on the left side of my face, and my heart beats firmly, but paradoxically, on the right.

www.ingramcontent.com/pod-product-compliance
Lightning Source LLC
Chambersburg PA
CBHW072058170626
46813CB00004B/1408